What (

The Soldier, the Terrorist and the Donkey King :

The Soldier, the Terrorist and the Donkey King

The Other Perspective

Cover Photo: Danielle Poisson
Map on page 8: Edward Li

Essence Publishing is a Christian Book Publisher dedicated to furthering the work of Christ through the written word. For more information, contact:
Phone: 1-800-238-6376 • Fax: (613) 962-3055.

THE SOLDIER, THE TERRORIST & THE DONKEY KING

THE OTHER PERSPECTIVE - A FIRST CENTURY NOVEL

DAVID KITZ

Essence
PUBLISHING

Belleville, Ontario, Canada

The Soldier, the Terrorist and the Donkey King
Copyright © 2003, David Kitz

First printing November 2003
Second printing September 2004

Scripture quotations marked NKJV are taken from the New King James Version. Copyright © 1979, 1980, 1982. Thomas Nelson Inc., Publishers.

Scriptures marked NIV are from *The Holy Bible, New International Version*. Copyright © 1973, 1978, 1984. International Bible Society. Used by permission of Zondervan Publishing House. All rights reserved.

Scriptures marked NBV are from the *New Berkeley Version*, Hendrickson Publishers, Inc.,1969.

Scriptures marked TEV are from *Today's English Version*, American Bible Society, 1966

Scriptures marked CEV are from taken from the *Contemporary English Version*, American Bible Society, 1995.

National Library of Canada Cataloguing in Publication

Kitz, David, 1952-
        The soldier, the terrorist and the donkey king : the other perspective : a first century novel / David Kitz.

Includes bibliographical references.
ISBN 1-55306-708-8

        1. Jesus Christ--Fiction. I. Title.

PS8571.I895S64 2003   C813'.6   C2003-905851-4

To Timothy and Joshua,
the two young warriors raised in my own house.

Foreword

What would it have been like to live in the centre of the world during the first century, when donkeys and camels were the cars and trucks; conversations over a goblet of wine were the newspaper, T.V., phones, e-mails; and religious conflict influenced every facet of life? What would it have been like to constantly live under the pagan political domination of Roman tyranny, while also under the oppressive ritualistic control of hypocritical religious bigots? What would it have been like to live in the very week that this dark confused world was being invaded by heaven—a week when history would shift years from BC to AD?

This gripping story, written by David Kitz, offers its readers a front row seat from where we can view the action. It's a hidden camera on the helmet of a primary witness of the history altering drama when the Sovereign of the Universe, quietly riding on a lowly donkey, overthrows the pomp and power of the most powerful empire this world has ever known. More than that, it's a look into the mind and heart of a man, not unlike you or me, who was wrestling with the questions of the meaning and purpose of life.

As you read the thoughtful eyewitness accounts of The Soldier, the Terrorist and the Donkey King, as told by Marcus the Roman Centurion, you'll feel his anxiety and anguish, as well as exult in his ultimate answers, because, despite the time and cultural differences, his story is our story.

Pastor Barry Buzza
Northside Foursquare Church
Port Coquitlam, B.C.

Jerusalem 30 AD

Road to Caesarea

KIDRON VALLEY

Road to Jericho

☩ Golgotha

Fish Gate

Antonia Fortress

Sheep Gate

Governor's Palace

Gethsemane Olive Grove

TYROPOEON VALLEY

Temple Compound

Golden Gate

Road to Bethany

Mount of Olives

Aqueduct

Pinnacle of the Temple

Gennath Gate

UPPER CITY

Herod's Palace

KIDRON BROOK

Herod's Family Tomb

Hippodrome

LOWER CITY

Pool of Siloam

Water Gate

Serpent's Pool

Aqueduct

HINNOM VALLEY

Road to Bethlehem

1

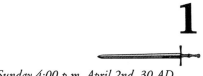

IT WAS NEVER LIKE THIS BEFORE.

I have been posted here in Jerusalem for ten years now, but in all that time I have never seen a Passover crowd like this.

It was not the numbers. I had seen that before.

What made the big difference was the person at the center of it all. You see, there had never been a central figure before. The Passover pilgrims just came plodding into the city in reverent caravans. Some of them would be chanting psalms. Others were silent, looking bone weary as they trudged like fretful herdsmen with children in tow. Undoubtedly, many were relieved that their holy city was finally in view.

But this year it was different. There was this man at the center of the whole procession. Every movement within that huge throng seemed focused on him.

Squinting in a futile attempt to get a better view, I gave Claudius a backhanded slap to the shoulder and demanded, "What are they doing?"

"They're climbing the trees, sir."

"I can see that!" I snapped impatiently, "But what are they doing?"

"They seem to be tearing off the palm branches, sir."

"What is going on here?" I said it more to myself than to any of the men standing near me. An uncomfortable feeling crept into me as the procession advanced.

"They don't usually do this?" Claudius questioned.

"No…. They've never done this before." There was worry in my voice.

Claudius had been recently assigned to this place, the festering armpit of the Empire, and I was at a loss to explain what was happening before us. We were standing on the wall above the gate of Jerusalem, and there, less than a half mile ahead of us, we could see the jubilant pilgrims surging toward us in numbers that were alarming.

"They're laying the palm branches on the road in front of that man—the man on the donkey."

Until Claudius said it, I had not noticed the donkey. Its small size, and the frenzy of activity round about, must have obscured this detail in the picture before me. What an odd way for this man to come. I could make no sense of it.

"They're throwing down their cloaks before him."

The sweat-glistened bodies of several men were clearly visible. Outer garments were cast down as a sign of homage before this man. At the same time the rhythmic chanting of their voices became more distinct.

What were they singing? Could I pick up the words?

"Hosanna to the Son of David!
Blessed is he who comes in the name of the Lord!
Hosanna in the highest!"[1]

That is when it hit me like a barbarian's club. I realized what I was witnessing. It was a triumphal entry—the entry of a king.

It was the words. The words they were now boisterously shouting. He was their Messiah. The son of David! The one they were waiting for! The one who would rid them of the Romans. He would set up his glorious Jewish kingdom, here, in Jerusalem! This is what I had been warned about since the day I first set foot on this cursed Judean soil.

And we, I and my men, and the garrison in the city, were all that stood in their way.

This crowd of thousands swept down the Mount of Olives into the Kidron Valley toward us. They advanced like a huge human wave about to collide with the rock-hewn palisades on which we stood.

Would they sweep us away?

My initial curiosity had grown into worry. In an instant, my worry turned to alarm. Instinctively, everything within me shouted, "Stand! Resist! Be a Roman!"

We had soldiers posted all about the city, especially along the pilgrim route. My own hundred men were among the first to be deployed. During Jewish feasts like this we made certain we were highly visible. I dreaded what might happen if this crowd ran wild. Rioting could erupt, and with an impassioned throng such as this, riots have a way of quickly turning deadly.

For several moments a debate raged in my mind. Should I order the gate closed to keep this rabble with their pretender king out of the city? Or should I let everything proceed—let it proceed as though, somehow, we hadn't taken note of what was going on?

"Stand! Ready for orders!" I shouted above the swelling din. The sentinels on the wall snapped to attention.

I hastily scanned the crowd for any sign of weapons, any hint of armed treachery. To my surprise I saw none. They were paying no attention to us. Everyone was caught up with hailing this man, the man on the donkey.

The front edges of the crowd had now reached the first platoon of eight men that I had positioned by the roadside about four hundred yards before the gate. But they ignored them, sweeping past the clump of soldiers without so much as creating a ripple, like a round stone in a swift-flowing stream.

At that moment I knew it made no sense to lower the gate. It would only enrage this crowd that was already fully aroused and moving as one.

Let them come. We will handle them and their king inside the city.

Their king. On a donkey. I could only shake my head in disbelief.

I had watched many a triumphal entry while growing up in Rome, and the conquering hero always rode a gallant war horse. And as a boy, I too had dreams of personal glory. But a donkey? It could only happen here, I thought with an incredulous grin.

I could see him clearly now. Donkey or not, he had the look of a man who knew exactly what he was doing. Those about him might not have known or understood, but he knew. He had a destination in mind, a purpose. You could see it on his face.

"Hosanna to the Son of David!
Blessed is he who comes in the name of the Lord!"
Hosanna in the highest!"

There was something else different about him. At the time I did not know what it was. I could not put it into words for a long time. I think I noticed it because I had watched all those other men come into Rome in their triumphal processionals. They were conquerors; still, they were hollow men, feeding off the adulation of the crowd, thirsting but never satisfied. You could see them vainly drink it in, hoping it would somehow fill their empty souls.

He was not drinking from the crowd. I somehow sensed he was full already, and what he had within must have come from a different source.

"Hosanna in the highest!
Hosanna to the Son of David!
Blessed is he who comes in the name of the Lord!"

Just at that moment a strange feeling seemed to rise within me. Maybe it was the joy of the crowd. I had expected anger. Maybe it was the children waving the palm branches, or the spontaneity of the singing? I do not know. For one moment it all seemed to come together. It seemed right somehow. Like heaven and earth had finally, for a moment, come into agreement—an agreement that had never been achieved before.

"Hosanna in the highest!"

He was much closer now.

"Hosanna to the Son of David!"

He was now within the shadow of the gate.

"Blessed is he who comes in the name of the Lord!"

At that moment he looked up. For an instant our eyes met. Then I heard a voice—clearly heard a voice say, "I have a future for you."

I was confused.

I turned to Claudius and said, "What did you mean by that?"

"What did I mean by what?" He had a blank look on his face.

"By what you said about—about the future?"

"I didn't say anything about the future, sir. I didn't say anything."

I was completely baffled. Was I hearing voices? This whole thing was making no sense, no sense at all. Passover pilgrims are not supposed to come into the city this way. Here we have a revolutionary on the loose—riding a donkey. And now I was hearing things?

I rubbed the sweat from my forehead, hoping for some clarity to emerge out of all this.

I had a hundred men whose lives were in danger from this Jewish messiah, and his horde of followers. That is what mattered now.

By this time, the donkey man had passed under the gate and was heading in the direction of the temple in the heart of the city.

I signaled for Claudius to follow as I raced down the stairs of the gatehouse. As I emerged onto the street, I grabbed the first two-legged bit of Jewish scum I saw. Pressing him against the stone wall I demanded, "Who is that man?" I pointed at the retreating figure on the donkey.

The poor wretch was in shock and seemed quite unable to get out a word.

Claudius reached for his sword.

"Je–Jesus of Nazareth!" the man stammered and then quickly added, "The prophet from Nazareth in Galilee."

I loosened my grip.

Then in a voice loud enough for all near to hear I announced, "Well, there is one thing I do know. We're going to have to keep an eye on that man."

2

Monday 1:00 a.m. April 3rd, 30 AD

SLEEP WAS IMPOSSIBLE. THE EVENTS OF THE DAY KEPT PLAYING through my mind.

He worried me. Donkey man. The Donkey king. Jesus of Nazareth.

He could have turned that mob against us. They were in his hands. Why did he not act? Perhaps it was the women and children in the crowd. Maybe it was a lack of weapons.

He must have been waiting for his support to build. He obviously had his supporters from Galilee with him. Maybe he felt he needed to build his base of support here in Jerusalem before he attacked us.

I rolled over. The room felt unusually hot for a spring evening. Maybe it just was not his time. He was a man with a purpose. I could see that. Of course, that was it. He was working according to some plan, some script I could only guess at. What was his next move?

The deep rhythmic breathing of Zelda, my wife, told me she was fast asleep. She knew none of my worries. It was best that way. Our two young sons were also sleeping in the adjoining room. Let them dream on.

But, by the gods, it is hard to sleep when you feel your life is threatened.

I had doubled my men on duty for the nightly foot patrol through the city; put an additional man on as house guard. Maybe that idiot Arius would not fall asleep if he had some company. I could faintly hear feet shuffling in the courtyard from time to time, so I knew they were on duty.

At least I knew our would-be messiah was not in the city. As the sun was setting, I had watched him leave by the same gate by which he had arrived triumphant an hour earlier. Word on the street had it that he was going to spend the night with friends in Bethany. So an overnight coup was not in the works.

Then there was Claudius to worry about, my sister's son. I was so pleased when he first arrived from Antioch. I remembered him as a curly-haired boy back in Rome, but when he stepped off that galleon, I was looking at a man. I did not even recognize him at that moment, though now I can see he has my sister's eyes.

Yes, there was Claudius. What would he step into, if this thing erupted?

Hellbent Zealots! I hate them! I could feel my body tense as the pictures raced through my mind.

There was Andreas, one of my lead men, dumped like a sack of refuse. I found him lying on the blood-drenched cobblestones. His throat was cut.

Then there was young Hermes, pinned to a wall by his own spear. His entrails hung down to the ground.

Terrorists! Bloody terrorists! That is what they were. And there was no telling when they would strike. The incident the month before was still fresh in my mind. Barabbas the zealot, the ringleader, would pay for this!

These were isolated random attacks by a few fanatics. For us Romans, the constant threat of terror was demoralizing. Each incident marshaled its own set of fears. But this prophet, this Jesus with thousands adoring him and singing his praise, what could he do? Anything seemed possible. He put all of Jerusalem in a stir. And it was only the first day of Passover Week. There was no doubt in my mind that we were in for a killer week, and it would be us, or them.

I rolled over. My pillow was wet with sweat.

Then there was Flavio.

All this would not have left me so fuming frustrated if it was not for the leadership crisis. Late in the day, when I and Renaldo reported all we had seen to Flavio, our tribune, our commanding officer, he was drunk. Drunk again. So there we were on the cusp of a mass rebellion, and our commander was so intoxicated he could not draw his sword to butter his own bread.

I threw back the flimsy cover, quietly pulled on a tunic and slipped out the door.

Standing on the balcony, I could see the two guards start at my sudden appearance above them. One quickly moved to the street gate, anticipating a rebuke.

The still night air was refreshing as I drew in several long breaths. I reached for the balcony rail to anchor me in the darkness. It was a clear moonlit night. The stars were glorious.

I just needed time to think. All was quiet except for the incessant chirping of crickets. I needed a plan.

How long I stood there I have no idea. Then it started to come. Slowly at first, and then my mind raced along.

I groped my way forward till I reached the stairs. With the assurance of familiarity I hurried down them. Beneath the stairs was a storage closet. The hinges creaked as I opened the crude door. I stooped to enter, turned a sharp left, and with fumbling hands reached for a small wooden trunk that I knew would be on a shelf straight ahead of me at chest height. I smiled into the blackness as my fingers fell on a well-worn handle. I shifted the trunk's weight onto my hip and ducked back out the door. Moving out of the shadows I set my trophy down in the centre of the courtyard.

Arius shuffled toward me from the gate and in whispered tones inquired, "Sir, do you need my help?"

I waved him off.

The clasps gave way before me and the tight lid squeaked open. I pulled out the robe and held it up to the starlight. I did the same with the carefully folded prayer shawl. The pungent cedar smell of the chest had permeated the fabric. The scent revived me. I hastily stuffed both back in the trunk, and carried my treasure with me back up to my chamber.

For what was left of the night I slept.

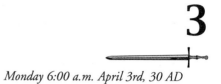

3

Monday 6:00 a.m. April 3rd, 30 AD

THE FIRST STREAKS OF DAWN WERE JUST BEGINNING TO SPREAD across the eastern sky when I left the house with the trunk tucked under my arm. In moments I was at Renaldo's gate. The gatekeeper immediately recognized me and granted entry.

Renaldo was a fellow centurion and a trusted friend. Our wives spent untold hours together, as our cramped Roman villas were joined one to another. For Zelda, female companionship of the Roman kind was hard to find in this outpost of the Empire, so our wives found in each other a kinship that might never have flourished back home.

In the dim light I caught sight of a familiar toga-clad figure seated on the steps stroking the head of a large dog. At the sound of my footsteps, Brutus swung free from his master and bounded about me in two great circles, his tail wagging furiously.

"He's such a great watchdog," I said in mock admiration. In fact, I knew he would be just that if a stranger entered.

"You're off to an early start," Renaldo remarked as he rose and straightened. We clasped forearms.

"Yes, well it's not a regular week."

"No, it's not a regular week," he agreed, then shook his head. "What a show that was yesterday. Holy Jupiter! I thought we were history. That dog on the donkey could have had us trampled and served up as Passover lamb. That was too close. Way too close!"

"Don't I know it!" I nodded my full agreement.

"We have to do something. This Jewish prophet is too scary—too dangerous."

"Well, that's why I came over. I have a plan. It came to me last night."

"What about Flavio?" Renaldo shrugged as he resumed stroking Brutus. The dog's silky ears twitched beneath his gentle hand.

"Forget Flavio. He'll be drunk for the rest of the week. Herod's coming down about midweek. There'll be a big wine swilling bash for the upper crust. He'll sober up just long enough so he can bow and scrape for Pilate at the right moment. Forget him. We have to save our own hides."

"All right. So what's this plan?"

"Well, it's not some great master scheme, but I do have a few ideas."

"Get on with it," he said with obvious interest.

"The way I see it, we have way too little information on this man, Jesus of Nazareth. We need to be aware of his every move. If there's some Passover plot being hatched, we need to be the first to know about it. Not like yesterday. I don't like surprises. Especially Jewish messiah surprises."

Renaldo scowled in agreement.

"So why the trunk?"

I had set it down after our greeting, and now it was Brutus, sniffing about it, who brought it to Renaldo's attention.

"This is one way I can get some information."

I opened the trunk and pulled out several items of clothing, among them a Jewish prayer shawl and several phylacteries. Holding up one of the fringed garments to myself, I announced, "Today I am Benjamin. Benjamin from Alexandria, and I've come to celebrate the Passover here, in the holy city, Jerusalem."

All this was done with a thick Aramaic accent, and a mock reverence that left Renaldo slapping his thigh in laughter.

"Marcus, Marcus! Only you could pull this off!" Then he added in a more thoughtful tone, "I could look in on some of our usual sources. They're bound to know a thing or two about this donkey man."

"Now you're thinking." With a glance to the eastern sky I added, "Look, we don't have much time. The sun's almost up. All my men know their assigned duties, so if you could just look in on them at the barracks that would be great. I should be back in uniform by noon, and I could meet you there to discuss what we've found."

"No problem... Benjamin!" he said shaking his head and grinning as he contemplated the sight of me in religious garb.

I began to place the clothing back in the trunk and then I turned to my friend.

"Oh, by the way, Renaldo, could you check in on Claudius at the Golden Gate? I expect our visiting prophet will be coming back into town by the same way today. Claudius might need a hand."

"No problem, Marcus." Then he added in a more serious tone, "Now, you be careful."

"Yes, well," I sighed, "I think we've all got to be careful."

I swung the trunk up under my arm. With a quick wave of my free hand I said, "I'm off for an appointment with Jesus of Nazareth."

4

IN A FEW SHORT MINUTES, BENJAMIN OF ALEXANDRIA WAS ON
the streets of Jerusalem outfitted in flowing robes and phylacteries.
He appeared at ease, in his element, like a devout fish enjoying a
swim in a bowl of holy water.

At least, I hoped that is how I looked to others. I was far less
at ease within. I was making my way to the same city gate on which
I had stood just the day before.

I felt naked. Twice naked. First, I was on the street without my
breastplate, my sword and armor, and secondly, I was beardless.
Beardless in the bearded Jewish world. I had wrestled over this fact
for sometime the previous night. But then, clean-shaven Jewish
men are not so rare at Passover. Just the day before I saw two such
wretches, looking as I now felt. It's part of their purification rites,
purification from the polluted Gentile world.

The city was beginning to stir. Camels. The reek of camels was
everywhere.

I wish by the gods they would keep those smelly sullen beasts
out of Jerusalem. I swear every Jew in town must have eight
brothers who come with three camels each to stay at his house for
Passover Week.

Just ahead of me a boy of about fourteen was collecting dung
from behind one of many beasts in his charge. The father, overseeing his efforts, overflowed with instruction. Suddenly, the man
turned in the narrow street and we were face to face.

"Ah, a naked Jew!" He gestured at my face with a grin. "Shalom,
my friend!"

"Shalom," I responded. His greeting put me at ease.

"Tell me, friend, do you know the best way to reach the Golden Gate from here?"

"Well, I am going there now." I cast a hesitant glance at his camels. "You could follow me now or I could give you directions."

"Micah, get your brother to help you water the camels. I'm going with this gentleman. I'll be back for breakfast with Uncle Zachariah."

I had company, if I wanted it or not.

He turned again to me. "Did you see that prophet from Galilee come into the city yesterday?"

"I saw him. But who really is this man? See, I'm from Alexandria. I don't know anything about this man or why he caused such a stir."

"I'm Timaeus from Damascus." He put an arm to my shoulder in greeting.

"Benjamin." I nodded my greeting.

"Well, Benjamin, your accent tells me you're not from here, and neither am I, so we can talk like foreign experts."

We started to walk.

"As for this Jesus of Nazareth?" He shrugged. "I know only a little more than you. My brother here in Jerusalem knew nothing about him. Had never heard the name. But I heard of him once, about a year ago, in Damascus."

"In Damascus?"

"I'm in the linen trade." He put his hand to an elaborately embroidered sleeve and stroked the pattern. "We supply market stalls in Galilee. One of our sellers there told me of this prophet. He had seen him in Galilee."

"So, what did he say about him?"

"Actually, he told me quite a lot, but I don't know how much I can believe. He said this Jesus worked miracles, drove out demons, healed the sick."

"Miracles? What do you mean—miracles?"

"Well, he told me about one time when he went out to hear this prophet, if that's what he is. He was on a hillside. Thousands had come to hear him speak. Matthias—that's the man's name—he said that he had never heard anyone speak like him. 'It was like heaven talking,' he kept saying. 'It was like heaven talking.'" He spread his arms heavenward in mock imitation. "Poor Matthias!" He shook his head.

"So was that the miracle? The way he talked?"

"No, no. It's not that, though Matthias kept going on about 'the kingdom of God.' Whatever that is. I suppose he got that from this Jesus. Anyway, after they had been there all day—he said there were more than five thousand people—this prophet told them all to sit down in groups of fifty or a hundred. Then he prayed and started breaking bread. He fed that whole crowd. Every last one of them."

"So, what's so miraculous about that?"

"Well, Matthias said he only had five loaves and two fish when he started. He was watching him, and Jesus just kept on breaking bread until the whole crowd was fed. Five thousand people."

"Five thousand people?"

"More than five thousand people." He shrugged incredulously. "Look, I wasn't there. I'm just repeating this fool's story. Matthias kept saying, 'It was like he was giving himself to us! Like it came from inside him!'"

It was my turn to be incredulous. I paused in my walk and asked, "What did he mean by that?"

"I swear by the altar, I have no idea."

"So what do you make of this Matthias and his story?"

"Matthias? He's a nut case. And he's from a fine family in Capernaum." He frowned, shaking his head. "I know them well. It's hard to believe he'd get into something like this. He's following this prophet around the country. It's all he talks about. He was probably up some tree yesterday breaking off palm branches," he spat out the words in utter disgust.[2]

"And Jesus of Nazareth?"

He raised a stout index finger and waved it in my face. "Now there's the real nut case! There's no nut like a religious nut! And this kingdom of God talk. It'll end in disaster."

He glanced about to see if other ears were listening.

I continued in a more hushed voice, "How do you mean? Do you think the Romans will get involved?"

"Look, I'm no prophet, but by the throne I swear." He looked me square in the eyes. "You don't preach about a kingdom in this place and get away with it. Rome will see to that!"

"Well, I was hoping to hear this prophet myself. Now I'm wondering if I should."

Timaeus sighed. "Go. Go hear the man," he said flatly. "Judge for yourself. I have better things to do with my time."

We were approaching the gate now. There was a pause in our conversation. It seemed we had no more to say.

Suddenly, Timaeus recognized a familiar face among the dozen or more men standing idly on either side of the customs booth. He waved and called the man by name. They clapped one another on the back, and together I watched them shuffle back into the city with a heavily laden donkey in tow.

About thirty paces from me, Timaeus spun around, waved and gave a quick nod in my direction; then he was gone.

5

Monday 8:00 a.m. April 3rd, 30 AD

As I waited for Jesus to return to the city, I had time to collect my thoughts. I was feeling less naked, more at ease in my role.

I was on familiar ground now. This gate, the Golden Gate, was my own gate. Its security was one of my responsibilities. Yet here I was, incognito, wiling away the morning hours waiting for a would-be messiah. The whole thing seemed preposterous. If I thought too much about it, my stomach knotted.

Nevertheless, in light of the risks as I saw them, I felt justified in my actions; after all, the Golden Gate was alternately called the Messiah Gate. According to legend, or prophesy, the Jewish messiah would one day arrive and make his grand entry there. Perhaps he already had. The crowd the day before seemed convinced Jesus, this Galilean prophet, had done just that.

I felt my tactics were paying off. Meeting Timaeus was like finding a gold ring in a boar's snout. I could hardly believe my good luck! A dozen paid informers could not have netted me more information. The gods must be smiling on me, I reasoned. Why not press on?

As the rays of the early morning sun cast long shadows into the valley below, I could see the first of many people making their way down the Mount of Olives on their way to the city. I had seen it a thousand times before. There was nothing unusual about it. This was not the frenzied pilgrim crowd of yesterday. It was more what you would expect on a market day, a busy market day, because this was Passover Week, after all.

Soon the customs booth was particularly busy. Jonas, the tax collector, was in an almost jovial mood. His greedy eyes were smiling, though he struggled valiantly to maintain his tax collector's scowl. His eldest son and even his wife had been pressed into service, though she stayed in the back.

I was buoyed by the success of my conversation with Timaeus. My disguise had proven effective. I began to loiter about the entrance as I had seen so many other Jewish men do, on so many other days. And I was not alone. Other men and sometimes entire families were obviously waiting to rendezvous with relatives, friends or business partners. There was a good deal of hugging and greeting when these events occurred, and in most cases the party would then move on into the city.

I was pleased to see my men carrying out their duties as prescribed. I had put Claudius in charge of the gate shortly after his arrival from Rome. He had a good mind and seemed to instinctively know what made for good security. In addition, he knew how to handle men—when to bark, when to bite and when to wag his tail. Only time would tell if he also had a good nose for sniffing out trouble.

The sentries were in place, two on either side of the gate house exterior by the outside wall, two on the interior, or city side of the gate, and two by the customs booth. I avoided eye contact with these men for fear of recognition. I tried not to worry too much about this possibility. My experience has taught me that most sentries have mastered the art of sleeping with their eyes wide open in broad daylight.

In addition to the sentries a two-man foot patrol was now on a morning stroll down the Kidron Valley. Claudius also had dispatched four, two-man patrols from this gate onto the city streets. Of course, there were the usual manpower assignments above the gate and along the western wall. All this was according to my instructions of the previous day.

But what about this prophet from Galilee? Would he be back?

Within an hour or so it became apparent that I was not the only one asking that question. The trickle of people arriving at the gate began to swell. Soon it became a crowd. Many of these people were in the previous day's pilgrim throng. Others were like me—the curious from the city. The entrance area of the gate became clogged with humanity.

Claudius came halfway down the gate stairway and bellowed, "Move on out! Move out!" Simultaneously he made a sweeping gesture with his arms as though shooing chickens out of the yard.

It worked. The crowd repositioned itself along the outside wall on either side of the gate. Within minutes the gateway was clogged again with new arrivals and Claudius descended once again for a repeat performance. There was a distinct sharpness to his voice this time.

Again the crowd responded well. The people on the outside wall made room for the newcomers and all eyes were fixed toward the road coming from the Mount.

Would the prophet appear?

I was now in the thick of this wall crowd. The anticipation was palpable. More people were arriving every minute. Whole families appeared. A mother to my left busied herself organizing her brood of six to ensure none would be lost in the press of bodies. To my right a father hoisted his young son onto his shoulders for a better view.

I glanced over my shoulder and up at the palisade above the gate. There, Claudius was in animated conversation with Renaldo. Claudius must have called Renaldo over from his position at the Sheep Gate, to see if anything should be done about this unexpected gathering. I knew he was worried.

Then someone ahead of me pointed and yelled, "That's him! He's coming!"

Necks craned. I raised my hand to shade my eyes. Just over the brow of the hill a figure in white rabbinical robes was beginning his descent into the Kidron Valley. It soon became apparent that he was not alone. A clutch of young bearded men surrounded him, and trailing on behind was an assortment of wives, children and barking dogs, of both types, canine and human. The whole entourage may have numbered a hundred and twenty. There was no donkey, and, to my relief, no thronging thousands. I am sure there was a collective sigh of relief above the gate as well.

The near giddy anticipation of these spectators was something I had not expected. I was surprised to find myself caught up in it. The front edges of the crowd by the wall now surged forward to line the roadside. Meanwhile, others continued to pour through the gate.

The man to my left stepped forward planting his foot on my toes. I grunted in pain and instinctively pushed my thumb and knuckles into his ribs. This brought the desired relief, and the man turned to face me. It was the man with the boy on his shoulders.

"My toes!" I gestured.

"Sorry, my friend."

I felt slightly embarrassed by the gruffness of my response. "You're waiting to see Jesus," I offered, stating the obvious.

"Yes. The kids are crazy about him." He nodded in the direction of the brood to my right. "It's all they've talked about since we came yesterday."

I could tell from his accent that he was from Galilee, so I continued. "Do you know much about him? I'm a Passover pilgrim from Alexandria in Egypt. All I know is what I saw yesterday."

"That was incredible!" he enthused. "Did you see him come in on the donkey? That's fulfillment of a prophecy."

Then he took on a more distant thoughtful look and he began to quote. *"Rejoice greatly, O daughter of Zion! Shout, O daughter of Jerusalem!"* And now his eyes brightened, *"Behold, your King is* coming to you; He is just and having salvation," and now he slowed for emphasis, and with his free hand stabbed the air with each word, "Lowly, riding on a donkey, a colt the foal of a donkey."[3]

It has always amazed me how these people memorize their scriptures.

"So, do you think he's…" I hesitated, "the Christ?"

"Shh!" He gestured with a finger to his lips, and a glance to the wall, "Or the stones will hear."

He continued. "There is no one like him. He drives out demons. He heals the sick. Even the dead have been raised. And yesterday," his voice raced with excitement. "Yesterday, I saw this with my own eyes, he healed a man born blind."

Seeing my interest, he pressed on.

"In the morning, we were leaving Jericho, the whole throng from Galilee, and by the side of the road was this blind beggar. He was yelling, *Jesus, Son of David, have mercy on me!*[4] Jesus stopped and touched the man's eyes."

He made as though he would touch my eyes.

"And he was healed!" His own bright eyes beamed at me as he smiled broadly. The boy on his shoulders also joined in his father's enthusiasm as for the first time he smiled down at me.

We began to reposition ourselves for the object of our conversation was now drawing near.

He nudged my shoulder, "And when he speaks, it's like God is talking to me. None of the Rabbis speak like him. It's like he has seen heaven and heard the voice of the Holy One."

A girl in her teens near the front edge of the crowd shouted, "Hosanna to the son of David!"

Soon others joined in. The masses surged around him and together we squeezed through the Messiah Gate and pressed on toward the temple.

6

Monday 9:00 a.m. April 3rd, 30 AD

IT ONLY TOOK A FEW MOMENTS TO REACH THE TEMPLE grounds. The Golden Gate grants the most direct access to the temple compound from outside the city. I remember being impressed by the sheer magnificence of this structure when I first arrived here ten years ago. The grandeur, the massive stones, the extensive gold ornamentation—taken together they create an awe in the beholder, that even now I find hard to express.

The West Wall, which I and my men patrol daily, directly overlooks the temple compound, so I know this place like the back of my hand. I know it, but yet I do not. I feel there is something veiled from me. Something I may not see, or maybe, I dare not see. The *'may not see'* part I vaguely understand. I am a Gentile. I may only enter the Court of the Gentiles, or outer yard of the great temple. To go beyond is to risk death. The inscriptions in Greek and Latin warn all who go there of that. But the *'dare not see'* of this veiling goes much deeper. I do not have time to speak of it now.

There was another way in which entering the temple compound left me feeling exposed. This has to do with jurisdiction. Within the temple compound I was truly in Jewish territory. This was the last vestige of the Jewish state. I was within the high priest's domain. No uniformed Roman soldier entered here. Armed Jewish temple guards patrol this precinct with the power to arrest at will. This was *their* place, and I keenly felt it.

Once again I felt naked. Fear of being exposed gnawed at my mind. At this point it was only the press of people around me that kept me moving forward. It was that, and a nudge from the Galilean father—the man with his son on his shoulders. He definitely wanted me to see and hear Jesus.

There were more of this prophet's followers awaiting his arrival within the temple grounds. Our numbers may have swelled to well over a thousand at this point. Keeping him in view from within this multitude of craning necks was a challenge at times.

We now poured into the Court of the Gentiles with Jesus taking the lead. It quickly became clear that he did not like what he found there.

The whole of this area had been converted into a market for the duration of the Passover celebration. There were currency exchange tables, caged foul available for sacrifice, and goods of various and sundry quality arranged for the pilgrim's perusal.

I can well imagine the eager anticipation among the merchants with the arrival of such a large crowd. But this prophet had no intention of leading a shopping expedition.

In a loud, anger-edged voice he declared for all to hear, *"It is written, 'My house will be called a house of prayer,' but you,"* his hand slashed through the air to encompass the assembled entrepreneurs, *"you have made it 'a den of thieves!'"*[5]

Then seizing the nearest table, he sent it, and all that was upon it, clattering onto the paving stones. The prophet swung around, and without stopping to admire the havoc he had caused, he grabbed a money changer's table and with one quick move he sent a thousand coins rolling in every direction. The next banker's hoard met with the same fate.

Pandemonium and panic now fully broke loose.

Benches stacked eight feet high with dove cages were next in line. Cages toppled. Birds flapped. Feathers flew. Within moments scores of birds had been released by the prophet's followers.

Frightened merchants rushed for the exits clutching all their arms could hastily gather. Within short minutes the entire Gentile court had been cleared of both buyers and sellers.

The transformation was astonishing, the effect upon his followers electrifying. They were in his hands. They loved the sheer power of the moment. With single handed raw courage he had swept aside the outward clutter of both wealth and religious tradition.

I was impressed. The man had convictions, and would act on them.

Timid temple guards skittered about the perimeter of the courtyard, dumbfounded by what they had witnessed yet fully knowing they were powerless to act before the prophet's adoring throng. This was a coup. In just moments they had lost control— lost it to the leader of a Galilean mob. Explaining this would not be easy.

The crowd now pressed in closer to Jesus, sensing he was about to speak.

"My house," and he gestured to the marble floors and columns that surrounded him, "*My house will be called a house of prayer for all nations.*[6] This is why there is a temple. This is why I have come… that we might draw near."

There was no anger in his voice this time, just the sincerity born of deeply held conviction. Then he turned from the crowd and faced the inner sanctuary, dropped to his knees, raised his hands to heaven and began to pray.

Since arriving here I have daily seen Jews at prayer. But at no time have I seen anyone pray like this man. It was not his posture or his words. I did not hear a word he said. It was something else. He was not praying for the crowd—to be seen or heard by them. I had this sense that he was praying to be connected. Connected to what lies beyond the great sanctuary doors, to what I am told lies behind the veil in the Holy of Holies. He was connected to that, that part of this place I dare not see and to which I would never dare go. It was as though he knew the One who was there, and was comfortable with him.

I found it odd how these thoughts came to me.

If he was comfortable, I most certainly was not! This was partly due to position. This prophet, Jesus, was too close. With all the movement and rushing to and fro as the merchants were evicted, by some quirk of fate it came about that Jesus stopped, and was now kneeling in prayer just six paces away from where I stood. He made me nervous. This reverence for God stuff gave me an awed, eerie feeling. I didn't know how to respond. I never felt this strange unease with the Roman gods.

I glanced at the Galilean father for some direction. But he was gone. I do not mean physically gone. He was, in fact, kneeling beside me, completely lost in prayer. I turned to see how others were responding. Some were kneeling. Others were standing with hands lifted. Still others looked just as stunned and awkward as I now felt.

I dropped to one knee to avoid looking conspicuous. How long I remained there, I really do not know. It could not have been long; it felt like eternity. I kept wondering what I had got myself into. This was not the conduct I had expected from a revolutionary.

The soothing murmur of a thousand spoken prayers filled the courtyard. Voices rose and fell like gentle waves on a shore. There was a quiet peace here, but I was afraid to let it touch me. The soft babble of voices reached a crescendo, then ebbed away.

Jesus rose to his feet. He turned to the multitude. He had the look of the satisfied on his face. Satisfied in prayer? That thought was a stranger in my mind.

Having witnessed the temple cleansing, there was such a strong sense of expectation in this crowd. "What would he do now?" I felt the unspoken question on everyone's mind.

In fact, for quite some time he did nothing. He simply stood there scanning a sea of faces. Then his eyes lit on a young lad, perhaps age twelve, standing to my far right. Their eyes engaged for a moment. The prophet gave a slight nod to his head—a signal for the boy to advance. He did so with haste. His right leg dangled loose like the limp rags he was wearing. The staccato scrape of his crutch on the stone floor echoed through the hushed courtyard. Eager determination marked his every move. In short moments he stood before Jesus. His right leg was easily six inches shorter than the healthy left leg. The absence of any muscle in this stunted limb was painfully obvious, even at a distance.

Like a father, Jesus placed his hands on the boy's shoulders, looked into his eyes, and in a firm voice commanded, "Stretch out your leg!"

The boy's leg began to twitch and stir. Then it kicked forward. Once, twice, three times. With each kick the stone pavement grew closer. The toes stretched forward; the heel pressed down. On the fourth kick contact was made. Two more kicks and he had a solid footing. Now he began to jump up and down, up and down, on both feet. Muscle—muscle that hadn't been there moments before, began to appear in his leg. The wooden crutch clattered lifelessly to the floor. He was free.[7]

With one voice the crowd began to cheer and applaud.

"Blessed is he who comes in the name of the Lord!"

The ecstatic smile on this lad's face, I will never forget. He glowed. He danced. He danced on the spot a few more times, as if to confirm the miracle was real. Then he buried his head in Jesus' chest and clung to him in a thank-you hug that lasted a full minute. When he raised his head to look into the Galilean's eyes, there were tears streaming down his face. Joy tears. Thank you tears.

"I can walk!"

"You can walk," Jesus confirmed.

In fact, for the rest of the morning he did very little walking.

He bounced, jumped, skipped, and ran, but only seldom walked.

I on the other hand, I, was astounded. I had never seen anything like this. I was seeing the impossible happen. It was happening in front of my eyes. I could not deny what I was seeing, but it was challenging my beliefs and everything I knew about the world around me. I kept rubbing my hand across the rough stubble on my chin. It was my way of checking in on reality. I was here. This was real. I was not dreaming.

A deep sense of awe began to invade my soul. I felt small. Smaller than I had felt for a long time, maybe even smaller than the crippled boy—the formerly crippled boy. He was, in fact, a familiar boy. I saw him about the city on other occasions. Sometimes he would prop his crutch along the stone wall and sit and beg at the Fish Gate.

I was shaken out of my thoughts by a nudge from the Galilean father.

"Didn't I tell you he was amazing!"

"I've never seen anything like this," I confessed.

"When the Christ comes, will he do more miraculous signs than this man?"[8] He shook his head to confirm the answer to his own question. Then, in hushed tones, he added, "I tell you, there has never been a prophet like him."

When we looked up toward Jesus again, another child had taken his place before the prophet. This was a younger boy, blind in one eye. Actually, from my vantage point there appeared to be no eye there at all, just a sunken hollow socket where the eye should have been.

Quietly, Jesus addressed the boy's father. "How long has he been like this?"

"Since age five." Then he added with an aching tone in his voice, "It was an accident." He would have said more to explain, but Jesus raised his hand to stop him. It seemed that no explanation was needed. The blaming, self-torturing thoughts could end.

Jesus placed his right hand on the boy's left shoulder. Then gently he placed his cupped left hand over the empty eye socket. He methodically took a deep breath, as though readying himself for some great exertion. As the breath slowly escaped his lips, he gazed down at the young lad and with authority he commanded, "Be healed!"

Anxious moments passed. Then slowly Jesus drew back his cupped hand. Eye lashes blinked and fluttered in the harsh brilliance of light. The eye was there, clear and bright.

Now, with two eyes, the boy gazed up at Jesus. Then he spun around to his father and yelled, "I can see, Daddy! I can see!"

His father was overwhelmed. With trembling hands he reached to touch his son's face—to see what wasn't there just moments ago. And seeing the miracle, he fell on his knees before his son and hugged him to himself. He rocked him to and fro; his strong frame shook with emotion. With stammering lips he cried out to Jesus, "Thank you, Master! Thank you!"

Jesus helped the man to his feet. But this man would not be silenced. He kept saying, "Thank you! Thank you!" over and over again.

A girl to my right began to sing, *"Hosanna to the Son of David!"* Soon all the children had joined in her song,
"Hosanna to the Son of David!
Hosanna to the son of David!
Hosanna to the Son of David!"

Their chant echoed off the marble columns of the temple. The whole of the temple grounds resounded with their spontaneous enthusiasm. The ragged beggar boy whose leg had been healed, began to skip and jump to the rhythm of their praise. A joyous pandemonium filled the sacred grounds. Everyone seemed caught up in it.

"Hosanna to the Son of David!
Hosanna to the Son of David!
Hosanna to the Son of David!"

I was, of course, reminded of what I had witnessed from the city gate just the day before. There was a power and an energy in this swelling crowd that sent a chill through my body. Where was this all going? The momentum was building. Where would it end?

The jubilation continued.

Glancing to the edge of the crowd, I noticed a stir. An official delegation from the high priest had arrived. Their long, flowing robes were an excellent match for their long faces. There was no joy in that camp. Undoubtedly, they had been fully informed of the eviction of the merchants and they had been assembled to come and to right that wrong. But now they were witnessing this mass hysteria, this indignity in the holy place. They were righteously disgusted by this public display of emotion and misdirected worship.

As the children's previously irrepressible enthusiasm began to wane, this high powered delegation made its way to the front of the throng where the prophet stood. With a pompous flourish their leader began, *"Do you hear what these,"* he scowled in the direction of the children, *"are saying?"*[9]

"Yes." Jesus of Nazareth nodded and smiled. *"Have you never read, 'From the lips of children and infants you have ordained praise'?"*[10]

The prophet's words, though they were spoken calmly, stung like a slap in the face. Of course this learned scribe knew the scriptures. To imply otherwise was an affront to his intelligence. But to insinuate that these children, the offspring of northern rabble now allied with some of the scum of the city, somehow intuitively knew what was right? Well, this was more then he could bear. The man turned purple with rage.

He began to sputter something about the ignorance of the masses, but then stopped mid-sentence when he saw the reaction of those same masses standing directly before him. He and his kind retreated hastily like humiliated dogs run out of town.

Seizing the moment, a young mother rushed forward clutching a limp form in her arms.

Upon seeing this mother and child, I was stabbed by pain. Remembered pain. The dark sunken eyes glazed by fever, the pallid skin, the wheezing cough and raspy breath; I remembered it all. The child was racked with consumption. And the disease was consuming her, consuming her body, and with it a mother's hope until none would be left.

The toddler did not stir a muscle as Jesus looked into her fevered young eyes. Experience told me this gaunt daughter would be dead within a week. It was the mother who trembled and pleaded—pleaded for her, who lacked even the strength to cry.

"Give me the child," Jesus gently urged.

The request took the mother completely by surprise. Instinctively she clutched the girl even more closely to herself.

"Give her to me."

There was tenderness in that deep voice.

The mother was now visibly caught in an inner struggle. I suppose she had held on so long and so tightly, that now, it was hard to give this frail object of her affection to a stranger.

Their eyes met for an instant. He gave a short nod to his head as if to say, "Yes, it has to be this way." And the struggle was over.

She eased her slumping burden into Jesus' arms. The child's head drooped against his chest. He wrapped a big hand round the girl's head, brushed a wisp of hair from her eyes, rocked her side to side. With slow deliberation, he turned from the multitude and faced the great temple doorway.

An intense quiet engulfed the assembly. Moments passed.

"Father... Father... "

That is all I heard him whisper. He raised his gaze to heaven, and then back to the little one in his arms. With the same slow deliberation he turned back to us.

The child was whole. Transformed! Completely healed! She squirmed in his arms—eyes bright and clear. Two little hands shot out, reaching for Mommy. The smile spoke ten thousand words.

The crowd was ecstatic.

"Blessed is he who comes in the name of the Lord!
Hosanna! Hosanna in the highest!"

Suddenly, for a second time, our eyes met. He knew me. I could see it in his eyes. I do not mean Jesus recognized me. I mean he knew me. Knew me from front to back, from inside out, from my first day till now. It was a dreadful feeling.

I turned abruptly from him. My heart hammered in my chest. I began fumbling my way through the crowd, desperate for an exit. I had to get away.

But my child… my daughter…

Why was she not healed? Why was she not spared?

7

"I KNOW IT'S HARD TO BELIEVE, BUT I SAW IT WITH MY OWN eyes. His leg grew a full hand span. It happened right in front of me!" For emphasis I gestured at an imaginary spot a few feet ahead.

"Are you sure it was Lucas?"

"Well who else could it be? What other kid hobbles along on a crutch, and has a bum leg a hand span shorter than the other?"

"Lucas?" Renaldo snorted as he shook his head. He was incredulous.

"Look, it was the same boy I've seen begging at the Fish Gate for the last six months."

"The one with the copper begging bowl?"

"The one with the copper begging bowl," I affirmed with a nod, and then added, "Don't believe me? Check it out yourself. The last time I saw him he was dancing around on both feet. He'll be back at your gate soon enough. But I don't think he'll be carrying his begging bowl, or his crutch."

Renaldo looked thoughtful as his eyes scanned the streets of the city below. We were standing atop one of the four turrets of the Antonio Fortress, the hub for military command here in the city. We had finished a light noon meal and then, for the sake of privacy, had climbed the stairs to the top of the northeast tower.

"Look, Renaldo, like I said, I wouldn't have believed any of this if I hadn't seen it myself."

"So, let me get this straight. This Jesus of Nazareth does miracles, and you saw him do them?"

"That's right."

"He kicked the money-changers and merchants out of the temple courts?"

"He went at 'em like a wild man," I responded.

"He defied the delegation from the high priest?" Renaldo questioned.

"Sent them scurrying for the exits like bugs under a rock."

"So, Marcus, what do you make of this prophet? This messiah?"

Now it was my turn to be pensive. I was so awestruck by what I had witnessed that I was having a hard time sorting through all my thoughts and impressions. The words came to me slowly. "He's not at all what I expected. He's not at all like a revolutionary."

"So he's not a revolutionary. Then we've got nothing to worry about," Renaldo concluded.

"I didn't say that." I paused, then added, "He's not *like* your common revolutionary."

"So, he is a revolutionary."

"Well, his revolution, if that's what he's leading, doesn't seem to be against us—against Rome—at least, not at this point." The vagueness of my answer left me feeling awkward.

"So who is he fighting?"

"Well, he's not exactly endeared himself to the religious establishment. Caiaphas is probably having a holy altar kicking tantrum right now. Those merchants pay good money to set up shop in there." I gestured with a sweep of my hand in the direction of the temple compound. "And they're going to be after him to get that northern hick town messiah out of there. Now!" In imitation of their tactics, I made a downward stab with my index finger, "and I mean now."

"So we let the high priest and his clan handle it. They've got the authority and the manpower."

"Not at the moment. Jesus and his followers outnumber those temple guards maybe a hundred to one. I tell you, he has the people—

the crowd—in his hands. They don't dare move against him."

"Marcus, it's still up to Caiaphas. It's his problem. Let the Jews sort it out."

"I suppose you're right," I tacitly agreed. "But he still scares me—scares me like no man ever has."

"Why?" Renaldo queried.

"Well, he's got power like no man I've ever seen." I shuddered inside at the thought of the unearthly nature of that power.

"This prophet really has you rattled, doesn't he?" Renaldo countered. "You're still worried, aren't you?"

"Yes," I acknowledged, "I'm still worried." Then, to justify my concern I added, "This talk about a kingdom bothers me. Besides, you didn't see what I saw today. It makes all the difference."

"Well, he had me scared spitless yesterday, so I hear you." After some moments of reflection Renaldo added, "You usually have a great nose for trouble. Let's hope we can head this one off."

I appreciated those words. I found this whole experience unnerving. I needed the steady hand of a level-headed friend. In this whole situation, I felt like I was in unfamiliar territory and losing my bearings. I had never encountered anyone like Jesus of Nazareth. At least Renaldo showed some confidence in me.

"So, how about you? Did you find anything out?"

"Marcus," Renaldo began with a mischievous grin. "You've got good company. Pedrum is worried too. Scared and worried about Jesus of Nazareth."

"Pedrum!" I scoffed. "What's Pedrum got to worry about?"

"Seems our prophet from Galilee is bad for business."

"Bad for business?" My curiosity was piqued.

"Seems he's got a way with women." With eyebrows raised Renaldo added, "He's been messing with Pedrum's girls."

"Messing with Pedrum's girls?" I was keen to hear the details. Pedrum ran Jerusalem's biggest brothel.

"It's not what you're thinking." Renaldo winked at me, as a broad smirk crossed his face. Then he began to elaborate.

"Apparently, Pedrum's lost two of his girls to this Jesus on his past visits to the city. Last night, he lost another one. That makes three now, and there may be more as the week wears on. Pedrum said, 'He messes with their minds. The girls get religion, and the next thing you know they're gone.'"

"Poor Pedrum!" I exclaimed in mock sincerity.

"'And it's the busiest time of the year!' he kept saying."

"My heart bleeds for the fat bastard."

"Well, there are more troops on the way with Herod coming down," Renaldo commented. "Those northern boys will keep Pedrum's girls busy."

"I don't think it's our job to solve Pedrum's prostitute problems."

"Ah, there you have it!" Renaldo grandly exclaimed. "Pedrum has a problem with Jesus. Our high and mighty high priest has a problem with Jesus. The two need to get together. I'm sure they could cook up a solution," Renaldo observed.

"Who knows, they just might do that," I remarked with a wry smile. "And what do we do in the meantime?"

"Nothing."

"Nothing but watch?" I asked.

"Nothing but watch," Renaldo stated flatly. On reflection he added, "I like what you're doing, Marcus. If Jesus is the people's messiah, we've got to watch his every move. Then we move if we must. But why dirty our hands if we don't need to."

"Yes, I guess you're right." I paused and then said, "I just don't have a good feeling about how this might end."

"As long as our hides aren't in the stew, what does it matter? By next Monday this will all be over. The crowds will be on their way home. In the meantime, Herod arrives tomorrow. As for you," he poked a bony finger in my direction, "there's Friday to look forward to." He spoke those last words with a lively nod and a wink.

"Yes," I concurred with a vengeful grin, "there's Barabbas on Friday!"

The remainder of the afternoon was taken up with planning and preparation for King Herod's arrival from Caesarea. A messenger had arrived confirming the particulars of his expected arrival time, and the size of the entourage. Two hundred horsemen, a hundred spear men and two hundred foot soldiers were to accompany a royal party of forty-eight. These details had, in fact, been known for weeks, but Flavio, in typical style, called a hasty meeting of the centurions under his command to work out how to accommodate this influx.

The mood among the centurions soon turned sour. Space in the barracks is always at a premium. There was also the problem of the stables. Flavio, of course, was expected to play the role of the gracious host, but how much do you inconvenience your own men to accommodate the troops of a visiting dignitary?

In the end, the horses won out over the men. I proposed tethering our mounts in a line along the outside of the east wall near the Serpents Pool. That would free the stables at the hippodrome for the arriving cavalry.

The men presented more of a problem. Flavio wanted each of us to shift fifty of our men out of the barracks and into our own villa courtyards. When something nearing revolt broke out over that proposal, the number of men was reduced from fifty to twenty. The remaining thirty men would sleep in the open air along the top of the city walls—a rather chilling proposal given that we had just passed the spring equinox. Of course, it was left to us to inform our troops, and our own wives and families, of these new temporary arrangements.

The bowing and scraping before the powerful had begun.

8

"YES, I SAW HIM LEAVE. IT WAS ABOUT AN HOUR AGO. JUST LIKE the other time, there must have been a hundred or more followers with the rabbi. They went back up the Mount of Olives," Claudius reported, and then he turned to me. "What's the story on this man? I've never seen anyone cause such a stir."

"He's dangerous," I stated emphatically. "More dangerous than any man I've ever met. Many think he's the messiah."

"The messiah? What's with this messiah notion anyway? Ever since I got here, I've heard people talk about it. What's it about?"

"It's rooted in history—history and religion. It seems religion touches everything here. It's really about regaining past glory. For a short time, the Jews were a world power. They had their Golden Age under King David and his son, Solomon. That was hundreds of years ago, but every Jewish child learns about it through their scriptures. It's like they've never forgotten what that was like. The power. The glory."

"And the messiah?" interrupted Claudius.

"Ah, the messiah!" My eyes glanced heavenwards in mock imitation of Jews I had spoken with on this topic. "The messiah will bring back the glory. That's the great hope—the hope promised in the scriptures. He will arise, the promised son of David. The people will rally round him, and together they will throw off the yoke of cruel oppression."

I could not help saying this with a certain melodramatic flourish. I was warming to the topic now, and pressed on.

"Oh, and the kingdom? He'll restore the kingdom! There will be peace and prosperity, and every man will sit under his own fig tree, and drink from the fruit of his own vine."

I paused in my theatrics.

"There's only one problem in all this." I cast my gaze on Claudius, inspecting him from head to toe, then turned on him in mock derision.

"Why, it's you! You're the problem," and with those words I gave Claudius a playful, but aggressive shove. "You pagan Roman dog! Get your crotch-sniffing nose out of here! This is our land."

After a snicker at Claudius' surprised reaction, I added, "Of course, they don't say that to your face, but that's what they mean. That's why you watch your backside. And why you watch prophets from Galilee. And why you have long ears like the jackass. You never know what they're plotting." I paused. "Terrorists sprout up like weeds in this Judean soil."

"They're not all like that," Claudius retorted.

"Of course not. But there's enough of that nationalist, chosen-people mentality to affect everything. They have a sense of national history, and national destiny. They're not like any other people we rule. They really are different."

There was a certain grudging respect in my words.

"The mistake I made when I first got here was thinking they were all out to get us. That just isn't true. When you think that way you're bound to make mistakes." I gave a slow, thoughtful nod and then said, "I tell you, Claudius, there's no joy in crucifying an innocent man."

I paused to let the weight of my words sink home before going on. "In reality, most men don't care one iota about who rules over them. As long as their bellies are full, and there's a woman in their bed at night, they're happy. It's the hungry young wolf you watch out for."

"So, this prophet, this rabbi," Claudius gestured with an open upraised hand, "is he one of these wolves?"

"What I saw and heard today makes me think so. He's the biggest, sharpest wolf I've ever seen. And that's why we're having this little talk. Tomorrow I want you to go and check out his teeth."

Eyebrows shot upward. I knew I had my nephew's full attention now.

"You're a new face around here. You're far less likely to be recognized. You'll wait at the gate like those pilgrims this morning, and then join with them as they head into the temple when Jesus arrives."

"Ah," he hesitated. "Are you sure I can do this?"

"I did it myself just this morning. I stood right down there." I pointed to a spot below us. "I watched you shoo the chickens out of the coop." I imitated the sweeping motion he had made with his arm. "And then I spent the morning with Jesus of Nazareth in the temple compound."

His mouth fell open. He was stunned by my words.

"Look, Claudius. We need to keep an eye on this man. Now, I mean what I'm saying. All our lives could be in jeopardy. You're a natural choice," I reasoned. "Like I said, you're a new face around here. You speak Aramaic very well—better than I do. And you've got a brain in your head. Right now, you're the best man I have for the job."

I could see he was thinking.

"Couldn't we just get some paid informants or something?"

"Ha!" I blurted. "In a case like this, paid informants will tell you whatever you want to hear, and collect afterward. How do you think I managed to nail Barabbas? It wasn't with paid informants!" I scoffed at the idea. "No, he'll feel the spikes on Friday because I went out and got the facts on him—myself." Determined to press home my point I continued, "Look, there are times in this business when you've got to put your own life on the line. You've got to dirty your own fingers. When good men like Hermes and Andreas go down, you don't sit and polish your brass. You get out there and sniff out the stinking truth for yourself. You owe it to your men.

I drew a deep breath and plunged on, "As for Barabbas, he's a tin pot hooligan. A brainless bloody terrorist!" I spat the words out. "Now Jesus—Jesus on the other hand, there's a different dog on the prowl! He's got followers. He's got a crowd around him. He's got heaven on his side. You don't let Jewish messiahs strut around under your nose and just ignore them."

"So how do I go about this?" Claudius questioned. There was a mixture of sincerity and trepidation in his voice.

"Tonight, you're coming home with me. Zelda will have some great Roman food waiting. I'll tell you all I know, and give you all you need for the job. Then tomorrow you're on."

Still sensing uncertainty, I paused and looked straight into his eyes.

"Look, Claudius, if by the morning you don't feel you can do this, or if I don't think you're up to this, I'll pull you off. I just want you to give it a try. I know this takes a lot of nerve. Not just anyone can do it."

There was a pregnant pause.

"Fine. I'll give it a try."

He said it with a smile and a nod, and enough conviction to give me considerable hope for success.

With the arrival of replacement guards, we headed home. We said little as we walked. As we rounded a street corner, our shadows became long titans striding across the gritty cobblestones. In moments the sun would set.

We passed the same sullen camels at the spot where I met Timaeus early in the morning.

On reaching the villa gate, the flitting movement of a sparrow caught my eye. It landed on a tangled nest among the lower level rafters. Tiny bobbing heads appeared with mouths agape.

Next thing I knew, two boys brandishing small wooden swords were charging at me.

"Papa's home!"

"Papa's home!"

9

THE DREAM BOTHERED ME. BOTHERED ME A LOT. IT HAD COME to me in that half awake—half asleep time before dawn.

At first, I tried to block it from my mind. But the pain of it cut through like a branding iron searing my mind.

Then I tried to analyze it.

Maybe it was the time of year. After all, Tara died during Passover Week, two years ago.

Maybe it was going into her room last night. I was showing Claudius his bed for the night. It was Tara's bed. A thunderstorm had swept in from the west, so Zelda suggested he stay for the night. The moment I opened the door to Tara's room, the memories just flooded back—memories both happy and painful.

I found it odd how she came to dominate my affections.

When each of the boys was born, all the pride common to every father filled me. Above all I wanted sons. Here were sons I could train. Sons who would be like me. Sons who were my own.

Then Tara came along. I was happy for Zelda. I greeted Tara's birth with a certain casual indifference. A third child. A girl.

But she won me to herself. It was her laugh. Her smiles. The way she watched my every move, her greeting when I came home, the curl in her hair, and the lilt in her voice. It all brought joy to me—brought happiness at the core.

When she got sick, I became desperate. The doctors were useless. The remedies seemed to make her more ill. As the months dragged by, her condition worsened. She was wasting away with consumption, too sick to cry.

I cried. I cried late at night.

I cried out to my Roman gods. I offered sacrifices at our household shrine.

Nothing helped.

Over and over again Zelda pleaded, "Ask the local god."

So reluctantly I went. I unpacked the wooden trunk. Retrieved it from under the stairway. Put on the local garb. Went to the temple.

I stood on almost the very spot I stood the day before, the spot where I had watched Jesus heal the children.

I cried to the God of heaven. The Maker of the universe. The one true God. The LORD God Almighty. I used all the phrases I had learned since coming to Jerusalem to this Jewish center of worship.

Quietly, I sobbed them out for my little girl.

She died the next day.

And now—now this dream—this cruel dream.

I was standing in the Gentile Court of the temple again. Jesus was there. He was talking with the woman I saw yesterday, the one with the sick child. But she was not holding her own child. She was holding Tara.

Jesus said, "Give me the child."

But she said, "No."

She pulled Tara even closer into herself.

How this woman got Tara, I have no idea.

Jesus gently beckoned with his hands extended toward her.

She was adamant. She would not give Tara up to him.

I was in turmoil. At first I tried yelling at her. But it was like she was deaf, unable to hear a word.

I was frozen to the spot. Transfixed, unable to move. Unable to even form the words. They would not come out.

This struggle seemed to go on in an unending loop. Me, unable to speak—to tell her to give up the child. And she, unwilling to do so.

Finally, she turned away from Jesus. She nonchalantly sauntered over to me, where I stood. Dumped the slumping child into my arms. Turned and walked away.

She was dead. Dead in my arms.

Tara was dead!

I awoke like a drowning man gasping for air.

10

CLAUDIUS GOT OFF TO A GOOD START. HE SHOWED THAT natural confidence that comes from being at ease in your own skin. Over the years I have come to believe that you cannot be comfortable being someone else until you first are comfortable being yourself. But Claudius demonstrated a certain inborn ease, and bearing that is quite uncommon among young men of his age.

Claudius had the further advantage of being raised, for the most part, in the Syrian city of Antioch, hence his fluency in the Aramaic language, commonly spoken throughout this region. The night before I had also discovered that despite his earlier questions, he is quite well acquainted with Jewish customs, thanks to the large Jewish community in that city.

Unlike myself, and the other centurions here, most of the regular Roman troops are Syrians. Only a minority are from Rome itself, the largest segment of these true Romans being the governor's own Praetorian Guard.

As for the Galilean prophet, he arrived right on schedule, and in the prescribed manner. If anything, the crowds awaiting his entry were even larger that day. Undoubtedly, word had spread about the miraculous healings.

From the safety of my gatetop vantage point, it was with a certain sense of relief that I watched Claudius disappear into the press of pilgrims bound for the temple.

Rather him than me.

Jesus so unnerved me that I could not bear the thought of going in there a second time with him. Everything about him set me on edge. The last straw came in that brief instant earlier when our eyes met. His eyes were double-edged daggers that penetrated my soul. It was as though my life was laid bare before him, as if he had grown up with me—knew me to that very moment.

What a stupid notion! Why was I even thinking these thoughts? Why did a momentary encounter leave me with such a soul-wrenching impression?

I was beginning to understand what Pedrum had said about the prostitutes: "He messes with their minds." I firmly resolved not to let this prophet mess with *my* mind.

Fortunately, there was a great deal to occupy my thoughts. Preparations for King Herod's arrival were now fully under way. The expected arrival time was late afternoon. The only thing still in doubt was the ceremonial route. Proper protocol would dictate that Herod be first welcomed to the city by Pontius Pilate. However, on his previous visits here, Herod Antipas had been notorious for giving the governor the royal snub. Stooping before Rome was not something any of the Herods did particularly well.

Pilate, from my perspective, appeared to be in a rather conciliatory mood. Wishing to play the role of the gracious host, a messenger had been dispatched to formally invite the tetrarch to supper at the governor's palace. Herod's response would determine the final leg of the ceremonial route.

In the past, Herod had always elected to proceed directly to his royal palace on the eastern perimeter of the city, making his grand entry through the Gennath Gate. But, should Pilate's invitation be accepted, an alternate fork in the road would be taken, and the king would make his entry through the Fish Gate at the north end of the city.

I had orders from Flavio to make a thorough inspection of both possible routes. Midmorning found me thus engaged, on horseback, leading a party of six cavalry men. Narrow, clogged streets presented a problem at the best of times, but funneling a royal party, and an armed contingent of more than five hundred men through Jerusalem's maze of streets required plenty of advance work.

All appeared fine until we entered through the Fish Gate. Suddenly, the narrow street leading to the Praetorium turned into an impromptu market clogged with sundry goods and bartering humanity.

I had never seen this street in such a state before. It must be cleared, I reasoned.

Apprehension was written on the faces ahead of us as we approached single file on our mounts.

Suddenly, I spun round in my saddle. Panic seized me. Instinctively my left heel dug into my horse's flank as I yanked sharply on the reins. Startled by my actions, my horse reared and twisted.

It now took all my strength and expertise to contain the beast beneath me, and to wheel it around in the confined space. After considerable stamping and snorting, I succeeded.

Astonished by the sudden rearing of my horse, and then this frantic turn, the mounted soldier behind me threw up his free hand in a silent questioning gesture.

"Retreat!" I ordered.

This was a feat not easily accomplished in these tight quarters. But to the credit of both the men and the horses, they mastered this tight reversal.

I felt like a cowardly fool in flight as the seven of us withdrew in awkward haste.

It was Timaeus. Timaeus the linen merchant.

I had suddenly recognized him directly before me at the first merchant's booth. The shock of recognition had thrown me into panic as he turned to face me. He was standing not more than three paces away.

58

Fortunately, my men, at least the ones farther back in the line, had supposed that my horse had been spooked by some sudden movement. In fact, they were right, but the movement had been my own.

I now reasoned that Timaeus probably had no inkling of my identity, helmeted and armor clad as I was. I might have been able to bluff my way onwards, but in that instant, there had been no time for second thoughts. I needed this informant, and I had no intention of blowing my cover in some accidental encounter.

We regrouped on the other side of the Fish Gate and then headed north on the Caesarea highway until we hit the fork heading to the Gennath Gate. It was a well-marked spot. Off to the right on a rock knoll, three roughhewn poles stabbed the sky: Golgotha, the place of the Skull, my Friday assignment, standing at the ready. It awaited the condemned.

We turned left at the fork and followed it down all the way to Herod's Palace. Aside from dodging the odd puddle from the storm the night before, there was nothing remarkable about this route, though it did provide more room to maneuver.

The next move lay in Herod's court. If he accepted Pilate's invitation, the merchants near the Fish Gate would have to be cleared. But that was not a mission I intended to lead.

11

IN DUE TIME, I AND MY PARTY ARRIVED AT THE ANTONIA Fortress. I was there to report on the morning's reconnaissance work, but first, I gave the six men with me their orders for the afternoon. To make room for Herod's cavalry, they were to begin setting up the tether lines for our horses along the east wall near the Serpents Pool.

After surrendering my horse to one of my men who took it to the stable, I climbed the first flight of stairs to the tribune's headquarters. The unmistakable smell of cooked cheese curd assaulted my senses. There was a certain familiar squalor to Flavio's briefing room. It was a fitting match with the state of the man. Only off in one corner was there a semblance of order. A handsome bronze Apollo stood upon the god shelf. A fresh offering of steaming food had been placed before it.

"Ah, Marcus, have a seat," Flavio called out to me when he spotted me at the door. Then he motioned to his personal servant and barked, "Get the man something to eat."

The tribune swabbed up a large glob of stringy cheese with a chunk of bread, stuffed it in his mouth, and slowly began speaking as he chewed. "So Marcus, Renaldo tells me… you have your eye… on a subversive."

"As a matter of fact, I do."

"Tell me more," Flavio prompted as he reached for another plump barley loaf.

"Well, it's a prophet, a rabbi from Galilee. Jesus, Jesus of Nazareth.

That's his name." I stumbled about for words. Flavio didn't respond, but kept right on eating, so I felt compelled to continue.

"He caused a huge stir Sunday when he came into town. Came in like a king. Like he owned the place. The crowds—there were thousands around him—treated him like some conquering hero. It was bloody ridiculous!" I said, gesturing with a sweep of my hand. "I've never seen anything like it."

"So, what did you do?" Flavio questioned.

"I talked with Renaldo, and we decided to have him followed. My nephew Claudius is on him right now."

I did not want to reveal my direct personal involvement since I had no idea what Flavio was thinking, or where he was heading with his questions. In addition, I was in the dark about what Renaldo must have already revealed to Flavio.

"I knew we needed to do something," I said, justifying my actions. My use of the word *"we"* was quite deliberate. I wanted to be clear that this prophet was worthy of a group response, and I had not acted alone. Renaldo had been consulted.

"Sometimes, I think you worry too much, Marcus."

"I worry because it's my job to worry," I shot back. "Barabbas is in prison because I worry."

Flavio appeared to consider my reply, swallowed another stringy morsel, and continued, "So what do you know about this prophet?"

"A lot of people think he's the messiah."

"May all the gods help us! Another Roman-killing messiah!" Flavio jeered in derision.

"This one just might be the real thing," I responded.

"Ha!" he scoffed. "Bring him on!"

He reached for his flagon. Finding it empty he bellowed, "Where's my wine? Bloody incompetent servants," he muttered. Turning to me, he asked, "Does he have weapons?"

"No, not that I've seen."

"Has he threatened us?"

"Not exactly."

"Assaulted the tax collectors?"

"No."

"Then leave the Jewish dog alone."

The servant arrived with a bowl of hot sticky cheese and placed it before me along with two small barley loaves.

"Wine! Where's the damn wine?" Flavio demanded of his harried attendant.

"He is preaching about a kingdom—the kingdom of God," I countered.

"So, let him preach."

"Who do you think will be the king of this kingdom?" I reasoned. When Flavio remained silent, I answered my own question, "I'm sure it will be none other than Jesus of Nazareth. I don't think there's room for two kings in this city, and a Roman governor, too."

"I see your point," Flavio conceded.

He wiped a greasy hand across his mouth, and then rubbed the three days of stubble on his chin. "So he talks about a kingdom?" Flavio offered.

"The coming kingdom," I clarified. "It's the whole point—the core of his message. So I'm told."

The servant arrived with the wine. Flavio helped himself. Drank two thirds of it in a massive gulp, then poured himself some more.

"And he has followers?" Flavio continued.

"Most of the Galilean pilgrims are firmly in his camp."

"Galilee?" Flavio questioned. "He's Herod's man." He paused to rub the tip of his nose. "I wonder what the Fox thinks of this messiah?"

"You may have a chance to ask him yourself."

"You're right on that." He straightened himself and cleared his throat. "I've been invited to the banquet." He spoke the words with a measure of hubris, and then added, "Now, we'll just have to wait and see if Herod, that crafty Fox, takes the bait. Did you check the routes, Marcus?"

"Yes, the Gennath route is fine, but a market's been set up along the Fish Gate route and it will have to be cleared if the governor's invitation is accepted."

"A market?"

"It seems that the merchants—the ones that our visiting messiah kicked out of the temple—they've set up shop right along there."

"Hmm!" Flavio huffed. "So he has caused quite a stir." Then after a pause he added, "Renaldo did mention that."

After another mighty gulp of wine he announced, "Our messenger should be back from Herod anytime now. As soon as we get the word, we clear the street. But there's no sense stirring that hornets' nest unless we have to. Herod may yet turn Pilate down. So, until we know, we let the traders trade."

"Renaldo could clear that street, couldn't he?" I volunteered. "After all it's in his sector. This afternoon I was planning to set up the tether lines for our horses along the east wall."

"Yes, I suppose he could," Flavio responded. "You can tell him that when you leave. Now about this messiah? Back off. He's picked a fight with Caiaphas, and that weasel is in our back pocket. Caiaphas is nobody's fool, especially when there's money involved. He'll nail that messiah's hands if he needs to. Don't forget, Marcus. He's the other big man in town."

As I broke bread, Flavio grew philosophical.

"It's all about money and power. This world runs on money and power. The two fit together like a man in a woman." He meshed his fingers together, and nodded. "Like a man in a woman." He thought this metaphor was particularly clever and repeated it for effect. "Don't forget that, Marcus."

Just then a messenger arrived from Pilate. In unison we fixed our attention on the young man standing in the open doorway. He cleared his throat and began, "His excellency the governor sends word that his majesty, Herod Antipas, Tetrarch of Galilee and Perea, has accepted an invitation to dine at the Praetorium today. The king will arrive at the fourth hour. Let all be made ready."

Flavio's eyebrows shot up. He turned to me with a satisfied smile. "Marcus, you see to it. I'm off to the bathhouse."

12

Tuesday 1:00 p.m. April 4th, 30 AD

"MONEY AND POWER. THIS WORLD RUNS ON MONEY AND POWER."
Flavio's words echoed in my mind as I left the fortress. That certainly was what Herod's trip to Jerusalem was all about.

It was the Empire's worst kept secret that Herod Antipas was engaged in an ongoing campaign to regain control of Judea. His father, Herod the Great, had built the magnificent gold-clad temple. The imposing palace constructed on the opposite side of the city was a further monument to his personal glory, or vanity, depending on your viewpoint. And it had all been lost after his death—squandered through constant family infighting and treachery. Now the tetrarch of Galilee and Perea was reduced to a mere fourth of his own father's realm. How demeaning!

Tetrarch. Herod Antipas loathed the title. He despised the implied subservience to Rome. King. Ah, King Herod, that was more to his liking, a title more in keeping with his heritage. Herod Antipas—King of the Jews. Now there was a title suited to the man.

But Herod was no son of David. He wasn't even a son of Jacob, the father of the Jewish nation. No. He was an Idumean, a descendant of Esau. But by some twist of fate, aided by nimble hands of murder and treason, his father had risen to the top. He had reversed the curse of a thousand years of Jewish history. This latterday son of Esau had come to rule over his brother Jacob.

And how sweet it was.

But then there was Pontius Pilate. For Herod Antipas, Pilate's presence in Jerusalem served as a constant reminder of what should

65

be his—what Rome had bequeathed to its own son, rather than to him, the rightful heir and successor to his father's throne.

And there was the temple. The temple was the fount of riches that had built his father's magnificent family palace. It had helped finance a thousand endeavors. Religion had its place. It had always served his family well. Now, the temple, this focal point of Jewish piety, lay beyond his diminished borders, in another man's domain, under a petty Roman governor. The fount of wealth was no longer his.

Antipas would not rest—could not rest, till justice as he saw it was done. A Herodian restoration was what was needed. Was not this, his chief ambition, his one great goal in life?

What motivated this Herod was apparent to anyone who had eyes to see, or ears to hear. Why, he had even financed his own party of followers to pursue these ends, to curry favor with the proper authorities and to lobby for the return of the whole kingdom.

A king in search of a kingdom. This was Herod Antipas coming to his Jerusalem, the capital that should be his own.

As for Pilate, what precipitated his unexpected move to improve relations with the sly Fox remained a mystery to me. Whatever it was, it undoubtedly had something to do with money and power. On that point Flavio was right. Despite his shortcomings, Flavio understood this world, and knew very well how it functions.

As for me, I was concerned about Claudius. I knew I had to speak with Renaldo, to tell him to clear the merchants, but Claudius and I had agreed to meet at the Golden Gate just after the noon hour. I felt that, at this point, he was my first priority.

From the fortress I took the first stairway to the top of the city wall and proceeded along it. Coming first to the Sheep Gate, I hastily checked if Renaldo was anywhere in view. Not seeing him, I made no inquiries, but quickened my pace hoping I would not miss my rendezvous with Claudius.

Another five hundred paces brought me to the Golden Gate, but Claudius was nowhere to be seen. I questioned the day's assigned gate-keeper, but he had not seen him. I had left very specific instructions with this man regarding Claudius, so he too had been expecting him. Since he was aware of this covert mission, he was also concerned. However, he pointed out that Jesus had not left the temple compound. Together we concluded that the prophet was still teaching his followers, and Claudius was so absorbed in the teaching that he could not pull himself away, or he was delayed for some other reason.

It was the possibility of some other reason that worried me.

At this point there was nothing further I could do about Claudius, so I turned my attention back to Renaldo. The mess at the Fish Gate still had to be cleared up, the tether lines had to be inspected, and Herod would be here in less than three hours. I was beginning to feel time pressure, and it was putting me in a foul mood. Worries about Claudius were not helping matters.

Who knows? Maybe Flavio was right. Maybe I did worry too much. But then, the drunken dolt needed to look after his own responsibilities. I resented picking up after him—covering for his drunken incompetence.

I hastily left instructions for anyone seeing Renaldo to send him my way. I was heading back to the Sheep Gate in hopes of meeting him there, and then proceeding on to the stables at the hippodrome.

As I retraced my steps, I brooded over Renaldo's apparent withdrawal of support for my initiative regarding Jesus. He seemed in full support when I began this investigation, and now it seemed he had pulled right back—had opposed me behind my back in his talk with Flavio. My point of view was not being heard.

Was I overreacting? I did not think so. I was convinced this prophet was dangerous. The closer I got to him, the more firmly I held that conviction.

This time, as I arrived at the Sheep Gate, I immediately asked if anyone had seen Renaldo. The gatekeeper reported he had been there a short while ago, but had left. Again I left instructions that he should report to me immediately for an urgent message from Flavio. I turned to leave.

"Marcus! Marcus!"

I spun around to see Renaldo emerging from the gateway stairway.

"Marcus! You were right. That boy really was healed."

He voiced the words with such bald enthusiasm that I was completely disarmed.

"I just saw him. He was here—here at the gate." He gestured down the gateway parapet to a point below us. "I saw him. I examined his leg. It's completely healed. Just like the other one. It's incredible!" he enthused. "He can jump! And run!"

"I told you. I told you, Renaldo," I said while shaking my head.

"Yes, but you don't expect it," he said as he justified his unbelief. "I mean, this child's been like this from birth. You see him the same way, day after day. And then one day… Boom! He's completely different."

"I told you. You didn't believe me?" I uttered the words with a certain smug satisfaction.

"Well, you don't expect it," he repeated. "I mean it's one thing to hear it, but it's quite something else to see it for yourself."

"That's exactly what I was trying to tell you. I said you've got to see this for yourself to understand." I sighed. Now I was beginning to realize why I was not getting through.

"So it was Lucas," I stated.

"It was Lucas!" Renaldo confirmed, shaking his head in a state of incredulity.

I changed the topic.

"Look, Renaldo, I would like to talk with you more about this, but we've both got some work to do. Word has just come into Flavio. Herod has accepted Pilate's invitation. He'll be going directly to the Praetorium. Arriving at four. The Fish Gate route needs to be cleared. You know those temple traders have set up shop in there, and you've got to get them out. And the sooner the better. Flavio says that's your sector, so you're on."

Renaldo took all this in stride and then responded, "Sure, Marcus. I'll get right on it."

I turned from him, but he called after me.

"Marcus. We need to talk more about this Jesus—this Jesus of Nazareth."

13

THE NEWS OF HEROD'S IMMINENT ARRIVAL SPREAD LIKE FLIES on a rotting corpse. It was not long and people were streaming out of the city and lining the imperial highway from Caesarea in hopes of catching a glimpse of the royal party. Here was a bit of pomp and excitement during this solemn, festive week.

Renaldo's assignment had gone smoothly, despite bitter complaints from the merchants. For the second consecutive day, they had been shunted aside by a would-be king. There was no joy among their ranks. In fact, the anger and hostility were palpable. Renaldo later told me you could sense it seething below the surface, ready to erupt—a volcano in search of a vent. But in the end, what could they do? They were not about to take on the Roman army.

My inspection of the tether lines was uneventful. The men had done a fine job, though I would have preferred having the stakes driven about a horse length closer to the east wall. This would have afforded at least an hour more shade from the afternoon sun. But there was no time to be fussy. There were plenty of other things demanding urgent attention.

I and the cavalrymen with me hastily returned to the stables that encircled the hippodrome.

My groomsman had done his job well in preparation for this event. The time had come to don our ceremonial apparel, and all was laid out in orderly fashion. He began by helping me out of my everyday uniform, a stiff multilayered linen cuirass with accompanying greaves. After stripping down to nothing but a loin cloth, I was ready to be outfitted in the best armor the empire had to offer.

First, I was handed a burgundy linen tunic. This served as a kind of foundation garment over top of which the armor itself was mounted. Next came freshly polished footware, followed by burnished bronze riding greaves. Believe me, the groomsman's help in strapping these on and assuring a comfortable fit was much appreciated. Watching the other men struggle unassisted made me thankful for an extra pair of hands.

Next came the highly polished muscled cuirass of brilliant brass. It was rather like strapping on a tortoise shell. It has double hinges on either side joining the breastplate to the backplate. The left half of this hinged shell is commonly left open, thereby granting access. Having by this means slipped inside the cuirass, my groomsman slid a leather strap through the two rings on either side of the first hinge. By drawing the leather strap tight he was able to align the two matching parts of the open hinge, and slide in the metal hinge pin, thus securing it. This process had to be repeated four times. One hinge lay just below the arm opening, followed by another one at the waist. Then there were two more hinges, one at the top of each shoulder.

The end result should be a tight yet comfortable fit, with the muscled cuirass fitting perfectly to the contour of the body. May the gods help the slovenly man who has put on weight.

The time had now come to strap on my belt or cingulum with its loin protecting strips of studded leather. The sword, with its highly ornamented scabbard, was also attached to the belt. The gold pattern found on the scabbard was incorporated into the hilt, the handle, and the pommel of the ceremonial sword.

Next, gold fringed epaulettes were fastened to the brass shoulder rings, which in turn were used to secure the scarlet riding cape. It was the epaulettes and cape that above all else served to distinguish a mounted officer from the rank and file cavalrymen out on the field.

Finally came the highly embellished helmet which, by my own choice, was capped with a jet-black horsehair crest. We took pride not only in our military might, but also in our ability to impress. After all, what glory is there in triumph if triumph is unseen?

Of course not only the horsemen needed ceremonial dress. The horses were also outfitted in the finest polished leather harness, embossed and adorned with silver studs.

I was just completing a walkabout inspection of my horse when, from behind me, I heard my name called. I swung round to see a very different looking Flavio, resplendent in burnished bronze armor, mounted on his white charger.

"Get on your horse, centurion," he ordered. "We've got work to do."

The time had come to put into effect the decisions reached the day before in our joint meeting.

"Do a final inspection of the route from the Praetorium back to the Fish Gate," Flavio continued. "I'll lead the cavalry out to their positions along the highway, and then I'll come back to meet you at the gate. Together, we'll ride out to greet the old Fox."

Having said this, Flavio headed off in the direction of the parade grounds, where three hundred cavalrymen were already beginning to assemble.

I mounted my horse and, taking a contingent of ten horsemen with me, I headed directly to the grand stairs at the east end of the Praetorium. From there we followed the main street leading north to the Fish Gate.

Three hundred foot soldiers had been deployed at regular intervals on both sides of the street. Their job was to ensure the street was free of traffic, and secondly, they were to limit the spectators to a single line on either side of the narrow street. Excess people were either ordered off the street, or told to move outside the city gate, where there was far more open space. In addition, every street intersecting with the tetrarch's route was blocked by two cavalrymen.

About half way along the route, I spotted Renaldo on horseback in conversation with two such cavalrymen. I approached.

"All looks well," I commented, motioning down the street with a jerk of my head.

He nodded.

"It's a far sight better than when I saw it this morning," I added.

"Now, if we can just keep it this way till that pompous little jackal gets through here," Renaldo dead panned.

"You do just that!" I urged. "I'm counting on you."

I and my party moved on. Upon reaching the gate, I waited. Flavio's cavalrymen had taken their positions at regular intervals on either side of the highway stretching off into the distance for about half a mile. The curious lined the route, up to five deep in places.

After a brief pause, I approached the closest cavalryman and inquired about the tribune's whereabouts. He reported that Flavio had proceeded up the highway as planned, and should be returning shortly. Due to the curvature of the road, and the rise and fall of the terrain, he was quite out of sight.

It was drawing close to the appointed time.

At last, Flavio approached on his mount. "Marcus, is all well?" he inquired.

"Everything's clear, right up to the steps of the Praetorium."

"Then we'll be off to greet the king."

Except for the rhythmic clopping of the horse's hooves on the broad paving stones, we rode in silence, side by side, up the imperial highway. My contingent of ten cavalrymen trailed behind us. Opposite the victimless uprights of Golgotha, at the fork in the road leading to the Gannath Gate, we stopped.

The road ahead dipped abruptly into a narrow valley, then emerged again on a ridge along the horizon. Within moments a messenger arrived and reported that Herod and his party were just beyond the ridge.

Minutes passed.

Then the tetrarch's standard bearer appeared along the ridge, like a mirage in the shimmering heat of the sun. The foot soldiers appeared next, trudging in rows six abreast. They were followed by men on horseback four abreast, and then by spear men. Row on row they appeared upon the ridge, then descended into the valley before them. The king's litter was briefly outlined against the horizon. Then came a cluster of porters, retainers and court officials, more foot soldiers, more spear men, more cavalry.

By this time the standard bearer had arrived before us. A halt was called to the march. Herod's general, his legion commander, appeared before us on a fine chestnut steed.

Recognizing a familiar face, Flavio began, "Greetings Caius."

"Flavio," Caius responded and nodded his welcome.

"All has been made ready. The route has been secured. The governor awaits his majesty's arrival."

Again Caius nodded, then cast his gaze down the broad road leading to the city gate, lined with people, marked at regular intervals with mounted guards. He raised a furrowed brow. "Quite impressive, Flavio. I didn't think you were capable of this—this fine display," Caius conceded.

"Ah, you will know me better in the days to come," the tribune answered.

"Shall we inform the king of your fine welcome?"

"Let's," grinned Flavio, obviously pleased with himself, and the general's proposal. "Let's do that."

Leaving my ten cavalrymen behind, Caius led Flavio and me, back up the highway to his master. We squeezed our way down the right side of the road past the general's weary troops.

Herod's litter was truly a sight to behold. Borne on two stout fourteen-foot long poles by twelve semi-naked men, the luxurious compartment itself was six feet long. In it, both Herod and Herodius reclined, facing each other. The roof of the litter rose from each of the four Doric columned corners to form a peak in the center. On the crown of this peak rested an exquisitely carved, gold ruby-eyed cobra. Each top corner of the litter was spiked with the upturned sweep of a golden horn. Royal purple brocaded silk was used throughout, and it was accented with gold fringe.

The gold-fringed and tasseled drapes were drawn fully open when we arrived, and from the litter itself dangled two short hairy legs—legs belonging to Herod the Tetrarch.

"Get on your knees, you sons of harlotry!" he bellowed.

The litter bearers promptly responded.

"Now, let's have some wine for my queen. And get the crest dusted off."

From behind the litter the wine steward quickly appeared, bearing a gold chalice for Herodius. A young female slave used something resembling a feather duster on a long pole, to brush off any offending road dust from the gold cobra on the roof.

It was an odd choice for an adornment or family symbol. It was a choice that appeared even more incongruent because of the religious tradition of this ruler's subjects.

Now the clatter of our horses' hooves drew the king's attention. Spotting a familiar face among the three horsemen before him, he inquired, "Ah, Caius, are we near?"

"Indeed, your majesty. The city lies directly before us."

The king poked a balding head out of the litter, but seeing little he yelled, "On your feet, you swine."

In unison the litter bearers struggled to their feet from the kneeling position.

Herod again peered out, but still seeing very little, he yelled, "Higher you swine!"

Now with valiant effort the hapless slaves lifted the carrying poles from above their shoulders, to a position above their heads. To go any higher they would have needed wings.

Still seeing nothing, Herod shook his head, and in utter disgust he glared at his attendants.

By way of explanation, Caius felt compelled to intervene. "The city is in plain view, from the hill just ahead, my lord."

"Who asked you to speak?" Herod snapped. With an upward wave of the back of his hand, he ordered, "On with us, then!"

Shaking off this rebuke, Caius barked out his command, "Forward… march!"

The caravan responded, slowly at first, as the message was relayed to the front of the column. We, too, moved forward, keeping pace with the royal litter.

I felt awkward—out of place. By not acknowledging our presence, Herod had left us hanging—ignored by the king. Flavio in particular must have felt the sting of this.

In a few moments the hilltop was gained. Caius called a halt. The king stuck his head out and peered down the highway to the city.

"Hm!" He drew in a long satisfied breath as he assessed what lay before him.

He slumped back into the litter, and then began barking out a stream of rapid fire orders to his attendants.

"My crown. Bring my crown."

"The jeweled robe. Get the jeweled robe."

"Get dressed, Herodius."

Then realizing the litter was still in midair, he ordered, "Down! Get me down, you swine!"

The slaves once again descended to their knees, then leaned fully forward, bringing the litter lower yet.

Herod hopped out slipped out of a flimsy purple robe, and into a beautiful, jewel-encrusted, gold-trimmed, fabrication. When the crown arrived, he snatched it from the cushion before him. Placing it on his bald head, he wailed, "The mirror—get the mirror! You harlots!"

Looking into it, he seemed suitably impressed with what he saw. And satisfied with his appearance, he perched himself on the edge of the litter, and looked up.

Seeing his opportunity, Caius again ventured to speak. "The tribune, Flavio here," he motioned with his hand, "has arrived with greetings from the governor, my lord."

"Yes, your highness," Flavio bowed. "His excellency sends greetings. He awaits your arrival at the Praetorium. Marcus here," he nodded in my direction and I bowed to the king, "has himself inspected and secured the route. We are at your service, ready to escort you to his excellency."

For a moment Herod gathered his thoughts. Then he fixed his eyes on Flavio and began, "Appoint ten of your own men to go before us as heralds. Let them cry out, 'Make way for the king!' Many of my own subjects are here for the Passover, and to them I am king." He spoke these last words as a kind of bitter justification.

Then looking to Caius he asked, "Are the trumpeters ready with their fanfare? And my own heralds near the litter here, see that they cry out, 'Bow before the king!'"

"I'll see to it," Caius responded, and rode ahead a few paces to fulfil these orders.

"As for you two," he spoke with a kind of shrill intensity, "you'll ride alongside the litter. If I cry halt, you will halt. If I say proceed, then proceed. There will be common riffraff along the way. If they touch the litter, kill them. If they touch me—you will die. I'll see to that myself. If a hand reaches out with a beggar's bowl, cut it off. I haven't come here to feed the dogs. Do you understand that?"

We both bowed stiffly from the waist. A moment of stunned silence followed. Flavio was first to recover. "By your leave, my lord the king, I will send Marcus here with the orders for our heralds. When he returns, we may proceed at your pleasure."

"Fine. Be off then," he sneered.

A distinct chill crept through my being, as I spurred my horse to a brisk trot. My mind raced. How could I ensure Herod's requirements were met? Brute force may work, but there were no guarantees. Any deranged idiot could get through to the litter if he was determined enough. We had nowhere near enough men to form a wall along the entire route to prevent any such breakthrough.

My chief concern was that none of our troops knew of these new stringent crowd control requirements which Herod had just dictated. I knew the ten men I was about to meet with could form part of my response, but I needed twelve.

My cavalrymen were waiting at the front of Herod's column, just as Flavio and I had left them. I ignored them and rode past. I then beckoned the first two mounted guards beyond them, to meet me in the middle of the highway.

"You have new orders. You are now messengers. Hear me now. Quickly move along the route from here all the way to the Praetorium. Order each of our men to keep the people off the road —on the threat of death. Have them announce it immediately. Tell them to chase any beggars away. Order them out of sight. Herod wants any hand reaching out with a beggar's bowl cut off. So chase the beggars off. Why should we be that jackal's butcher?"

Then looking intently at them I said, "Did you get that? Repeat it back."

When the man on my left succeeded in repeating the essence of the message they were to transmit, I sent them off.

I then returned to my own ten cavalrymen and gathered them around me. "You are no longer armed escorts. Herod wants you as his royal heralds," I reported.

This news was greeted by some with looks of disdain. "You are to call out, 'Make way for the king! Make way for the king!'" Even more looks of disdain.

"Now, you need to do that. Call it out. But your real job here is to make sure no one gets on the road, or steps out of line back in the city—not so much as a young child wandering onto the route. I have orders to kill anyone who touches the royal litter.

"And no beggars," I continued. "If Herod sees a hand reaching out with a beggar's bowl, he wants it cut off. So watch for them. If you see even one beggar tell them, 'Herod's men will cut your hand off. Get away! Out of sight, before he comes!' If they refuse to listen, or move, draw your sword and chase them off." Once again I added, "I don't want to be Herod's butcher. So do your job well. Now, I want you to advance in groups of two when we start out." I signaled this with two fingers raised. "Leave about twenty or thirty paces between each pair."

"Have you got all that?" I had one of them repeat their instructions, and then had them arrange themselves in teams of two. I wanted no room left for error.

"I'm going back to Herod. When he's ready, he'll give the word, and you'll start." I pointed to the first two conscripted heralds in the processional.

Giving all these instructions had taken more time than I had anticipated, so I stormed back to Herod's litter, fully expecting a rebuke.

I arrived to find the slave with the duster, busy fussing over the gold horns on corners of the litter's roof. Another slave was combing and pinning the queen's hair. As for Herod, he was holding a mirror and cursing the young female slave who was trimming his beard. On seeing me arrive, he brusquely pushed her aside, then he followed that up with a well-aimed leering smile in her direction.

"Your majesty," I bowed forward from the waist, "the heralds have been appointed. All is ready. We await your pleasure."

"It took you bloody long enough!" he barked. Then motioning with his hand, he directed, "You'll ride there, on the left side of the litter, just a bit behind me. Don't block my view or I'll have you castrated. You hear that?"

"Yes, your highness."

I would soon discover that Herod's threats were not mere bluff and bluster.

I maneuvered my horse to the back of the litter. Flavio was already in his assigned position, slightly ahead of the open litter, right alongside the front set of litter bearers. I would ride parallel with the rear set of litter bearers. Immediately beside me a tall brutish looking foot soldier was posted, apparently one of Herod's personal bodyguards. A bodyguard of equal stature stood alongside Flavio. These men were closest to the edge of the highway, and served as the first line of defense should any unruly person from the crowd dare to advance toward the king.

On the right side of the litter the same pattern was repeated. Caius rode beside the front of the litter with an accompanying body guard to his immediate right. At the rear right of the litter rode a centurion under his command, flanked by the fourth bodyguard to complete the array. A further array of twenty-four swordsmen would walk with swords drawn immediately before and behind the litter in ranks six abreast.

The start of the procession was delayed, despite the urgent haste Herod had called for. Herodius needed more time with her hair, and a perfumer was called to anoint the royal couple. Soon the heavy scent of nard blended with the reek of human sweat.

To wile away the time, the muscular bodyguard to my left amused himself by slashing away with his drawn sword at some imaginary foe.

At last, the Herods were ready. The litter bearers stood erect, and Caius called out the order to advance.

"Now walk like men, not like camels, you swine," Herod hollered out to his bearers.

The first few hundred yards were uneventful. The trumpeters blew their fanfare. The heralds near the litter shouted, "Bow before the king!" And the cowed populace dutifully responded. There were no beggars in sight, and no one dared venture onto the imperial highway. I was confident my own advance men had done their job well.

About two hundred yards from the Fish Gate, Herod caught sight of a white-robed delegation off to his right. Perhaps it was the glint of gold embroidered thread and jeweled adornments that caught his attention. He called a halt to our advance. The litter was lowered, and three of the plumpest white robes were beckoned by the king to come forward. One of them I immediately recognized as Timaeus of Damascus.

I strained desperately to hear the full conversation, but since this delegation stood on the opposite side of the highway, I could only make out a few words. I overheard something about impediments to commerce, and so-called prophets misusing the great temple. To this Herod responded with the only words I heard distinctly, "I will meet with you Thursday."

In moments we were off again, only to be halted once more by another delegation on the right. We stopped just before the city gate. It was Caiaphas, the high priest himself, along with several of his family members. They made a great show of bowing low in their elaborate finery. Undoubtedly, they were here to welcome this Herod to the city; perhaps to invite him to visit the great temple his father had built.

Herod called them over. Try as I might, I could not make out a single word, though I could distinguish the high priest's voice from the others. His voice has always reminded me of the sound of rusty hinges. The creaking somehow cut through the other noises in the air. Yet I was still unable to decipher what was spoken.

The litter rose once again. We passed through the Fish Gate. I could feel my body relaxing somewhat from the tension. We were over halfway to the Praetorium without incident.

Suddenly just ahead, among the bowing throng, a small copper bowl flashed in the sun. I sucked in a shallow breath, and hoped it had gone unnoticed.

Herod's hand shot out from the left side of the litter, just a few feet above and ahead of my horse's ears.

"There! There!" he yelled. "Stop the litter!"

Flavio bellowed, "Halt!"

"Bring the boy over." Herod gestured to the bodyguard next to me.

The guard beckoned with his hand and the once crippled Lucas stepped forward. He wore a shy smile, but there was an eager glint in his eye.

"Is that a beggar's bowl in your hand?" the king inquired.

"Yes, sir."

"I didn't come to feed beggars," Herod said coldly.

"Now, teach this boy not to beg from a king." Herod again gestured to the guard.

With one hand the guard grabbed the boy's free hand. He raised his gleaming sword above his head.

With sudden terror in his eyes, Lucas instinctively yanked back.

The blade flashed down.

The boy fell back into the crowd as the guard triumphantly raised the severed, dripping hand above his head.

"Well done, Cestas!" Herod cheered. "Well done!"

White-faced and stumbling, I saw Lucas flee, clutching tight the bleeding stump.

"There are no beggars in Galilee," the Fox announced to the crowd. "And if I ruled here, there would be none in Jerusalem."

The onlookers were stunned, riveted to the spot.

Herod paused, and after a brief search he pulled out the flimsy purple robe from among the cushions behind him. He made a great show of folding it carefully several times.

"Now bring me your trophy."

Cestas came forward—placed the small severed hand in the folds of the purple robe—bowed graciously to his monarch.

"Ah, tribute for the governor." Herod laughed coarsely. "Let's be off!"

The remainder of the processional was uneventful. Following the trumpeters' fanfare, Pontius Pilate and his wife, Claudia Procula, received the tetrarch graciously, with considerable pomp. The Roman governor politely inquired about the journey, and made flattering comments about Herodius and her attire.

As for Herod, he seemed perfectly jovial and invigorated. He commented about wishing to make a presentation of a small item at the banquet that evening. He committed the purple bundle to one of his attendants, and then arm in arm with Herodius, he accompanied the governor up the grand stairway to the Praetorium.

My duties as a royal escort had come to an end.

14

WHEN I RETURNED AFTER MY ASSIGNMENT WITH HEROD, I found Claudius at the Golden Gate. He was positively effusive. I had to slow him down so I could understand what he was saying, and I insisted he start at the beginning.

"Well, when we got into the temple compound, Jesus spotted some men carrying goods through the temple courts. He immediately stopped them. I think this was all just a ruse. It was just an attempt by those same merchants to set up shop in there again. He saw right through it, and sent them packing."

"Then he began teaching," Claudius continued. "I've never heard anyone teach like him. It was so different."

"How?" I asked. "How was it different?"

He thought a moment before answering, "Well, I guess it was the examples—the parables he used. I didn't always fully understand what he meant. I guess it's because I'm not a Jew, but when I understood, I really understood. I suppose it's because his parables would take a certain truth and make it simple, something you could grasp. He talked a lot about the kingdom of God."

"The kingdom of God," I huffed. "So, tell me about this kingdom of God."

I spoke the words with a certain disdain. After what I had witnessed in the past few hours, kings and their kingdoms had lost their appeal. I was in no mood to be regaled with accounts of conquest and might, not from some power-hungry would-be Jewish messiah.

Claudius could sense my reticence but, brimming with enthusiasm, he pressed on, "I'm really not sure that the kingdom he's talking about is anything like what we call a kingdom. Actually, the more I listened to him, the more I became convinced he's talking about something totally different."

"So what's so different about this Jesus and his kingdom?"

I could tell I really had him thinking now.

"Well, Jesus?" he struggled for words. "I've never heard anyone like him. It's like he knows God. I mean, really knows God—the God who made everything—like they sat down and planned the world together."

I could not help but chuckle at this notion, yet at the same time I understood exactly what he meant. I had watched Jesus pray. I had sensed both the power and the mystery of those moments.

"Did you notice that, too?" he inquired.

"I guess I did," I admitted. "But... he just gave me this eerie, uneasy feeling, like he was connected to someone, or something far bigger. And I was small—smaller than I've ever been."

"Hmm," he mused. "I know what you mean. I felt that way too," he reflected, but then he was struck by another thought.

"But he talked about God like a father—not far away, but near —near as the next breath. And as though he cares, really cares about us, not like our Roman gods. He said we shouldn't worry because our heavenly Father knows what we need. He even knows if a sparrow falls, and he knows the number of hairs on our head." He impulsively ran his fingers through his dark brown hair, and then added, "I heard him say that."

I fell silent. But I wanted to snap back at him. Snap back about what I had just seen happen to Lucas. Snap back about my daughter, Tara. Snap back about a thousand and one injustices that I have seen in this botched world. Caring? Where was this caring God? But after a long pause, I just changed the topic, "Yes, but this

Jewish dog talks about a kingdom. You still haven't told me about his plans for this glorious kingdom?"

Claudius could not help noticing the hard edge to my voice, so he began more tentatively, "Well, if I understood him correctly, it's where God rules. It's where His will—God's will—is done. I don't think it's so much a place, a physical place, as it is a state of the heart—a place where people know God, and love and obey Him. I'm really not sure that he's here to overthrow Rome."

"Then why is he here?"

"I'm not sure I really know," Claudius answered. "I guess he wants to somehow connect people with God—get them together. Connected—like he is connected with God."

"Hm!" I sniffed at this notion.

But Claudius went on. "One thing I do know for sure; those fancy-robed religious leaders don't like him much. Jesus taught for a while this morning, when all of a sudden the high priest, along with maybe ten other officials, came marching in. They demanded to know by what authority he was doing these things. He didn't answer them, but instead, he asked them a question. He asked them, 'By what authority did John baptize?' They talked it over, and then said, *'We don't know.'*[11] So, he said he wouldn't answer their question either. So they just turned around and left in a holy huff. You could really tell the crowd around Jesus just loved the way he handled these high and mighty holy types." Claudius abruptly turned to me and asked, "Who was this John anyway?"

"A few years back, he caused quite a stir. Thousands of people went out to the Jordan River to hear him. He insisted that people repent, turn from their sins, and then he would baptize them in the river. Even some of my own men went out to hear him.[12] In the end, Herod the Tetrarch had him beheaded."

After reflecting a moment on the day's events, I caustically commented, "You know, that bloody old Fox hasn't changed much."[13]

"Anyway," Claudius continued, "from then on Jesus would teach for a while, and then some new high-powered delegation would arrive to question him. They weren't sincere in their questions. It was like they were trying to trap him into saying something they could later use against him. That's all I think they were after. But in the end Jesus always turned the tables on them. He would expose their real motives. He could see right through them."

I felt a certain remembered discomfort when Claudius said those words. After all, Jesus' eyes had shone a light on the darkness of my own soul. I do not know why I felt so naked, so transparent before this man.

"But Claudius, what makes you so sure he's not here to kick out the Romans?"

"It was the way he answered one of those fancy-robed delegations. They asked him if it was lawful to pay taxes to Caesar. He called them hypocrites right to their faces. He accused them of trying to trap him. Then he asked for a coin. He demanded to know whose portrait and inscription were on it. When they answered, 'Caesar's,' he jumped on them—like a cat onto a nest of mice. He told them, *'Give to Caesar what is Caesar's, and to God what is God's.'*[14] Even at a distance, I could see their mouths drop, and their ears catch fire. They left like cowering dogs with their tails between their legs."

Claudius became even more animated as he said, "The crowd—the crowd loved it. You could really tell the people loved seeing those phony religious officials get a taste of a little humility. I'm sure they haven't tasted it for a good long while." He paused. "That's why I don't think he's a threat to us. He's not opposed to paying taxes. Nothing he said all day makes me think he's got a quarrel with Rome. But he's sure got the religious leaders worried and bothered. Later in the day he went after them full force. Called them hypocrites, blind guides, a brood of vipers!"[15]

"Ooo! I'm sure they were pleased," I commented sarcastically.

This assessment actually confirmed what Renaldo and I had been thinking. I had heard the same thing reflected back to me by Flavio. This latest evidence on taxes lent considerable weight to the conclusion Claudius had drawn. But I still felt uneasy. Jesus simply struck me as such a huge, larger than life figure—the kind of person you do not dismiss lightly, no matter what others say. I somehow felt all we had done thus far was scratch the surface. I'm not sure I really understood him at all. How could I begin to fathom what he was trying to accomplish?

But Claudius was not finished.

"You know, about this kingdom notion," he continued. "Jesus told another story, and it helped me catch what he was driving at. He talked about a landowner who planted a vineyard, and then went away. He rented the land out to farmers, but when he sent servants to collect the rent they would beat them up, or kill them. Finally, in desperation, he sent his own son to collect the rent, thinking they would respect him. But the renters said, 'Let's kill him and the land will be ours.' So they took the son outside the vineyard and killed him.

"Then Jesus asked the people around him what would happen to those renters when the owner came back. They answered that the landowner would kill those miserable renters, and give the vineyard to someone else who would pay him on time.

"Well, Jesus said they were right. And then he said—now catch this—" Claudius gestured with an upraised index finger, "'*The kingdom of God will be taken away from you and given to a people who will produce its fruit.*'[16] Those were his very words."

"What did he mean by that?" I asked quite mystified.

"I wasn't too sure myself, at first. But I knew he said this as a rebuke to the high priest and the religious establishment. Everyone there knew he was telling this story against them. But later I asked the man beside me what he thought Jesus meant by this parable. He said that the landowner was God, the religious leaders were the renters, and the servants who came to collect the rent were the prophets of the past. We just weren't sure who the son was. I suggested that Jesus himself might be the son. But he just looked at me like I was a complete idiot, shook his head and said, 'God doesn't have a son.' I kept my mouth shut after that."

"Well, then," I surmised, "this prophet, this Jesus, really has set himself up in opposition to the religious authorities. If he's publicly predicting the end of their rule, he has really picked a fight with them." I sucked in a long slow breath. "And Claudius," I said, nodding in his direction, "it'll be a fight to the finish." I continued as my mind caught the implications of my own words. "Jesus may have the people, or at least a good number of the common people on his side. But Caiaphas is nobody's fool. He's got money and power behind him. The son in that story, if that's who Jesus is?" I gestured my question with an upraised open palm. "Well, he might yet be taken out and killed."

15

Tuesday 7:00 p.m. April 4th, 30 AD

MOST OF MY CONVERSATION WITH CLAUDIUS HAD TAKEN PLACE as we slowly ambled along the top of the city wall from the Golden Gate, past the Sheep Gate, and onto the Antonia Fortress.

An official reception, complete with a hearty meal, had been planned for the arriving troops. While Pontius Pilate entertained Flavio, Herod Antipas and the tetrarch's general, Caius inside the governor's palace apartment, the common soldiers were feasting in the central courtyard of the fortress. Huge cauldrons of thick stew had been simmering over charcoal fires for a good part of the day. By the time we arrived they were almost empty. Their contents had been ladled into the soldiers' pewter bowls, and the men were now scattered about the courtyard, some sitting on crude benches, while others ate, bowl in hand, standing in diverse clumps.

Claudius hurried off to retrieve his own bowl from within the barracks, while I made my way to a kind of second-level dais overlooking the courtyard from the north side. That is where the centurions dined.

A long table had been set up, and on either side of this table the centurions were already seated. Most had just begun their meal which, unlike that of the common soldier, consisted largely of roast lamb.

I took a seat at the only spot left open. It was at the far end of the table, across from one of Herod's centurions. To my left sat Marius, one of the centurions from our own legion.

There was a fine bit of good-natured banter going on when I

arrived. At a suitable moment, Marius introduced me to the two men across from me, and I bowed in greeting.

There was something vaguely familiar about the man across from me, but at first I didn't recognize him. Perhaps it was due to the lighting. By this time the sun had gone down. Even as we arrived, torches were being lit and then fastened to brackets in the stone walls along the perimeter of the courtyard. Due to his seating position, this centurion was turned away from one of these torches and very little light hit his face.

Soon a servant arrived with my meal, and I began to dine.

Wine flowed freely. Voices became more boisterous. Bouts of hearty masculine laughter echoed through the night air.

At one point, the man seated across from me turned his head sideways, so I clearly saw his profile. I recognized him as the centurion who rode escort duty across from me and the litter bearers during Herod's entry just a few hours earlier.

The conversation around me grew more course as discussion turned to women and their ways, then onto feats of strength, then feats in battle. I was attentive, but brooded in silence, distracted by the events of the day.

Then with his lips loosened by ample wine, the bellicose man across from me piped up, "Did you see Cestas today? He sliced off that little beggar's hand like he was cutting through butter. Sure taught him not to beg. Did a damn fine job! I couldn't have done it better myself. Taught a real fine lesson. A mighty fine lesson."

My left hand shot out across the table. I seized him by the metal collar of his breastplate, yanked his body fully across the width of the table, slammed my right fist full into his face, and then flipped the stunned brute off the side of the table.

I pinned him to the floor and yelled, "I'll teach you to keep your bloody butchers out of our town!" I hammered him once more. And I would have done it again, but Marius restrained me, shoving me back on my heels.

I shot to my feet, and pressed forward shaking with blind rage.

Voices yelled all around me.

I shook free of Marius and his hold on me. Then I stormed down the stairs and out of the military compound.

Out... out into the night.

16

Wednesday 1:00 a.m. April 5th, 30 AD

AFTER KNOCKING REPEATEDLY, ARIUS THE GATEKEEPER FINALLY arrived and opened the barred wooden gate.

"Master!" his voice betrayed a measure of surprise. "Welcome home."

I acknowledged him with a hasty nod, then began briskly striding across the courtyard. Suddenly, I stumbled and nearly fell over the feet of a sleeping soldier.

Ah, yes. Thanks to Herod, or was it Flavio, I had twenty men camped out in my villa courtyard. In the moonlight, I threaded my way around them to reach the stairway leading to the family bedrooms on the second level.

I passed by our own bedroom, and quietly moved to our sons' room. Gently taking a hold of the worn leather strap that served as a handle, I slowly eased the door open. I was actually amazed that, for once, the hinges didn't creak. I lightly inched my way into the room.

The boys slept on two separate beds on either side of the room. There was a broad open window directly ahead of me, through which a brilliant full moon was visible. I listened for their steady breathing, and waited a few moments for my eyes to adjust to the light level. Then, with slow, deliberate steps I moved to the bed on the right side of the room. I stooped, and ever so gently grasped the hand of my older son, Julius. I heard him swallow, but he did not wake. His breathing continued with that soothing rhythm common to a sleeping child.

His hand was warm… small… a perfect hand. Perfect fingers. A perfect little hand resting on the palm of my own large, rough hand.

93

I let go of his hand, straightened, turned, and with the same slow deliberate steps I moved to the other side of the room.

I took my younger son's hand, Andrew. Held it in mine. Felt its warmth and life. Laid it gently down.

I turned to go, then felt impressed to stop in the middle of the room between my two sons. I raised both of my hands about shoulder height, palms open, much as I had seen Jewish men do. While slowly raising my head, I whispered, "God of heaven, take care of my sons. Take care of my sons."

I eased the door shut behind me, and through the dark shadows, shuffled my way to my own bedroom.

This time the door creaked when I opened it.

"Marcus?" Zelda whispered into the darkness. There was worry in her voice.

"Yes, it's me." I sighed. I began to undress.

"Marcus, I was so worried. Are you all right?"

"Yes, I'm fine." I paused a moment or two. "I nearly killed a man, but I'm fine."

"Marcus!" Now I really knew she was worried. She threw back the covers and bounded out of bed. She was at my side in an instant, pulling me close to herself.

"Are you sure you're all right? Come to the window so I can see you."

She tugged lightly on my sleeve.

"Just let me get this off," I said, referring to my tunic.

I knew she wouldn't be satisfied without a full inspection, so I pulled the garment over my head and tossed it on a bench. I was glad to be free of it after such a long day.

"Come. Come now to the window," she urged.

"See, I'm fine." I began to speak the words before we even arrived at the window, before she had a chance to look.

She reached her hand to my chin, and turned my face from

side to side in the moonlight, searching for the bruise or cut that was not there.

"Your *'all right,'* isn't always all right," she chided.

"Well, I'm fine. See," I said, reaching out to place my hands on her shoulders.

"You're fine all over?" she inquired quite in earnest.

"I'm fine all over."

I drew her close and wrapped my arms around her as a form of proof.

"I was so worried," she continued, looking up at me. "You said you would come home with the other men. They started coming, and you weren't with them. Claudius didn't know where you were. Nobody knew. You know I don't like being alone with all those rowdy men down there."

There was more than a hint of anger in her voice, and she drew back a step.

"I know. I know," I said trying to be reassuring. "I just had a horrible night—a horrible day. It was awful."

"So you got in a fight?"

"I guess you could call it that. I beat somebody up."

"Well, I hope he deserved it."

"Oh!" I nodded my head. "Oh, he deserved it. Deserved far more than he got." Changing the topic, I added, "You know I'm getting cold standing by this window." I hugged her warm body close to me again. "And further more, I'm tired, very tired. I think we should go to bed before I collapse in a heap."

"Ah, you poor man," she said with a deep melodramatic sigh.

We crawled under the covers. And she received me gladly. We loved one another. In her arms I found happiness.

It was the only good thing about the day. Like so many other days, she and the boys were often the only good things about this life.

17

Wednesday Morning, April 5th, 30 AD

IT BEGAN TO RAIN ABOUT TWO HOURS BEFORE SUNRISE. I HEARD curses—men cursing in my dreams. It took a while to realize the curses were coming from the men downstairs in the open courtyard. It seems soldiers are never fond of getting soaked while they sleep.

The rain had started sporadically at first. It almost stopped, but then began in earnest. That is when it roused all the men. Arius had had the good sense to open the kitchen door and let some of the wet and irritated soldiers sleep on the floor in there. More room was found in a storage shed near the gate, and even in the hallway of the servants' quarters. Nevertheless, when I got up in the morning, I found four men sleeping on mats on the second level balcony just outside our door.

The rain was steady and the sky uniformly gray from horizon to zenith, and down to the distant horizon again.

Our household cook was summoned. He reported that as planned, breakfast was ready. Any men still sleeping were roused. A thick heavy porridge was dispensed into tin bowls using a wooden hand paddle. The men ate in grim silence.

Together we slogged off through the pouring rain to the barracks at the Antonia Fortress. My men assigned to sleep along the top of the wall were already there.

They had not fared much better in the rain. When the downpour started, most of them had left the wall and had crowded into the city gates at ground level. Until sunrise, they were forced to make do with the meager shelter the gates afforded.

Due to the weather, it was an equipment day. Swords were sharpened. Spears were repointed. Shields were oiled. Bridles and halters were tended to. Footwear was repaired and clothing was mended. The legion's smiths and cobblers were a busy lot.

I called for an equipment inspection in the early afternoon, all the while hoping the rain would stop and the sky would clear. It was a faint hope. This weather had all the earmarks of a two or three-day general rain, something we had not yet had that spring. With their crops freshly planted, there would be many a happy farmer in the land, but I was left feeling anxious.

What worried me most was a chance encounter with Herod's centurion, the one whose face my fist encountered the night before. I worried about a revenge attack, or worse yet that he might bring the matter before Caius, or, may the gods have mercy, before the gold-crowned Fox himself. The threat Herod made yesterday still rang in my ears. Over the years I have become affectionately attached to every part of my anatomy. I would fight any loss to the point of death.

I was beginning to think that I liked the pretend-king on a donkey far better than the pretend-king carried on a gold encrusted litter.

I had planned to send Claudius back into the temple compound to continue his undercover education at the feet of Jesus of Nazareth, but the rain killed that plan. Hardly a soul stirred from their homes, and the temple area with its broad open-air courtyard was largely deserted.

I busied myself in the stable workshop attaching some silver adornments to my horse's ceremonial bridle. It was the kind of work I could have easily left to my groomsman who was employed alongside me, tending to other cavalrymen's needs. Yet, throughout my twenty years as a soldier, I have always enjoyed this type of leatherwork, and I was occupying a spot where a chance meeting with my prime rival from Herod's ranks was highly unlikely.

Due to the menial nature of the work, I soon found my thoughts turning back to the events of the previous night. For a time after my fight with Herod's centurion, I had wandered aimlessly about the city streets. I was so filled with rage. I could barely control myself. I clenched my fists over and over, digging my fingernails into the palms of my hands. Even now, I could still see the red marks left in my palms. I knew I needed time to calm down or I would kill someone. I was incensed. I needed to get out of the city, to be alone.

I had wandered out of the Golden Gate and down into the Kidron Valley. There is an olive grove down there running along the slope of the Mount of Olives. In the Aramaic language they call it Gethsemane. I have gone there before to think, or to clear my mind after a particularly difficult day. I felt drawn there now.

Fortunately, there was sufficient moonlight to guide me. I avoided the dark shadows and moved slowly, not fully trusting my footing on the uneven path that led into the grove. Soon, off to the right I heard male voices speaking in quiet tones. Instinctively, my right hand came to rest on the pommel of my sword. I need not have worried. Possibly a dozen men were sitting or reclining around a white-robed figure in the shadows about twenty paces off the path. They ignored my passing as I hurried by.

I made my way farther up the slope, finally stopping at a bare rock outcropping from which I could faintly perceive the outline of the city walls and the silhouette of the great temple on the opposite slope. Here I sat down.

Just getting out of the city brought a measure of calm to my spirit, but almost immediately anxious thoughts flooded in. Beating up a fellow officer in an unprovoked fight, as I had just done, could result in dire consequences. There were consequences I didn't even want to think about. If I were called to account for my conduct, running off, as I also had just done, would do little to advance my case. All these thoughts troubled me.

For a time, I seriously considered returning to the city, considered getting thoroughly drunk to forget my troubles, considered visiting Pedrum's brothel for a little physical pleasure to ease the anguish in my soul. Briefly, I even considered ending it all by jumping from the pinnacle of the temple, that high point on my section of the wall that drops cliff-like into the Kidron.

I got up to do one, or all of these, when I suddenly remembered Jesus. I remembered the words Claudius had attributed to him—about the Jewish God knowing if even a sparrow falls, and about Him knowing the number of hairs on my head.

Was this God watching me now?

Did he care even one wit about what happened to me? About what had happened to Lucas? About what had happened to Tara?

The crickets chirped. A million stars illuminated the sky. Every breath I drew was filled with the moist fresh scent of life—the life of spring. A gentle breeze stirred the leaves of the nearby trees. Even in this darkness, stark quiet beauty surrounded me—assaulted all my senses.

I thought of death—thought of life—thought of family. I thought about all the apparent contradictions in this life, thought about this God who cares, and how yet, terrible things happen to innocent people.

How could this Almighty God, working through a mortal man, heal a crippled boy one day and on the very next day, allow the same boy's hand to be cut off by some demon in human flesh? I shook my head in bewilderment.

Then I thought about the deep contradictions in my own life, about my own actions, the darkness in my own past.

Does anything ever make sense?

I sat down again. I prayed, bowing forward in the direction of the temple. Poured out all my troubles, all my frustration. Prayed for the beggar boy. Prayed as though someone would hear.

After a long while I got up and went home.

I did not understand it. I did not understand life, or God, or this man called Jesus. I understood the mess I was in, and it felt good just to speak out my frustration.

Maybe I did not just speak my words into the night air. Maybe someone in the broad starry expanse above did hear me. In any case, I left the hillside strangely at peace, more willing to face the next day and whatever anguish or joy it might bring.

"So how's our banquet table warrior?"

It was Renaldo's voice cutting through my thoughts and bringing me sharply back to the present.

"Oh, I'm fine," I answered with a quizzical grin as I looked up from my work. "Banquet table warrior? Is that what I'm called now?"

"That's your new name, Marcus. Banquet Table Warrior. Marius thought up your new title. We all think it has a certain ring to it, a certain flare." He gestured grandly with his right hand as he beamed. He was obviously enjoying some good-natured humor at my expense. He added, "You did a mighty fine job on that bigmouthed idiot. A mighty fine job! All our men were quite impressed."

"Well, I wasn't trying to impress our men. It was Herod's man who needed his brain rearranged."

"Oh, you did a fine job of that. A fine job. I couldn't have done better myself."

I had not expected this jocular admiration from any of my fellow centurions. But Renaldo continued, "Look, those strutting cocks needed their tail feathers kicked good and hard, and this sooner the better. If this hadn't happened, they'd be running this place by the end of the week. They need to know their place. They're our guests, not our bloody masters."

"So, what happened after I left?"

"Well, that bigmouthed idiot screamed for your head. Marius told him he'd be dead before sunrise if he opened his mouth about this to Caius. He told him he was in our fortress now. Told him to sit down and shut up. And he did. He sat down with his fat bloody lip and drank until he was so drunk that in the end they had to carry him down the stairs. I don't expect we'll see him at all today. If he's smart, he'll keep his head down all week."

My eyebrows shot up when he said these words. I nodded and smiled knowing that a camel's load of worry had just been lifted from my mind.

"No, Marcus, you did us all a big favor last night. A huge favor. The whole week will go better because of it."

"Well, do you know why I clobbered the idiot? It was because of Lucas. They cut off his hand yesterday. During the entry."

"Cut off Lucas' hand?"

"Yes. Cut off his hand," I spoke each word with slow emphatic deliberation, making a downward chopping motion with my right hand, as though I was hacking off my own left hand at the wrist.

"They did it right in front of me. Right in front of Herod. It was at his orders. The bloody butchers! Thought it was great fun. It was Cestas—Herod's bodyguard. He did the job. Then that boneheaded centurion bragged about it last night at the banquet. That's when I let him have it. Bloody butchers!"

"The man's lucky he's alive." Renaldo's eyes narrowed. "I'd have cut him to pieces," he declared through clenched teeth.

I had no reason to doubt his declaration. Renaldo knew Lucas far better than I did. On occasion, he had used him to run small errands, despite his stubby crippled leg. Afterward, he would drop a copper coin into his beggar's bowl.

"I can't believe it." Renaldo shook his head. "What kind of bloody idiot would cut off a kid's hand! Why? Whatever for?"

"Because Herod hates beggars—hates the poor," I seethed. "He told me, 'Cut off every beggar's hand, everyone with a beggar's bowl.' I sent ten of our men ahead to chase off the beggars, but they must have missed Lucas. Maybe he wasn't even there when my men passed by. Anyway, Herod spotted him. And wham! It was over."

Again I made the slashing motion with my right hand as though chopping off my hand. Again, my blood was beginning to boil. The rage I felt the previous night came surging back. I turned from Renaldo and hammered the flat of my fist down on the work-bench behind me. Tools and rivets bounced and rattled. The sharp pain of this action shot through me.

At least I had a hand I could abuse.

Renaldo was silent for several moments. I turned back to face him. He stood with his head bowed. He pinched his eyes closed several times, sighed deeply and repeatedly clenched his right fist. I half-expected him to do the same as I had just done. Instead, with a determined, calm voice, he asked, "What did Lucas do after this happened to him?"

"He just ran off, holding the bleeding stump. It happened so fast. There was nothing I could do."

"He'll be at Pedrum's," he responded, "if he didn't bleed to death—if he's still alive."

"Pedrum's?"

"Yes, Pedrum's." He sighed and rubbed a big hand across his chin, "His mother is one of Pedrum's girls. After his father died, they lost everything. Some money lender, a Pharisee, took it all. They moved into the city, and she got a roof over her head by selling the only thing a woman like her has left to sell."

Again, he pinched his eyes shut, shook his head and said, "Lucas will be there."

He turned from me and began walking away. But he called back, "I'm going to get him. I'll have the legion doctor take a look at him."

He stepped out into the rain and was gone.

I stood in silence. The steady patter of rain on the crude workshop roof seemed to calm my mind. After a few moments, I let out a deep sigh and then shrugged. Maybe on the hillside the night before, my words did not just drift into the still night air. Maybe they were heard?

Maybe....

18

"BELIEVE ME. HE'S ONE TOUGH KID." RENALDO LET HIS BREATH escape with a low whistle. "He took it like a man—like a true soldier. I told him to, and he did. Took it a far sight better than many men I've seen."

Renaldo was responding to my question regarding Lucas and his treatment at the hands of the legion's doctor. We were relaxing around the pool at the Roman bathhouse at the close of the day.

"There's no way he would have survived if I hadn't got him out of there. No way! Pedrum said he wrapped the stump the moment he got to the house. His mother was busy with a customer, so he said he did the best he could. Wrapped some dirty rag around it and tied it tight with twine. Because it was tight, I guess it probably saved his life. But an amputation like that needs proper care. Not what you get at a brothel." Renaldo sniffed in disgust.

"So, what did the doctor say?" I probed.

"Well, after he cauterized the wound—and wow, that really was quite the ordeal!" Renaldo shook his own left hand repeatedly as though he himself had endured this assault to his flesh. "The doctor soaked the stump in some good strong wine, and he told me to bring the boy back tomorrow. He said he'll probably pull through, but he needs proper care, and good food. The wound needs daily cleansing with wine and later with oil."

He paused and combed his fingers through his wet hair before he continued. "I took him home. He's at our house now. Junia managed to get some broth into him before he fell asleep. Tomorrow she'll give him a bath and I'll take him back to the doctor. That brothel is no place for him."

"I won't argue with you on that point. What did his mother say? Did you talk to her?"

"Yes. I think she was relieved. She cried the whole time. I told her we'd look after him until he was better. But she just cried harder. I think it bothers her that she can't really do anything for Lucas. I said she could come see him at our house if Pedrum would let her come. Pedrum agreed, and that seemed to settle her a bit. When I picked Lucas up in my arms to leave, she fell at my feet, bawling. She said, 'Thank you. Take care of him.'"

After a moment's reflection, Renaldo remarked, "I guess time will tell if she comes to see him."

"Or if Pedrum actually lets her leave," I added caustically. "I wouldn't trust that slithering snake. Remember, for him and his kind it's the busiest time of the year. He'll let her go see Lucas if it's to his benefit to let her go, not because of some great sense of compassion."

"Sometimes I think you're too hard on dear old Pedrum. He's probably got a heap more compassion than the Pharisee that seized their land. At least he doesn't cover up his greed by standing and praying in the marketplace by day, and then sneak off at night for some fun with the nearest harlot." Renaldo turned to face me as he continued. I could tell by the intensity in his eyes that he was warming to his topic. "You know that Pedrum tells me some of those fancy-robed religious men are his most regular customers. They're Jewish experts in the law by day, and then come dressed as Gentile whore hunters at night. A real fine bunch! If there is a hell in the afterlife, like these Pharisees so confidently claim, I'm sure it was made just for them."

"Oh, oh, oh!" I laughed and waved a cautionary finger in his direction, "How can you say that? Why, I always thought they were holier than God himself?"

"Holy! If that's holy, I'll drink all this bath water! It's all show and you know it. From start to finish! If you're rich and can parade around in fancy clothes, heaven's gates are open wide." He gestured by throwing his own strong arms wide open. "But may the Almighty help the poor working dog. They'll cheat him out of the rags on his back, steal the crumbs off his table, and then they'll stand and brag about it in front of all the other fat swine. Fat swine!" he spat out the words and shook his head in disgust. "That's all they are. Fat swine in long-fringed robes showing off their fat phylacteries."

"You're beginning to sound like Jesus of Nazareth," I responded.

"Jesus?" he questioned. "What did he say about them?"

"Called them a brood of vipers. Called them blind guides and hypocrites. Said it right in the temple courts. That's what Claudius told me."

"Well, then, there's one Jew who's got them pegged. There are no bigger hypocrites in this world. Say one thing, and then do the opposite. That's what they're all about." He drew a deep breath and grew reflective. "You know, I half believe in their one true God. It makes more sense than our Roman concoction of deities. But I won't bow before Him so that pack of bloodsuckers can lord it over me. Besides which, to them we're just Gentile dogs, the filth of the world, untouchable and unclean. They would never take us in if we even wanted to follow their God. Worse yet," he scoffed, "if they did accept us, we might become just like them."

"You know, Renaldo," I quickly scanned his towel-clad frame, and then winked as I said, "I think you would look really handsome in some fancy-flowing robes."

He whipped the towel from around his waist and gave it a vicious flick that cracked against my hip. I laughed, stepped back and planted my feet ready to counterattack with my own towel, but a second assault never came.

I waved a hand in surrender and said, "Look, I understand what you mean."

Though he smiled weakly, I could tell he was genuinely annoyed by my levity. To show my sincerity I added, "I've been thinking about my own beliefs since that donkey-riding prophet rode into town. He seems to have a way of getting my attention."

"Hey, Marcus, you've got to tell me how that prophet healed Lucas. How did that leg grow like that?" He gestured in bewildered amazement with an upraised hand.

"Well, it was incredible! It was just like I told you the last time. Jesus signaled for Lucas to come up. He put his hands on the boy's shoulders and then told him to stretch out his leg. It was like that limp rag of a leg came to life. The leg started to move. It was as though Lucas kicked downwards, and with each kick the leg grew longer. Then he was touching the ground, and he started to jump—to bounce up and down."

I found myself mimicking these movements. I reached down and ran my hand along the back of my calf as I said, "Suddenly there was muscle in that leg—muscle that wasn't there just a moment ago. It was incredible! Just incredible!"

Renaldo shook his head and then he rubbed his hand across his brow as he absorbed this account. "You know, Marcus, all Lucas would say while the doctor was working on his stump was 'I wish Jesus was here! I wish Jesus was here!' He whispered it over and over again. I think it's what kept him going through the agony of that treatment. I honestly think the boy believes Jesus could heal his hand. I don't mean heal his stump. I mean give him a new hand. Grow it right onto that stump."

I threw up my hands in a questioning gesture. "Who knows? Who knows what Jesus can do? I thought I knew what was possible and what was impossible, but I don't anymore. Not after what I've seen."

Renaldo hung his head in thought, then raised it to look me in the eye. "So do you think he could heal him?"

"I said I don't know. I don't know a lot of things I was sure of before. There's a power there I've never seen before. It's a power that's not from this world. I'm not even sure if he's from this world." I paused and then added, "And I have no idea where this will all end."

I sat down again beside the pool and let my feet dangle in the tepid water. Renaldo put his hand on my shoulder as he eased himself down into a similar position.

"What do you mean by that? How do you think this will end?" he inquired.

"This Galilean prophet's days may be numbered. He's stirred up a hornet's nest by kicking those merchants and money-changerss out of the temple. He's offended and humiliated the high priest and his clan. He's cut off a major source of their temple revenue. He called the Pharisees a brood of vipers. And if that's not enough, he predicted that their power, their kingdom as he calls it, will be taken from them and given to others."

I paused and kicked my right foot out straight, scattering a shower of drops onto the flat surface of the water. "You don't say and do those kind of things without creating some enemies. I'd say he's sealed his own fate."

With a furrowed brow, Renaldo asked, "Where'd you get all this information?"

"Claudius. Claudius told me. Yesterday I had him sit in on one of the prophet's teaching sessions. It was quite an eyeopener. Jesus doesn't just heal the poor; he takes a skewer to the bloated rich. He's publicly opposed the rich and powerful in this town, and his opposition has been right to their face. If nothing else, the man's got courage."

I drummed my fingers on the poolside tiles and then continued, "I tell you, Renaldo, they won't stand for it. They're probably hatching some plot to do away with him right now as we're sitting here talking."

"Yes, but he healed all those kids," he objected. "Doesn't that show that the God of heaven is working through him?"

"The God of heaven? Do you honestly think that matters to them? This is all about money and power. Those are their real gods. Jesus is a threat to their money, and their positions of power. Healing a few poor kids, the offspring of the unclean—that isn't going to mean a thing to them. You're right. You hit the nail on the head. They're puffed up swine who care only about themselves. There isn't a drop of mercy in them." With scathing irony, I added, "But they're right. They're always right. Right to the letter of the law."

"So what do you think they'll do?"

"I'm not sure. But I know what they won't do. They won't arrest him with that crowd around him. They know better than that. They'd have a bloody riot on their hands. There's no doubt about that."

Thought after thought raced in as I considered the implications of my own words. "They might wait till after Passover when the crowds leave, but then Jesus would probably leave with the crowds and head right back to Galilee. Then he'd be out of their hands. No," I hesitated, then briskly snapped my fingers, "I think they'll try to act now, if they can. He's humiliated them in front of the people. They won't stand for that. Caiaphas won't stand for it. Jesus has co-opted the high priest's authority right within the temple courts. Blood will flow because of it. Mark my words. It will flow."

"But what could they do to him? What crime has he committed?" Renaldo reasoned. "You know the Jews can't condemn a man to death. They can't have him crucified. They'd have to bring him before Pilate."

"Yes," I responded, "but accidents happen in the dark of the night. And Renaldo, I think you underestimate the old Weasel. If anyone can twist the law to his own liking, Caiaphas can. That Weasel can kill his prey in more than one way. The big question is, can he get his hands on the prophet?"

"So you really think there'll be a confrontation?"

"Absolutely. Actually, from what I saw on Monday the confrontation has already started. It started when Jesus kicked out the merchants. Later, when I was there, the high priest's men questioned him, but he wouldn't back down. Then, yesterday, according to Claudius, he humiliated Caiaphas and his delegation right in front of the crowd. Like I said, he called the Pharisees and the teachers of the law a pack of hypocrites and a brood of vipers. I'd call that a confrontation. And he didn't do it out in the desert. No. He did it right in front of them, in front of the pilgrims and right in their holy place. I tell you. The man's got guts. But," I paused to emphasize my point, "I'm just waiting for the other side to strike back. And they will." I made a long sweeping motion with a pointed index finger and then stabbed down spear-like into my friend's bare ribs. "I'm sure they will."

Instinctively, Renaldo recoiled, shrugged off my antics and then countered, "But you don't think he's a threat to Rome?"

"Not from what I've seen or heard. But he is a threat to Caiaphas. Right now he's their problem. And that's where I want to leave him. If blood's going to flow, I don't want it getting on these hands." I gestured with my hands extended, palms up.

19

MY FEET FEEL THE SHARP BITE OF COLD, WET SNOW THE INSTANT I dismount. Our military objective is spread out before us, nestled along a wooded valley beneath lead gray skies. A light haze of wood smoke hangs over the village, hinting at places of warmth in this bleak winter world. The clustered huts are now surrounded. Their fate is sealed.

With an upraised wave of my sword, I signal our position and our readiness to my centurion commander stationed on the dark-forested slope on the opposing side of the valley. His own signaled response calls us forward.

The noose is in place. Now we draw it tight so none can escape.

In unison we rush forward, swords drawn, bucklers held at the ready, swift but silent. Surprise is our sharpest weapon.

Our orders are clear. Spare none. Vengeance must be swift, utter and complete. Barbaric justice for Barbarians, nothing else will do.

I round the corner of the first hut, and all but collide with a child—a girl.

Thhuuck! My sweeping blade catches her just below the ribs, slicing three quarters through her slim torso. Her blond head snaps back in shock. Questioning blue eyes shoot upward, looking me full in the face. I feel a hot red gush cover my sword hand.

I sat bolt upright in bed. Trembling. Sweat-drenched. Chest heaving. Heart pounding.

I fumbled to bring my two hands together, expecting to find blood there. But I could feel none—none that I could see in the blackness of our bedroom.

Zelda's hand touched my shoulder. I pulled away, swung out of bed and stumbled to the window.

Again I wiped my left hand across the palm, and then across the back of my right hand. In desperation, I squinted and strained as I tried to focus. But even here at the window on this dull overcast night, only the faint outline of my hand was visible.

I brought my trembling right hand—my sword hand—to my face. I touched my nose and mouth. I anticipated feeling the warm stickiness of blood. There was nothing. It was dry. My shoulders heaved. My breath came in enormous gulps. I sank down clutching the window sill for support.

"What's wrong? Marcus, are you all right?"

Zelda was at my side. She touched my brow. Wiped away the sweat. Said my name again: "Marcus?"

Though present with me, Zelda seemed far away, beckoning me from another world.

"It's… It's Germania!" I gasped.

She cradled my head in her arms.

For Zelda and me, Germania had become a code word. It signified everything that had gone wrong in my past as a single young man. It was the living hell I had endured for eight long years as a common soldier.

Germania was cold destitution wedded with the hot depravity of war. All of it had ended in futility with the agony of defeat, and a shameful withdrawal across the Rhine. These were wasted years, years spent in the brutality of slaughter. I saw young men—my companions, close as brothers—hacked to death. And for what?

For no lasting purpose. Germania. The lost province. I lost more than a Roman province there.[17] I lost peace. I lost innocence.

I lost a province, a part of my being, at the very core of my own soul.

During saner moments, in daylight hours, I could console myself over Germania. Germania brought promotion. It brought rank. I was now a centurion because of my conduct, my combat experience in Germania. But at night when the blond-haired girl visited, this meant nothing. Less than nothing. Rank, position, and this world's honor turned into dross, mere dross, discarded, soul-searing dross.

For long minutes Zelda rocked me, both of us sitting on the floor with our backs against the wall, my throat stinging, my eyes moist.

"Tell me what happened?"

I shook my head. Shook it hard. Shook it over and over. How could I tell her? What could I say? The stain was on my soul, though I could not find it on my hands. Nothing in this world could remove it. And heaven knew about Germania. Heaven knew about the blond-haired girl. Heaven knew about me. Knew all about me. Knew me to the core.

Wasn't that why my own girl—my daughter—my Tara was dead?

20

AT THE FIRST HINT OF MORNING LIGHT ZELDA OFFERED HERself to me. She loved me. She has always loved me, even in the worst of times. Why, I'll never know. I drank more deeply from her than ever. It was an aching feast of pure pleasure. Her love was a blanket covering my guilt-ridden night of despair.

If there is a God, and He made me to experience a woman like this, He must be good. He must be very good.

But why did He make us to know pain?

I lay exhausted but satisfied by her side. She was the anchor that held me. Loving her sustained me. In times like this she kept me from falling into the chasm at the center of my own soul, a chasm that had opened up in Germania and had grown wider ever since.

I met Zelda in Rome after my eight hellish years in Germania. My mother and her mother were close friends. It was not an arranged marriage. It was a suggested marriage. My mother suggested I meet Zelda. After that first meeting I was the one who did all the suggesting.

As I dressed, Andreas came to mind. Why, I don't fully know. Maybe it was the memory of all the blood spilled in that nightmare. Maybe it was because he was simply another good man lost, and my hideous dream had reminded me of all those other good men lost in Germania? But Andreas was a good young man lost right here in Jerusalem.

I'll never forget finding his body dumped on the street, just a few steps from our front gate. An early morning wake-up gift, courtesy of our local terrorists. Bloody zealots!

I had worried about my sons discovering the huge blood stain on the cobblestones, so I covered it with sand and then had Arius sweep it up. Even so a discolored patch remained. Perhaps all this rain finally washed it away.

Remembering Andreas reminded me that I had Friday to look forward to. Tomorrow, Barabbas would finally get his due. I had the blacksmith make a special set of spikes just for him. I personally planned to do the honors. Both Andreas and Hermes would be avenged. Rome would answer back, blood for blood. We would have the last say.

Breakfast was a more cheery affair. The rain had stopped during the night, and there were breaks in the cloud cover. Our twenty-man crew from the previous night had been reduced to only eleven as additional shelter had been found in every nook and cranny of the Antonia Fortress. The same had been done within our villa. The previous evening the courtyard was still being soaked by an intermittent drizzle, and there was a sizable puddle in a depression near its center, so space had been found for the men indoors.

My two sons were up early, and they made a happy nuisance of themselves as they plied the soldiers with questions. Claudius was great with the boys. They soon were the center of attention, a position my older son, Julius, particularly enjoyed.

The boys followed us out onto the street as, once again, we set out for the Fortress. I gave each of them a boost so they could see into the sparrow's nest. The bobbing bald heads of the hatchlings peeked out, expectant mouths wide open.

I sent the boys back to their mother and turned to quickly scan the cobblestones where Andreas had fallen. The dark stain was finally gone.

The day was looking far more promising, but within me I felt a certain unease. I could not put my finger on it at first, but then we passed a gaudily clad man. It was Timaeus as he emerged from his brother's home. I immediately remembered where he was going. He was on his way to his prearranged audience with Herod.

Perhaps this was the cause for my unease?

As I fully expected, Timaeus turned and headed in the direction of Herod's palace. There was no fear of recognition this time. I was on foot with my men and he paid scant attention to us. He was intent on his destination.

Was the noose being drawn around the prophet from Galilee? I could not help but think so. I expected Timaeus to get a sympathetic hearing before Herod. When money talked, Herod always listened, and Timaeus represented money, international trade, commerce—all the fine things this life offered.

I could well understand the linen merchant's frustration. For the first two days of the week Jesus of Nazareth had co-opted his market space—the best market space in town. On the third day, the Roman army shut down his street stall so Herod Antipas could parade into town. Then yesterday, the Almighty joined the conspiracy against him by sending a deluge. And today? Today was the first day of the Feast of Unleavened Bread, the day to slaughter the Passover lamb. Everyone was occupied with the preparations, hardly a suitable day for much buying and selling.

From a business standpoint, the week had already been an unmitigated disaster. Only Friday remained before the Sabbath, and Timaeus and his associates were determined to get the temple compound back into business for Friday, thereby salvaging at least a small portion of this wreck of a week.

Only this Galilean prophet, this rabbi of the rabble, stood in their way.

I knew Timaeus would never go before Herod alone. He would

be part of a well-dressed, well-prepared delegation. They would make their case before the Fox, and as sure as the sun rose that morning, the Fox would lament that if he were king here in Jerusalem this travesty would never have taken place. His righteous indignation would be stirred. But that is all he could stir since he had no authority here. It was Pilate's playground.

But Jesus was from Herod's jurisdiction, and the conniving tetrarch was well aware of the prophet's effect upon the masses. He had heard of his miraculous powers, and had hoped he might somehow harness them to serve his own kingly purpose. If the reports he had heard were true, then this roving rabbi could turn water into wine. If this were so, perhaps he could also turn lead into gold. If he could feed five thousand, why could he not feed an army bent on conquest? If he healed the lame and the blind, and it had been the talk of the whole region, why not have this miracle worker heal those wounded in battle? The possibilities seemed limitless.

Herod's desire to meet Jesus was genuine, but that desire extended beyond mere curiosity. After all, what good is a royal subject if he is not subject to his king? Perhaps this prophet would be useful. As in everything he did, the Fox had a purpose, an overriding purpose, a kingdom-gaining purpose.

A flock of bleating sheep came streaming toward us, distracting my thoughts and bringing me back to the present Passover realities. Four foul-smelling shepherds directed their flock down the street at the north end of the temple compound. The male yearling lambs were on their last journey. Their fate, too, was sealed.

The morning was uneventful. I had Claudius back in uniform at the Golden Gate. I had him watching for the arrival of the northern messiah. But there would be no covert activity today. For the second consecutive day, the prophet was a no-show. Even if he had arrived, I fully resolved to leave Jesus to the temple authorities. He was their problem. I had enough problems of my own.

As I descended the stairs of the gate, I caught sight of Jonas and his son, unoccupied at the customs booth. With a quick wave of my hand, I signaled my intention to speak with him, and after taking the salute of the sentinels at the gate, I headed straight to the booth.

"Good morning, you old goat!" I called out as I approached.

"Well, if it isn't the top dog himself," he shot back.

"It's always good to see a man standing around doing nothing. It sets me at ease," I quipped.

"Ease?" His eyebrows shot up. "Oh yes." He nodded emphatically. "It's been a week of ease all right. I've had my feet up all week." Of course just the opposite was true, and it was true for both of us.

"Do you think we could have a short word?" With a jerk of my head I motioned in the direction of the road leading down the Kidron Valley.

"Sure," he answered, and then with a glance and a nod to his son, he transferred responsibility to him.

A light mist still hung over the lowest reaches of the valley, but the early morning sun promised to burn it off. The swallows nesting along the crevices in the city wall were engaged in a full-throated competition with the songbirds in the trees along the brook. Early morning traffic to and from the city was just beginning to stir.

When we had gone a few paces beyond the gate, I spoke. "I just wanted to say thanks for the help with the Barabbas case."

"Oh, don't mention it." There was relief in his voice. "I thought you were going to warn me about some new plot."

"No, there's no new plot." I hesitated. "Let me rephrase that. There's no new plot that I know about. You never can be sure what's being hatched in this crazy city."

"Yes, you're right about that. I guess we learned that with Barabbas." Jonas nervously bit on the corner whiskers of his mustache, and then continued, "Now, that Galilean prophet? I've been losing sleep over him all week."

"Harmless as a dove," I reported. "Harmless as a dove."

"How do you know?"

"I checked him out on Monday. Checked him out myself, right back there in the temple courts." I gestured with my thumb over my shoulder. "Then, on Tuesday, I had Claudius in there with the prophet."

"You Romans have more nerve than brains." He kicked a loose pebble off the pathway, looked up at me with a quizzical grin. With an incredulous shake of his head he repeated, "More nerve than brains! That's all I can say."

"If we didn't have nerve we wouldn't be running this place. Or any other place for that matter."

He shrugged, furrowed his brow and then cocked his head to one side. It was his way of reluctantly conceding my point.

"So he's harmless?"

"Harmless to us." I pointed first at Jonas, then at myself, and then back again. "He's not harmless to Caiaphas, but he is harmless to us. Caiaphas, on the other hand," I paused for effect, "now there's a man who I'm sure hasn't slept well all week."

"So you think the old rusty gate has lost some sleep? Over what?"

"Money. Money and prestige. It can't look too good having some roving upcountry rabbi come in and take over your temple at the religious high point of the year."

"I suppose not," Jonas acknowledged. But then he added, "You know this prophet, Jesus of Nazareth, he's been here before. He kicked out the money-changers a few years back. Caused quite a stir then. But nothing like this. He's got the temple guards running scared. That's what my uncle told me."

"Well, your uncle's right. I saw that firsthand on Monday. So, what else do you know about this Galilean?"

"Well, my wife tells me he's a friend of tax collectors and sinners. She told me one of his disciples was a tax collector before he met the prophet."

"Ah, tax collectors and sinners?" I responded with a wink and a nod. "Maybe there is hope for the two of us yet."

Jonas smiled back at me. "So, Marcus, where is this all headed? Some people think he's the messiah. You know that, don't you?"

"Yes, we're well aware of that. But he doesn't oppose paying taxes to Caesar." I gave my tax collector a supportive thumbs-up signal. "And he hasn't spoken a word against Rome since he's been here."

"Well, that's not a surprise. He knows better. You and your boys would have him nailed up on Golgotha the moment he did."

"You're right about that," I agreed. "But I honestly don't think he's got a quarrel with us. He's going after the parading hypocrites, those killjoy Pharisees and teachers of the law. You know the ones, the religious police who run this place."

Jonas blew a sharp breath of air through his graying mustache. "Oh, I know the ones. The pure ones! The ones who kicked me out of the synagogue the moment I got this job. But they'll travel Roman roads to seize a widow's house in the next town. They'll expect Roman soldiers to protect them from bandits on the way to Jericho. They'll connect their fancy homes to the Roman aqueduct and every evening they'll bathe their stinking arses in its water."

I nodded in agreement. My words had obviously struck a nerve. But Jonas wasn't finished.

"Every day they'll curse the Gentiles and their influence. With their mouths they lust for the good old days, the days before Rome." He gestured expansively and then shrugged, "Ha! They don't talk about the rotten poverty of those good old days, 'cause while their mouths talk, their filthy hands rake in the money, the money the empire has brought in here. Oh, I know the ones! Believe me. I know them well."

"Spoken like a true son of the empire," I said with an exaggerated nod.

Over the years Jonas and I had developed a working relationship that allowed me to speak to him in a certain way. I could say things that I would never repeat to another Jew. He was observant—a Jew with his religious blinders off. He put his life on the line when he took on this occupation. I respected him for it.

"Look," I declared, "Jesus of Nazareth is the high priest's problem. He's not ours." Jonas and his family were fully included in the scope of my statement. They fell under our protection. They were part of us. "If we're lucky this will all blow over, and the prophet will be back in Galilee sometime next week," I added. "Then he'll be Herod's problem."

"Herod?" Jonas huffed. "There'll be another head on a platter soon if he gets a hold of him."

"Well, Jesus and what happens to him is out of our hands. But Barabbas isn't, and tomorrow he'll get what's coming to him. And it's thanks to you," I spoke my appreciation with genuine sincerity. "We would never have landed that fish without your help."

"I didn't expect catching Thaddaeus would lead us where it did. I mean he's just a petty tax thief. I really had no idea Barabbas was the ringleader behind all this stuff—the theft, the tax booth vandalism, the murder of the soldiers." Even now Jonas gestured his surprise. "I thought he was harmless. A little hotheaded, but harmless. It wasn't until you showed me that weapons stash—that pile of swords you found in his house— that's when things began to fall into place." He gave a snort and shook his head, "I guess you can't tell what's in the soup until you taste it."

"Well, if Barabbas is the soup we're talking about, I'd say there's a good sized dash of poison hemlock in there. It's too bad Hermes and Andreas had to taste it. Oh well. Tomorrow I'm going to spill

121

that soup all over Golgotha. And the world will be a better place because of it."[18]

We reached the Brook Kidron. There was a lively babbling flow thanks to all the rain. I've often seen it bone-dry. I glanced back up the road to the city. "I guess it's time we headed back. You've got taxes to collect. I've got a tribune I should see."

21

BACK AT THE FORTRESS, TRUE TO MY PREDICTION EARLIER IN THE week, Flavio was nowhere to be found. None of the centurions had seen him since Herod's arrival. Caius, on the other hand, had been active and visible, providing leadership for his troops both within the city and the fortress.

Just before noon a red, bulgy-eyed Flavio put in an appearance at the fortress. He brought word that Herod intended to tour the temple area. The high priest's invitation, offered during the tetrarch's arrival on Tuesday, had been accepted.

Flavio hastily convened a council of centurions. After some debate, it was decided that Renaldo and Marius would provide the manpower needed to secure the route from Herod's Palace on the western edge of the city on through the heart of the capital, to the temple compound on the east side. Here was a route fraught with hazards—a security nightmare. After my previous experience with the tetrarch, I was eager to avoid any personal involvement. I volunteered my men to provide cover duty so Renaldo's men could be reassigned for the task.

As before, we assumed Caius and his troops would lead the march. A messenger was dispatched to Caius outlining the outcome of our deliberations and offering our services. The general was staying with his master at the Herod family palace.

We received a reply that was both prompt and curt. Reading from a prepared statement the messenger intoned, "His majesty, the tetrarch of Galilee and Perea, will not traverse the city of

Jerusalem, but, rather, following the custom of his father, Herod the first, he will take the southern perimeter route and enter the temple compound through the glorious Golden Gate. His own soldiers will provide escort. We have need of no others."

Here was a royal snub. That is how Flavio perceived it. His neck and face turned beet red. For a moment I thought he might kill the messenger.

"We might just as well kneel before the king—the bloody Fox —and kiss his stinking feet!" he raged. "Why not hand him the city on a silver platter? Silver? Pah!" he spat. "That wouldn't be good enough for him. Gold. Only gold will do!" With acid in his voice he added, "Oh, I forgot. Silver platters are for prophets' heads! And beggar boys' hands!" His teeth clenched, he rapped his knuckles three times on the table before him. "What do we do?" he glowered as he shook his head.

It was a question no one dared answer. But then, Flavio did not expect an answer from us. The tribune turned from his assembled centurions, took a few steps to the nearest window and looked out across the tile roofs of the city. He stroked his chin, then with both hands grasped hold of the window ledge as he gazed straight ahead.

After a few moments, he turned to the fidgeting messenger. He yanked the rolled parchment from the messenger's hand, seized a writing quill from the table, and began jotting furiously. In due time he spoke.

"We'll meet the Fox at the Golden Gate. He won't walk in there alone. This is our city, not his. He'll see us first." Flavio rolled the document up once again and handed it back to the waiting messenger.

"Off with you," he scowled.

But the tribune was not finished with his dispatches. He again seized the quill and, with an air of urgency, began writing on a fresh sheet of parchment. His final strokes were executed with a confident dramatic flourish.

My curiosity was intense, but neither I nor any of the other men present dared speak.

"Messenger!" Flavio bellowed.

One of our young recruits straightaway stepped into the briefing room.

"To the governor! With haste," Flavio ordered as he handed the soldier this new missive. Turning to us he continued, "We'll see what Pilate says about Herod's sudden turn to religion."

I was actually relieved about the news of Herod's chosen route to the temple. There were no crowded streets, encounters with beggars were less likely and, best of all, there was little direct responsibility on our part. The true reason for this circuitous route was obvious after a moment's thought. The route through the city would bring the Fox to the backside of the temple compound. From there he could choose one of several rear or side entries. But this was no way for a king to come. He would enter by the main gate, the Golden Gate, or he would not enter at all.

If the route was no cause for alarm, Herod's apparent rapprochement with Caiaphas certainly was. Herod would leverage any friendship, any alliance with the rich and powerful to his own advantage. Caiaphas certainly was both rich and powerful. His mansion spoke volumes. I have repeatedly been told that the opulent interior makes the governor's palace apartment look shabby.

Once again, the litter-bearers would be pressed into service. In my mind's eye I could again see the regular cadence of their steps, smell the sweat from their bodies, hear Herod's curses over some imagined misstep. The tetrarch's actual arrival was, however, at least two hours off. Until then, there were ample preparations to be made, and Flavio tapped me for service.

Tuesday's arrival procedure for Herod would again be employed. There were, of course, some obvious differences. The distance our troops would be covering was vastly reduced. Herod would be following a U-shaped route, starting from the Herod family palace on the west side of the city, traveling south past the Serpents Pool, then east across the southern perimeter of the city wall, or bottom of the U, and finally heading north to the Golden Gate at the top of the U. Flavio and Marius would greet the tetrarch as he turned north on the final leg of the journey, just opposite the Pinnacle of the Temple. The Pinnacle is the high point on the wall at the south end of the temple compound. The fortifications at this point soar two hundred feet above the Kidron Valley below.

Once again I was asked to inspect the route before the king's arrival—the distance from the Golden Gate to the point on the road opposite the Pinnacle. Traveling along the top of the city wall, this distance amounted to only a few hundred yards, but at ground level the official route multiplied this distance by at least a factor of four. About four hundred yards from the Golden Gate, the road to the Mount of Olives was intersected by a north/south road running parallel to the Brook Kidron. Herod would be coming north along this road and then turning to face the Golden Gate and the massive gold clad temple directly behind it.

My groomsman was dispatched to bring my horse back to the Antonia Fortress from the tether lines near the Serpents Pool. In fact, all the horses were brought back and conscripted for duty. Once again we would give Herod a show. He would know who was in charge here.

I was just getting into my brass-muscled cuirass when my groomsman returned. With quick assistance from him I was in the saddle in a few short minutes. Again I called on a half dozen cavalrymen to accompany me on the brief reconnaissance mission. It took only a few moments for us to ride from the fortress to the Golden Gate.

A constant stream of bearded men channeled in both directions through the wide arched gateway. Most of those leaving through the gate were carrying freshly slain year-old lambs. With their throats cut, the bloodied heads dangled limply. The Passover lamb would be made ready for the great feast.

Aside from the heavy traffic there were no particular security concerns that were readily apparent. From past experience I knew that at this hour the bulk of the slaughter had already taken place. Though the killing would continue until sunset, most families would try to have this job done by the early afternoon, even if it meant standing in line from the early morning. Here was slaughterhouse religion at peak performance.

With the heavy focus on the Passover celebration, my hope was that fanatics and religious zealots would have their minds fully occupied on this sacred event, rather than be distracted by Herod's sudden appearance, or by the activities of the Roman army near the city gate.

We continued down the road into the valley, the same road Jonas and I had walked in the early morning. Before reaching the Brook Kidron, I gently tugged right on my horse's reins, and with that my party turned south onto the road that led round the city. We had not gone far when we came to the bloody discharge. A veritable river of blood gushed from a three-foot diameter clay pipe that emerged on the left side of the road. It was the outflow from the slaughter in the temple. The red stream of gore flowed another two hundred yards before it joined the Brook Kidron. To be accurate, the stream was not pure lambs' blood. It was supplemented by water from the main city aqueduct; enough water to keep the solution moving freely.

A stream of blood—blood flowing between fertile grassy banks dotted with the flowers of spring. It was a disturbing sight on a sunny day, one not easily forgotten.

The air was thick with a constant buzz of flies. Swallows swooped low to enjoy the flying insect feast. There was a continual wheeling and diving in what amounted to a winged acrobatic frenzy. A colony of swallow nests lay thick upon the steep adjacent wall. I worried that their careening flight might spook the horses.

How the blood of a lamb could bring freedom to a nation remained a mystery to me. I heard the whole story; the plagues on Egypt, the death of the firstborn, the lamb's blood sprinkled upon the door of each home bringing escape from the Angel of Death. Jonas had told all of it to me. For me, there was a certain resonance to this tale. I was a firstborn son. Three years ago, before Tara's death, my family had eaten the Seder meal with Jonas and his family. He was a believer. Though the synagogue would not have him, this tax collector took us in and taught us the rudiments of his faith.

We reached the point on the road opposite the Pinnacle without incident. Two-way traffic on the road was more brisk and purposeful than usual. People by and large ignored us as they went about their business, and we went about ours.

We returned to the Gate. As I approached, I looked up to see Claudius looking down at me from atop the Gate. I returned his salute and was instantly reminded of Jesus of Nazareth. Though in reverse position, I was right now at that point where our eyes had first met. The words—the words I heard at that instant of meeting —they came echoing back forcefully into my mind.

"I have a future for you."

The voice was soft, even gentle, but somehow terrible.

I shuddered. I looked about me, half expecting to see him by my side. There was no one—no one but my own cavalrymen.

A gray-bearded man approached. He held the back legs of a freshly slain lamb as his son clutched the front legs. They walked by me with their burden, passing on the left. Behind them drops of blood dotted the paving stones.

It was my mind. It must have been my own mind playing back the earlier incident, I reasoned. That was why I heard his words.

But why did this man, this prophet, unnerve me like this?

We continued to the fortress, but my mind was on the northern messiah. His penetrating eyes haunted my thoughts. There was a power there I had no ability to fathom. I was reminded of Ruth's words. Ruth is one of our household servants, a Jewish girl. When at the supper table I told Zelda about Jesus and his miraculous powers, Ruth's eyes had brightened. I asked her if she knew anything about this man.

"Oh, yes," she said. "Almost a year ago he healed a blind beggar from the Lower City. Jesus made some mud, put it on the beggar's eyes and sent him to wash in the Pool of Siloam. When he washed, he could see. It was a miracle. I've seen this man myself. I know it's true," she earnestly avowed.[19]

When I asked her about this power Jesus had, and where it came from, she bowed her head and answered, "From God." But she seemed somehow uncomfortable with her answer. She added, "It must be from God. He does good things. But our leaders aren't sure. They think it may be demon power. But demons don't heal the sick," she reasoned.

Maybe the religious leaders were right. Maybe it was demonic power that made the blind see. It seemed preposterous. But why had I heard this voice? Why did this man trouble me so? Thinking of him seemed to stir up nothing but torment within me, and I did not even know why. I seemed strangely attracted to him, yet, at the same time, repelled.

Then there was this talk about the kingdom of God. Maybe Timaeus was right about this prophet. The words of the wealthy merchant came back to me: "You don't talk about a kingdom in this place and get away with it. Rome will see to that!"

Maybe we would see to it. Maybe we should see to it soon.

But his enemies were the same pompous self-serving leaders I despised. He had aligned himself with the common man, with the

129

poor, the oppressed, the sick and suffering. And he did not just champion their cause for personal benefit as some crass politician lobbying for the Emperor's favor. No, he healed them. He fed them. He walked with them, ate with them. He was one of them. He was their king, whether he wore a crown or not. I saw that clearly when he entered on the donkey. He was the donkey king. A horse would have put him above the crowd. A horse would have meant elevating himself like all the other egotistical men who lead in this upside-down world.

In his case others would have to do the elevating.

The meaning of his entry on Sunday came clear to me now. It was a perspective gained from my comfortable perch on the back of my own noble steed.

By the time I reached the fortress for the second time in the week, I resolved to shut this messiah out of my mind. He did not fit any of my categories for human behavior or religious thought. He was beyond understanding, an unwelcome intruder in my city and my thought life.

Flavio was already mounted and attired in gleaming brass. I immediately reported my observations on the route. He seemed little interested. The decisions had already been made. Our response to Herod's visit had been determined by a higher authority.

"Pontius Pilate will meet him at the gate," Flavio crowed. "They'll both know Rome runs this world."

By *both* Flavio of course meant the high priest and the tetrarch. Ambition and treachery formed a blend that pulsed strongly in their veins, too strongly to be left unchecked.

"He's already passed the Serpents Pool. He'll be here within the hour," Flavio reported. Then he added his orders. "It's your gate. You'll wait there with the governor until the Fox comes. I'll greet him at the Pinnacle and escort him to the gate. After that he's in the governor's hands. Off with you then."

I saluted and turned. Flavio wheeled his horse round to face the cavalry assembling on the parade ground. Within minutes they would ride out of the fortress and begin their deployment along the route to the Golden Gate.

I ordered the six horsemen who had accompanied me to join the ranks of the other cavalrymen. Then, with considerable haste, I returned to the gate. I dismounted and then clambered up the steps of the gatehouse. I ordered Claudius to quickly assemble all the men under my command from their positions along the wall. Within minutes I reported the unfolding events: Herod's expected arrival, Pilate's coming to greet the tetrarch, and the high priest's plan for a royal tour of the temple compound. In all my years on this assignment there had never been such an assemblage of the high and the mighty at this gate. I wanted everything and everyone looking their best, fit for a king, whether genuine or pretender. I was grateful for the troop inspection I had undertaken the previous afternoon. Armor and equipment had been freshened and repaired; nevertheless a frenzy of purposeful activity followed.

I returned to ground level and mounted my horse just in time to salute Flavio as he lead row upon row of cavalry past the gate and out along the route to the point opposite the Pinnacle. Renaldo and Marius were among the centurions who joined in the display of military might. Five hundred pikemen followed the cavalrymen. They formed up on either side of the final four hundred yards leading to the gate. They stood erect with the butt end of their spears planted in the ground directly in front of them. With their right arms fully extended in front of them, they grasped the shaft of their twelve foot long pikes. Arrayed in this manner they formed a bristling arch between which Herod's litter would pass. Finally, hard by the gate, the trumpeters held their instruments by their sides as they awaited the signal for the imperial fanfare.

When all were in position, I called for the lowering of the huge grate iron gate. From now on the Passover celebrants would be forced to use an alternate entrance or exit.

In short order, the toga-clad governor, Pontius Pilate, arrived on his gold ornamented chariot. The gate was raised. By the governor's side stood Claudia Procula lavishly dressed in full length scarlet. Her bejewelled opulence contrasted sharply with the poverty common to most women of this province. The chariot took a position allowing the ruling couple to look out to the Mount of Olives, in readiness for the approaching king.

The only missing player was Caiaphas. In due time his delegation arrived, and the enormous gate was hauled up once more on creaking chains, only to be lowered again when the priestly party had exited.

Pilate had been gazing down the road stretched out before him when Caiaphas arrived, and it was only the coarse rattle coming from the gate chains behind him that alerted him to the approach of the high priest and his delegation. He turned, stepped down from the chariot and briskly strode over to the dumbfounded cleric. The expression on Caiaphas' face said it all. He clearly did not expect to see Pilate there. He had intended a discrete private tour and consultation.

"You're expecting someone?" Pilate brusquely inquired.

An uncomfortable pause followed. Caiaphas cast a hasty glance at those accompanying him, adjusted the folds in his robe, cleared his rusty throat and replied, "Yes, King Herod requested a tour of the great temple."

"Did he now?" There was a coldness in Pilate's voice that betrayed the utter contempt he felt toward this Jewish leader. "Ahh!" He gestured grandly, "There is no king in these parts. I know of no king." Then, spotting me on horseback nearby, the governor turned and in mock sincerity called out, "Centurion. Is there a king around here?"

"We have no king here but Caesar," I answered joining in the sport.

"The centurion says there is no king but Caesar. Do you have some other king I'm unaware of? Perhaps I should meet this king."

By now the high priest was well beyond flustered. He had stepped into a trap. Surrounded by Roman troops and cut off from the safety of the temple's hallowed sanctum, he was being hectored by his chief political rival. It seemed more than he could endure. He began to tremble uncontrollably, whether from fear or anger I could not tell.

"Your excellency," he swallowed hard, "I was referring to the…tet-tetrarch of Galilee."

"The tet-tetrarch?" Pilate mimicked not only the high priest's tremulous stammer, but also the rusty gate scratch of his voice. "Is that so? Well, the tetrarch is no king. And he certainly isn't your king." With slow, icy deliberation, Pilate stated, "There is no king here but Caesar. Did you hear that?"

It was no rhetorical question.

"Yes, your excellency. I heard."

"Do you, any of you," Pilate scanned the delegation, "have any other king?"

The cowering dogs dutifully answered, "No, we have no other king."

Caiaphas, however, was silent, a fact well noted by the governor.

Pilate took a step closer to the trembling priest, pointed a bony finger in his face and hissed, "Now don't forget that, you old goat, or your blood will be running down the Kidron! Did you hear that?"

"I…I am your servant, your excellency," Caiaphas rasped.

"Ha!" Pilate laughed an icy laugh in a show of disdain for that remark. Then he turned on his heels and marched back to his chariot, where once more he joined his wife.

For a full minute there was stunned silence from the religious delegation, then suddenly they all began to speak at once in a huddle of hushed tones like schoolboys after a tongue lashing from the headmaster.

There was murder in the high priest's eye, nothing childish there. From my vantage point I could see that. He did not have the means, but he most certainly had the intent.

I am sure that if the gate had been open, the delegation would have returned to the safety of the sanctuary to plot their revenge, but that option was not open to them. They were trapped in this pocket, surrounded by hated foreign troops, subject to the whim and ridicule of their enemy, awaiting the arrival of their pretentious savior king.

Long awkward moments passed. They were saved from this interminable purgatory by Herod's arrival.

Caius and Flavio lead the procession with the royal litter following close behind. One by one, the pikemen drew back their extended arms bringing their long angled spears fully upright. This synchronized motion continued up the length of the column as the royal party advanced—a truly impressive display as viewed from on the back of a horse. For a moment I was envious of Claudius, who had an even better view from the top of the gate.

At last, the two mounted commanders arrived before Pilate's chariot. They were motioned to take their position on either side. After a brief confusion of feet, the royal litter was turned sideways so the royal couple could face the governor as he stood upon his imperial chariot. The trumpeters sounded the fanfare. When the last note had echoed off the marble wall, Pilate unrolled the parchment handed to him by an attendant. He cleared his throat, and began his oration.

"It was under the rule of the great and wise Emperor Caesar Augustus, that this magnificent temple behind us began to take shape. He recognized the desire of the Jewish people for a central place to worship. It was Herod the great Idumean king who oversaw the construction of this masterpiece of the empire, and it now stands as a symbol of Roman respect for the unity and diversity of all the peoples of the empire. It is only fitting that today I, as the emperor's representative, welcome the son of this master builder, Herod Antipas, the tetrarch of Galilee and Perea."

With a wave of his hand Pilate signaled the sounding of a second trumpet fanfare. As the first note was sounded, he stepped off the chariot and then graciously lent a hand to his wife. Thus accompanied by his mate, he swaggered over to the royal litter to personally greet Herod and Herodius, who both stood to meet them.

Greetings were exchanged, none of which I could discern from a distance. After a brief discussion, Claudia joined Herodius in the royal litter. Herod barked out orders. The litter-bearers stood and headed off in the direction of the governor's residence. Apparently the ladies would have their own time together.

At a leisurely pace Pilate then escorted Herod over to where the priestly delegation waited.

It was an unusual sight, these three hostile, inflated men exchanging greetings and meaningless pleasantries. Herod Antipas, Pontius Pilate, and Joseph Caiaphas; the Fox, the Badger, and the Weasel. All three were kings in their own right, within their own jurisdiction. All three craved more power, absolute power, while fiercely holding each other in check.

Pilate turned to me and gave a quick, tight nod. I signaled up to Claudius, and the great Golden Gate, the Messiah Gate, was hoisted granting entrance to the three—the three competing kings.

Only the fourth king, the people's king–the donkey king–only he was absent.

22

Thursday 7:00 p.m. April 6th, 30 AD

IT WAS ALREADY DARK WHEN I TRUDGED, LANTERN IN HAND, UP the stairs of the southeast turret of the fortress, the prison sector. Octavia the jailer greeted me warmly. He knew well why I visited. Each of the three prisoners on this particular level, the highest level, would be crucified the following day, and I was charged with their execution.

"So, you'll join me tomorrow on the Skull?" I asked.

"Of course," he responded. "I wouldn't miss that party for all the emperor's wine and women."

"Good." I smiled. "I'll need your help. It's been a while since I've been to a hammering. I guess you could say I'm a bit rusty."

"Marcus," he shrugged, "don't worry. You'll do fine. I'll bring my crew. They're experts now. We'll have 'em up there before they know what hit 'em."

"Sounds good to me."

His words put to rest some hidden doubts and misgivings. I usually avoided parties of the hammering kind. But this one, this was a party I was throwing. And I had a score I needed to settle with the head guest.

"Now, Octavia, I would like a little visit with our three fine friends."

"Let's go then, Marcus."

The heavy plank door creaked open and I stooped to enter the first dank cell. The combined stench of urine and sweat assaulted my nostrils. Barabbas was sitting with his back to the far wall. His

136

feet, which stretched out before him, were secured in a well-worn set of wooden stalks.

The fat pig had not lost much weight in spite of his prison diet. His eyes were as cold and belligerent as ever; no contrition there, not that I had expected any.

I handed the lantern to Octavia who had entered right behind me. I drew a five-inch, four-cornered spike from a pouch attached to my belt. I examined it carefully before the prisoner. I stood the head of the spike on my thumb and gently pressed its steel point into the fleshy ball at the tip of my middle finger. I drew the prisoner's attention to the sharpness of the point, admired the nail's considerable length, and then asked Barabbas if he thought it would be adequate for the task at hand.

He glared at me, rattled his chains and called down upon me all manner of curses in the name of Jehovah. When he began going on about the glories of the Maccabean revolt two centuries ago, I turned my back on him.

Narrow religious zealots like him make me sick. Here was an advocate for a brand of exclusive, race-based religion, that holds the rest of humanity in contempt. He would have us all back living in caves so he could preserve the pure faith. If he had his way, the streets would flow rivers of blood just so he could take us back to his narrow world. The stain on the cobblestones near my house had only been a small token of his intent.

Arguing with men of his kind is utterly pointless.

When his rant ended, I calmly smiled back at him and wished him a good night's sleep. The next day I would hammer home a few points of my own.

"I'll see you in the morning," I called out as I pulled his cell door shut.

Of course, this insurrectionist had not acted alone, hence the two other men on their way to the Skull. The Skull—Golgotha—

137

what a fitting name for the hill of execution. The bare, rounded, rock crown of the hill mirrored the ultimate fate of all who walked up its slope.

The man behind the next door went berserk the moment I stepped into his cell. He was a trapped animal spitting venom on any who approached. I needed no theatrics to gain his attention. He provided his own.

While this human sewer spewed curses, I placed the point of the spike at the base of my left palm, and shouted back at him. "Tomorrow! Tomorrow!"

He got the message.

He continued his raving and I slammed the cell door shut. This man was capable of anything. There was little doubt in my mind who of these three was the butcher, the henchman.

The last man presented a sharp contrast. Thaddaeus, dear Thaddaeus. His tongue had come loose under duress, which culminated in the arrest of the other two. He appeared reflective, even resigned to his fate. Or was it only fear that I saw stamped upon his lean and lanky frame?

He glanced up at me when I entered his cell, and then hung his head as though in shame.

"We're going to Golgotha tomorrow," I stated in a matter-of-fact manner.

He sucked in a short tight breath and squeezed his lips together as though I had punched him in the stomach.

"Tonight will be your last night…here."

I added the word "here" to soften the finality of my statement. His lowered head began to weave from side to side. I could clearly see his mind absorbing what his body would feel.

My announcement was no new revelation. The execution date for all three men had been set the week before, immediately after the trial. But I came confirming an eventuality which the whole of

138

this man's being wished to deny. It was plain that my words came as a staggering shock to his whole system. It was a shock that left him reeling.

After my encounter with the last two prisoners, I was unprepared for the long silence that followed. "Do you have any questions?" I asked.

He began to rock back and forth, head down, hands nervously clenching and releasing, clenching and releasing. He swallowed hard and then stammered, "Wi–will there be myrrh?"

"Yes. I'll make sure there's myrrh." I paused and then justified my answer by adding, "We're not Barbarians. It'll help with the pain."

He continued his rocking. A brief glance up at me and a quick tight nod was his way of thanking me. Then he was overcome. Unable to look ahead, to face me or the future, Thaddaeus turned from me, face to the wall.

I turned from him. I had nothing more to say.

The door creaked shut. The metal latch bar clicked down.

Tomorrow waited... Golgotha awaited. The Skull awaited its prey.

23

"MASTER. THERE'S A MESSENGER AT THE GATE WANTING TO SEE you. HE says it's urgent.

"Already? We haven't even had breakfast yet." I sighed, straightened, and reached for a towel to dry my dripping face. "Arius, tell him I'll be there in a minute. I still need to wash up."

Although I was freshly shaven, I wasn't yet fully dressed. I strapped on my sword, stuffed three dried dates in my mouth, and then slowly ambled across our villa courtyard, crowded with cranky, early-morning soldiers. They were reluctantly setting their day into motion.

A visibly agitated messenger saluted me as Arius opened the gate. It was the same young man I had seen Flavio send off yesterday with an urgent dispatch for Pilate.

"Sir, I have just come from the governor. You are to report to the Praetorium immediately. Jesus of Nazareth has been arrested. The high priest has brought him before the governor for judgement."

"Is that so?" I said in a state of consternation. "Who sent you?"

"The governor himself. Sir, he said you were familiar with the Galilean."

I blew a short puff of air through my nostrils. All of Jerusalem was somewhat familiar with the Galilean.

"So he wants me there immediately?"

"Immediately, sir." He shifted from one foot to the other, and then to justify this response, he added, "The high priest and a big delegation, maybe three hundred men, maybe more, arrived at the palace door at first light. They had the prisoner—Jesus—with them."

140

"Tell the governor I'm on my way." With a quick nod of my head I dismissed the messenger. Instantly, he turned and began his run back to the governor's residence. I took one step back inside the gate and began barking orders.

"You, you, and you!" I stabbed my index finger in the direction of the most dressed and prepared looking soldiers. "Strap on your swords and follow me. Now!"

Addressing the other soldiers I announced, "The rest of you, meet me at the Praetorium as soon as you are ready."

"Claudius," I nodded in his direction, "you are in charge. I'll give everyone their assignment for the day when they get there."

I stepped back through the gate and began covering the ground with long, quick strides. My three recruits had to run to catch up.

With each stride a new thought came jogging into my head. Stupid Arius! Why did he not tell me the messenger was from Pilate? I would have moved a good deal faster.

Obviously my concerns about the prophet had moved up the chain of command. Flavio must have informed Pilate about my worries and the actions I had taken, hence the unusual move—a direct summons by the governor. I harboured the hope that he would consult directly with me on the matter.

Three hundred men! Three hundred men at first light? The Weasel must have had a busy night. It takes a good deal of effort to set your troops in array. Caiaphas must have been hatching this plot for a long while.

But the Weasel caught his prey! What a sweet bit of treachery that must have been. I wondered how he pulled it off. Now the high priest would move in for the kill; we would see if he could slaughter his own Passover lamb.

The people! If the pilgrims, especially the Galilean pilgrims knew their messiah had been seized there could be a mass revolt. That must be why the Weasel did his dirty work in the dark of the night. Furthermore, he played out this drama at the zenith, the high point of the festival, while minds and hearts were on faith, home and family. Here was a cunning scheme worthy of the Fox, played out by the Weasel.

Undoubtedly, most of the population would still be unaware of these developments, even as I had been caught off guard—off guard but not surprised. I could smell it coming.

My conversation with Renaldo at the bathhouse came echoing back into my mind. It gave me an eerie feeling knowing I had spoken like some prophetic oracle. It made me wonder where that insight had really come from.

"By Jupiter! I forgot the spikes." I wheeled round while reaching out my hand to halt the soldier at my side. Addressing him directly I said, "I forgot them—the spikes. They're in a pouch hanging on a peg in my bedchamber. My wife, she'll know where they are. Ask her to get the pouch for you. Then bring it to me at the Praetorium. Oh, and tell the other men to hurry. This is urgent." I fixed my eyes on him to stress the importance of this last statement, and then added, "Now run."

I swung around and resumed my steady pace. The loping slap of his sandals on the pavement told me that he took my words to heart. The two men remaining with me sensed the gravity of the situation and quickened their own pace. In a few moments, we reached the governor's residence, the stately columned palace adjoining the rear or southeast side of the Antonia Fortress.

The sight before me contrasted sharply with what I saw when I had escorted Herod to this very location three days earlier. My early morning messenger had been wrong. There must have been five hundred men crowded into the street fronting on the fortress. A cordon of Roman soldiers had already been thrown around this crowd. The street was blocked in both directions. Pikemen, with their menacing spears lowered for attack, formed a solid wall before me. Only the foolhardy would dare approach.

Off to the right I spotted their commander. It was Marius. I signaled my approach with a wave.

"A fine mess we have here!"

"Yes, Marcus, a fine mess," he agreed. "The high priest has his man. I only hope we can keep the crowds away."

"Your boys are doing a fine job of that. Look, I've got twenty more men on the way. They'll be here in a few minutes. Claudius will be leading them. They can form a second line of swordsmen immediately behind your pikemen."

"That would be excellent, Marcus," he answered with a thumbs up signal. "Not a soul will get through here. I'll see to that."

There was determination in his voice—determination stiffened by a whiff of fear. He too remembered the surging crowds of Sunday adoring their messiah king. The latent power of the masses could break forth at anytime. At this moment, defensive vigilance was paramount.

"Tell Claudius and his men to fall in behind you, then," I declared. And then added, "The governor sent for me. I need to get through."

"By all means," Marius responded.

He stepped forward, faced his bristling pikemen, and with a short horizontal move of his right hand he parted them, allowing access for me and the two men who followed in tight behind me.

I moved to the Praetorium entrance as quickly as the milling throng would permit. They were packed in so tightly that progress was slow and fitful. I repeatedly yelled out, "Make way! Make way!"

They did make way when they saw they were facing a centurion, but due to the press there was little space they could grant me. I was sorely tempted to draw my sword, and then use the flat of it on the recalcitrant. But though I was armed, I could become an easy target in this inflamed crowd. I let that temptation pass.

143

At last we reached the stairs fronting the Praetorium. Here, again, a line of pikemen faced the crowd. Their spears, however, were raised upright forming a respectful barrier for this hasty, early morning assembly. The contrasting stance of this array of pikemen was striking.

A quick glance over my shoulder confirmed the composition of this crowd. These were the high priest's men. There were at least fifty temple guards present, some with swords drawn. Then there were perhaps two hundred priests, Sadducees, and members of the Jewish high council, the Sanhedrin. Finally there were the leading merchants and traders of the city, an irate bunch, thirsty for blood.

No women. No pilgrims. No disciples. No Galileans save one, and I had yet to set eyes on him.

I turned back and locked my eyes on the pikeman directly before me. I raised my hand as a signal and he stepped back smartly, granting access to the six long broad stairs leading to the governor's residence.

These stairs were empty, unoccupied, except for three men, Caiaphas, Annas, and Jonathon.

Jonathon was chief of the temple guards. I knew him well enough. We had words on more than one occasion. He liked to throw his weight around, considered me of no account; well below his own station. I responded by treating him in like manner.

Annas formerly held the position of high priest, and he was also the father-in-law of Caiaphas. Undoubtedly, he was here as an adviser on points of law and protocol.

Then there was the Weasel himself. His long narrow face was made longer yet by his grizzled beard. I always thought he had a hungry look. He seemed rather satisfied this morning. The hint of a smile was on his face.

At the top of the stairs, on either side of the grand cedar doors, twelve sentinels stood guard. Pilate was nowhere to be seen. The great doors emblazoned with the imperial eagle crest remained firmly closed to the restive horde out front.

Leaving my two men on the first step, I approached the doors. I nodded a greeting in the direction of the three temple officials as I passed them. I had reached the fifth step when both the doors directly in front of me burst open. Pilate strode through flanked by Flavio and an assessor, a lawyer well acquainted with Roman law. Instantly the sentinel's arms shot upward in salute.

I froze in my tracks, and saluted.

Pilate's furrowed brow marked his surprise at seeing me here on the stairs. He swept by me, but with a quick beckoning motion of his hand, he indicated that I fall in behind him, something I was quite willing to do.

Pilate was dressed in his procurator's robes, the robes of judgement. In his left hand he held a tightly wrapped scroll. I was curious as to its contents. He took his position on the fourth step before the three-man temple delegation. Flavio and the assessor took their position on either side of the governor, while I stood to the left of my commanding officer.

A hush fell over the throng. This is what they came to see. Every ear strained to hear the proceedings.

The governor peered over the heads of the men directly in front of him. He scanned the assemblage on the street, took in the significance of it all, and then cleared his throat.

"Where is the man?"

Jonathon turned quickly. On reaching the first step, he beckoned beyond our pikemen to three of his own temple guards, who then advanced with their prisoner—Jesus of Nazareth.

He was a mess, almost unrecognizable. His hair was matted. He had been spat upon. The spittle was drying in his beard. There were red welts on his face and neck, a blood-oozing gash above his left eye, a discernable limp to his gait. It was apparent that during the night they had their way with him.[20]

He was escorted to a position directly before me. Intuitively, I knew he was my man now, my charge.

A twitch of Pilate's eyebrow hinted at his surprise with the condition of the man.

"Loose him," he directed with a slight wave of his hand.

Two temple guards hastened to unfasten the leather strap binding Jesus' arms to his torso. The third man freed the prisoner's hands. With a second wave of his hand, Pilate dismissed the temple guards who repositioned themselves on the first step and stood facing the proceedings.

Pilate took a seat on the throne of judgement which had been brought out for him by two attendants. Raising the scroll in his left hand he inquired, *"What charges are you bringing against this man?"*[21]

It was clear from this gesture that he was referring to the charges written on the scroll he now clutched in his hand. Undoubtedly he had read these charges himself and, in all likelihood, had discussed them with the assessor standing to his right. But he wanted the high priest to articulate them.

"If he were not a criminal, we would not have handed him over to you,"[22] Caiaphas huffed.

A rather cheeky response I thought.

"Take him yourselves and judge him by your own law,"[23] Pilate answered.

Here Annas interjected, *"But we have no right to execute anyone."*[24]

Now here was a devious response if there ever was one. The temple, in fact, routinely acted as both judge and executioner in religious matters, and had been granted full authority to do so. Death by stoning was commonplace. I had witnessed Annas himself cast the first stone at some hapless adulteress within the first week of my arrival here ten years ago. No, the temple had the right to execute, and these crafty fellows could surely find grounds on which to execute this man. They just did not want the blood on their hands. They did not want to be blamed for the death of this rabbi. For many, he had become the hope of the nation. No, they wanted us to do the job, to act as their executioners. They wanted him judged and executed under Roman law. What Caiaphas said next made this abundantly clear.

"We have found this man," he aimed a bony finger at Jesus, *"subverting our nation. He opposes payment of taxes to Caesar and claims to be Christ, a king."*[25]

Now here was a capital offence—a capital offence under Roman law. The Weasel had backed the Badger into a corner, and he was relishing the moment.

These charges would need further examination. But Pilate would not proceed in full view of a gloating high priest, urged on by his consorts and a handpicked audience. He retreated.

He abruptly arose from his throne, fixed his eyes on me, and said, "Bring the man." He motioned with a jerk of his head toward the great doors behind us, and then marched off into his residence.

I stepped down to escort Jesus, but he was already in motion. It became clear that the steps were painful for him. I put my hand to his elbow.

I found it strange that despite the pain he moved with the quick determination of a man with a destination in mind—the very thing I had noted on his arrival to the city.

I avoided his eyes. By the gods I avoided his eyes! I could not help think that out of some great mercy he was avoiding my eyes too.

For some strange reason there was the fading smell of fine perfume about him. It hinted of far better evenings than the last.[26]

Just before passing through the doors, I looked up and saw Pilate's wife, Claudia Procula, granddaughter of Augustus Caesar, gazing down at us from a second floor window. Undoubtedly, she had been watching the unfolding events of the morning with considerable interest. In the dance of life, she knew only too well the missteps her husband was capable of making.

When we entered the judgment hall, the dark-eyed Badger was seething. He knew he was being used by Caiaphas. He had said so to the assessor. He let fly with a string of profanity. "He has me trapped!" he snarled, "trapped like a rat in a stone water jar." And with that he tossed the list of charges onto his desk.

Then he turned to Jesus in the center of the room. He looked him over, walked fully around him. Pilate sighed, and nervously ran his fingers through his thinning hair. He made a smacking sound with his lips and asked, *"Are you the king of the Jews?"*[27]

"It is as you say,"[28] came the unequivocal answer.

This answer left the governor rocking on his heels. He brought a finger to his lips in pensive thought.

Jesus was not making an acquittal any easier.

But after a moment Jesus continued, *"Is that your own idea, or did others talk to you about me?"*[29]

"Do you think I am a Jew?" Pilate shot back with an ample measure of haughty contempt. *"It was your people and your chief priests who handed you over to me."* He continued the questioning, *"What is it you have done?"*[30]

"My kingdom is not of this world," Jesus responded, and to drive home this point he added, *"If it were, my servants would fight to prevent my arrest by the Jews. But now my kingdom is from another place."*[31]

Certain words that Claudius had spoken came echoing back into my mind. He had been convinced that this kingdom Jesus spoke of was somehow different from kingdoms as we know them. Now I heard it from the messiah's mouth. He was no armed insurrectionist and he had offered the actions of his followers as proof.

But Pilate seized on the use of the word kingdom. *"You are a king, then!"*[32] Pilate deduced.

With calm, clear deliberation the prophet spoke, *"You are right in saying I am a king. In fact, for this reason I was born, and for this I came into the world, to testify to the truth. Everyone on the side of truth listens to me."*[33]

It almost seemed from this response that Jesus was operating from, and speaking on, some higher plain—a dimension from which I had witnessed him operate during the healings at the temple. He was inviting Pilate to join him in discovering this higher ground of truth.

Pilate would not be moved. They were speaking past each other.

"What is truth?"[34] Pilate shrugged. The question was rhetorical. He had no intention of being dragged into a philosophical discussion with this prophet of the Jewish masses. Just as Caiaphas did, the Badger retreated.

Grabbing the list of charges from off his desk, he motioned for us to follow him back outside.

I quickly scanned the crowd as I emerged into morning sunlight with Jesus at my side. The crowd had not grown. Marius and his men had kept the general public at bay. His ranks had been augmented by a contingent of my own men. I spotted Claudius off to my far left. I felt more at ease.

In due course, we all resumed our previous positions. At this point I fully expected Pilate to pronounce the prisoner guilty of high treason. After all, this messiah had freely confessed to being a king. But I can only guess that Jesus words did have an impact on the governor. Upon taking his seat he announced, *"I find no basis for a charge against him."*[35]

A murmur arose from beyond the pikemen.

Caiaphas was livid. He let fly with a torrent of accusations, the last of these being that Jesus had threatened to destroy the temple and then rebuild it in three days.

Showing extraordinary patience Pilate let the high priest rage.

When his fury was spent Pilate turned to Jesus and asked, *"Don't you hear how many things they are accusing you of?"*[36]

But Jesus answered him not a word. His silence itself became a challenge. He had been cleared by Pilate. Why should he answer to these further allegations?

Though stunned by this silence Pilate repeated his position, *"I find no basis for a charge against this man."*[37]

Once again discontent began to rumble through the crowd on the street.

At this point I expected the trial to end, and the prisoner to be released. Let the crowds rage. Rome had spoken.

But Annas stepped smartly into the breach. *"He stirs up the people all over Judea by his teaching. He started in Galilee and has come all the way here."*[38]

"Is he a Galilean?" Pilate asked. "Under Herod's jurisdiction?"

"Yes," the flustered Caiaphas confessed, not knowing where this questioning might lead.

"Then to Herod he should go," was Pilate's prompt response. "Why drag me into this?" He sneered at the high priest.[39]

The governor seemed weary of the whole affair and, for the third time that morning, he found a way to dodge and retreat.

This trial was over.

The dark-eyed Badger rose from his judgement seat. He walked over to Jesus, the accused, and with a rather cunning smile and a nod he said, "Off to Herod you will go, man of truth."

24

Friday 7:10 a.m. April 7th, 30 AD

PILATE CALLED FOR A SCRIBE. HE DICTATED A SHORT DESCRIPTION of the early morning proceedings. He explained that when he discovered that the accused was from Galilee he felt it only proper that the tetrarch should judge the man. "Since he is your subject, I defer to you in this matter," he stated.

He included this letter with the roll of charges that the high priest had prepared. After affixing the imperial seal to this missive he handed it to me.

I viewed these developments with growing alarm. I had no desire to parade our prisoner across the city to Herod's palace in full public view—a public which would surely include a large number of pilgrims, fellow Galileans, and disciples of this man. I could think of no better way to advertise his arrest, and thereby foment turmoil. I could easily envision a pitched battle out on the street between the messiah's followers, and the high priest's temple guards supported as they were by the Weasel's merchant class allies.

"Now, Marcus, take this," Pilate said referring to the scroll, "and your man here, to Herod. I'm sure Jonathon can accompany you. The high priest certainly won't."

In a flash it occurred to me—Herod was not at his palace across town. He was here. He and Herodius had spent the night here with the governor and his wife. The governor's next words confirmed this sudden insight.

"He's in the guest apartment. You and the tribune Flavio can work out the details with these gentlemen." He motioned with a jerk of his head in the direction of the three-man delegation. He showed little concern for these details. The messiah was, after all, the high priest's problem. With that, he turned from me and strode back into his residence.

The dark-eyed Badger had scurried off. Of course, behind his back we did not call the governor the Badger without cause. Initially, it was because of his eyes. He had dark brown eyes. By that, I do not mean the color of the iris of the eye. They were a rather standard, unremarkable brown. No, it was the skin about the eyes that had a dark brown hue. This was his distinguishing feature. It gave him his badger look.

It now became clear to me that Caiaphas and his crowd out front were not moving anywhere. Caiaphas, Annas and Jonathon were in a hushed but heated discussion a few feet away. They were clearly caught off guard by these sudden developments.

Flavio turned to me. "You may yet have a fourth man on Golgotha," he remarked. "Herod won't take kindly to a second king—a man from his own domain."

I sniffed and then scowled at the thought of his expected reaction. "No, he won't," I confirmed. Visions of brutal torture galloped into mind.

"This thing may get very ugly." I motioned beyond my prisoner to the throng on the street. "I have twenty of my men backing up Marius and his pikemen. I may need all of my men if Caiaphas gets a conviction."

"You're right there, Marcus." Flavio nodded. "We need to keep this contained. I'll send a messenger and have them brought up. They can form a second line around the perimeter of the crowd." Then, to my relief, he added, "I won't be moving from here until this matter is settled."

Flavio showed a measure of early morning sobriety I had not witnessed in weeks. Maybe heaven was working on our side in this. He stepped back into the shadow of the Praetorium entrance, and in short order dispatched three messengers. The entire legion was placed on high alert, troops were redeployed, street patrols were doubled.

Seeing the three temple officials still in discussion, I beckoned my three man party on the first step to come forward. My third man, with the retrieved nail pouch in hand, had rejoined his partners.

I accepted the pouch and said, "You three will be coming with me. We'll be taking the prisoner to Herod inside the fortress."

Throughout this time, Jesus stood in sublime silence. I could only imagine what was going through his mind. Terror would be logical. But it was not to be seen in his face or his posture. He puzzled me—no, troubled me. Once again, he was beyond my understanding.

Flavio returned. Motioning to me, we approached the temple delegation.

"The centurion here has the written charges you have brought against the man, and he has the letter from the governor. He will take them and the prisoner to the tetrarch inside the fortress."

"In the fortress?" Caiaphas objected.

"Yes, in the fortress," Flavio responded. "The tetrarch is here." He motioned over his right shoulder.

This news was greeted with dismay. The high priest would not enter the fortress, even as he would not enter the Praetorium. If he did so, he would become defiled—unclean during this the high point of the Jewish calendar. That he would even venture out onto the street was an indication of the gravity which he attached to this matter.

Again, they huddled to discuss this among themselves. It was clear that Caiaphas was furious because Pilate had not simply ratified the decision of the Jewish High Council, or Sanhedrin, and then ordered Jesus crucified. I am certain that he believed Pilate had acted out of spite, and perhaps he had. Now, Caiaphas was forced to rely on Herod's erratic judgement to convict the man who had dared to challenge his authority. This recent news meant he would now be unable to personally present his case directly before the king.

Things turned out just as Pilate had predicted. Jonathon was chosen to accompany me. But Caiaphas and Annas elected to stay and await the outcome. In their place, they selected two men from among the coterie of priests and teachers of the law assembled behind our line of pikemen. Jonathon called on his three guards, who once again bound the prisoner. Together now, as a party of eleven, we set off.

It is only a few paces from the front steps of the Praetorium, around the southwest turret of the fortress, and then on into the fortress itself. But the milling throng did not make our passage easy. The moment they saw us move Jesus in that direction, there was a corresponding surge from the crowd toward him. It was clear they wanted blood. I hastily pressed a half dozen pikemen into service. They worked a certain magic. When their spears came down, aiming directly ahead, the way suddenly opened before us. Even so, I was relieved to reach my sanctuary—the fortress.

The guest apartment to which Pilate referred formed the entire second level of the southwest turret. It is connected directly to the governor's residence by a canopied catwalk, but there is also a second entrance from the inside of the fortress. This is the entrance we used.

I reasoned that there must have been a dramatic thaw in relations between the governor and the tetrarch. Perhaps the first ladies had something to do with this. Claudia Procula often invited Roman friends and relations to her home. These guests, like Claudia herself, came from the upper echelons of Roman society. For weeks on end, they would stay in the lavishly furnished tower suite. But this overnight stay was a first for the Herods. In my mind, it was an ominous development.

We reached the steeply rising stairs leading to the apartment. Without a moment's hesitation, I again reached out a hand to support the limping messiah.

He nodded his appreciation. A wisp of a smile crossed his lips.

It is strange how the mind works. In an instant, I was transported back to my childhood. In a moment of rough play, my younger brother had stumbled, snapping his ankle. It was the kind of accident that could have just as easily happened to me. For weeks I supported him. I became his living crutch while the bone mended. Every night I helped him up the stairs.

It was like that now. In my mind I was back helping my brother. For twelve steps I supported him, the messiah.

On the balcony above, Cestas, Herod's brooding bodyguard, waited. His well-muscled arms were folded across his chest. The brute's encounter with Lucas flashed into mind. There he stood, guarding the entrance to his master's suite.

A mixture of anger and loathing welled up within me. I fixed my eyes on him, and then addressed him. "We have come with an urgent message for the king, from his excellency the governor, and the high priest," I spoke with a glance toward Jonathon.

"He's not to be disturbed," Cestas replied impassively.

"I said it's urgent." There was insistence in my tone.

"Well, I said he's not to be disturbed."

He didn't flinch, or look me in the eye.

Seeing the impasse, and the anger beginning to burn in my eyes, Jonathon intervened, "Look, man. We have just come from the high priest and his excellency the governor. This is a matter of importance."

Cestas was unmoved.

"We have a prisoner. A Galilean," I interjected. "The king is to render judgement."

The word prisoner seemed to spark this butcher's interest. What this man did with prisoners I dreaded to imagine. He stared at Jesus. A thin smile crossed his lips.

"Who is the prisoner?" he inquired.

"Jesus, the prophet from Nazareth," I answered.

"Jesus of Nazareth?" His eyebrows shot up. He snickered. "Yes, my master will see him." Then, with a full grin he volunteered, "He has wanted to see him for quite some time."

He turned and rapped his knuckles three times on the door.

No response.

He rapped again.

"Cestas!" came the gruff response. "Send them away!"

He knocked once more and said, "They have a prisoner. Jesus of Nazareth."

I could hear the muffled sound of movement from within. The door latch clicked and then opened. It was Herod, blurry eyed, unkempt. An open purple robe hung loosely around his shoulders. In all other respects he was naked. Not only the robe was hanging loose.

"You have a prisoner," he growled as he looked beyond me.

"Yes, your majesty," I answered with a bow and then continued, "we have just come from the governor, and the high priest. The accused is with us: Jesus of Nazareth. Here are the charges against him." I bowed again and offered him the rolled parchments. He ignored them completely.

"Bring him in," he ordered. He stepped back inside and adjusted the robe about him.

"Herodius!" he bellowed. "We have a guest. Jesus of Nazareth."

It took a few moments for my eyes to adjust to the dim light of the room, and then to fully realize where I really was. This was the royal bedchamber. On the far side of the room Herodius lay on her side in an enormous four-poster bed. She propped her head up as she watched our men bring in the prisoner. A magnificently carved table, inlaid with ivory, stood in the center of the room. Off to the wall on the right stood two enormous thrones of a similar style. On the left, a doorway lead to what I guessed were the servants quarters.

Jesus stumbled slightly as he crossed the threshold. This rather large room soon became small with the arrival of eleven men.

"Untie him," Herod instructed as he perched himself on one of the thrones.

Jonathon's men expeditiously followed through.

I instructed two of my soldiers to wait outside, and the last man to wait just inside, at the door. Jonathon followed the same formula with his men.

Addressing Cestas, Herod said, "I will call you if you are needed."

I was relieved with Cestas' departure, and I sensed a certain reluctance on his part to leave.

"Jesus of Nazareth," the Fox pompously intoned. "The prophet of Galilee. I've longed to see you, my most noteworthy subject."

With that, Herod arose and, holding his robe shut, he approached the messiah. He inspected the taller man, walked fully around him. Noticing the welts and the dried spittle, he looked my way and inquired, "Is this your work, centurion?"

"No, your majesty." My eyes darted to Jonathon and back again.

"Ah, the high priest's work!" the Fox remarked grandly as he turned to Jonathon. "I didn't think you temple boys were capable."

This bit of sarcasm drew an acknowledging nod and a slight smile from the chief temple guard. Here was a backhanded complement from the pretentious Fox.

"Your majesty, I have here a letter from his excellency the governor, and certain charges brought by…"

The king halted me with an uplifted hand and a shake of his head.

"That can wait, centurion." He paused, and with a certain dramatic flourish he began, "We have here a man of rare talent. He makes the lame to walk, the blind to see, has cured the leper. I have heard reports that he has raised the dead." Spotting a gold chalice on the inlaid table, he seized it by the stem and with relish declared, "He has even turned water into wine."

He lifted the chalice before the messiah and grandly inquired, "Isn't that so, Jesus?"

The messiah did not answer him a word.

If Herod was perturbed by this silence, he did not show it. "Joanna!" he hollered. "Joanna!"

An attractive young woman entered from the door on the left, and with short quick steps she made her way before the tetrarch. She bowed low.

"Fill this chalice with water, and bring it back."

He stared after her as she left. I noticed Herodius following his hungry gaze.

"Soon we will see if this prophet can perform the works of which we heard." He nodded his head with an eager enthusiasm. Then, addressing Jesus, he inquired, "Tell us of your magic arts."

The messiah fixed his eyes straight ahead. He looked beyond the Fox and did not answer him a word. His silence was challenging enough.

Herod's eyes flitted to me, to Jonathon and his men, back to Jesus, over to Herodius.

Joanna returned, brimming chalice in hand. This time, as she bowed, he bowed too. His eyes played with hers. He received the chalice. He cradled, and then fondled it gently in his open hand as he watched her retreat.

Herodius cleared her throat and made a great fuss of repositioning herself on the bed.

Herod stepped back in front of Jesus. With great show, he lifted the gold chalice to his lips, took a sip and swirled it around his mouth and then he coughed it full force over the front of the messiah's robe.

"It's water!" he cackled. "It's water," he repeated as he coughed again to clear his throat. He found great humour in this, and began to laugh uncontrollably.

Herodius joined in. Jonathon chuckled. I smiled just enough to be polite.

"I haven't drunk any damn water in so long… " He broke off into more laughter. "I forgot what the damn stuff tastes like."

He fought to bring himself back in control. Forgetting himself, his robe fell open, exposing all. This set him off cackling wildly again. He turned from us.

I saw a repeated pattern of four brown stains along the back of the purple robe. Recognition was immediate. These were blood stains—blood from the severed hand of a beggar boy. I sucked in a sharp breath, as though punched in the stomach.

The demented cackle continued.

The messiah stood in silence, a quiet silence that despite all, came to fill, even dominate, the room. Strangely, he was master here.

The Fox was unable to face him. King Herod was unable to face the donkey king, to look him in the eye.

I understood perfectly what was happening. I, too, had tasted of this unease in the messiah's presence. Back in the temple I had put feet to my own fear.

Having laughed himself to lunacy, Herod gasped for air. Then with his composure suddenly regained, he wheeled around and held the chalice up to the *Christos*, the messiah's face. With his eyes pinched shut and his voice almost breaking, he hissed, "Now, change it to wine!"[40]

The messiah looked past him. He uttered not a word.

Herod, with eyes still shut, gasped three times and as if counting, on three he hurled the contents of the chalice in Jesus' face.

Looking up he cackled, "It's water! It's only water!"

There was genuine relief in his voice. He had feared it might be wine. And so he set loose again with a further bout of hideous laughter.

Now, for a moment, I dared look at Jesus' dripping face. I saw a noble serenity there that Herod, that small shrewd monster, would never know.

The tetrarch saw it too and it was driving him insane. He made no pretense of covering his nakedness now. He pranced about laughing, a raw fool on display.

Glancing at Jonathon, I could tell that he, too, found no humour here. His troubled eyes spoke of growing discomfort, if not alarm, at the king's antics. Where this was heading defied prediction. Clearing his throat, he began, "Your majesty, there are certain charges the high priest has brought."

"Charges. Ah yes, charges," he moaned as though aroused from a drunken stupor. "What are these charges?"

"I have them here," I answered, and once more bowed and held the rolled parchments out to him.

He ignored them. He approached, put his mouth to my ear and screamed, "Read them!" He snickered and coughed, and he began to tremble violently until he collapsed into his throne.

With my left ear ringing I opened the roll and began, "From his excellency the governor… "

"From his excellency the governor," he mimicked. "Hang the governor!" he screamed as his face contorted like one possessed. "There are charges. What are the charges?" He held his hands up above his head, with his fingers fully spread, as though he would try to capture the parts of his head if it should explode.

Completely flustered, I blurted out, "He's charged with being the king of the Jews."

The reaction was instant.

Herod's head snapped back. It whacked the back of the throne with such force that it split the wooden backboard.

His body convulsed once more and slid to the floor.

His eyes rolled back in his head.

His face contorted.

From a kneeling position, a demonic voice—a voice not his own, erupted from deep within his being, "He is the king of the Jews! The Christ! The holy one of God!" A low guttural hissing sound followed. The demonic manifestation was now complete. His body rocked and convulsed. Rocked and convulsed. Every muscle rippled and twitched. He had become a tautly coiled human cobra, spitting venom.

The Messiah for the first time looked to him.

"Be still," he whispered.

It was a whisper so quiet that I would have missed it had I not seen his lips move.

But his words brought an instantaneous reaction in his opposite. The pretender to the Jewish throne fell forward in obeisance to the said true king. His body convulsed once more, and then became still.

Still as death. Long moments passed.

He stirred. Then the tetrarch lifted his head, and in his own calm, flat voice stated, "He is the king of the Jews."

He struggled awkwardly to his feet.

Taking the bloodied purple robe off his back, he approached the messiah, naked and whimpering. He tied its sleeves around the neck of the people's king, so that the stained fabric hung cape-like over his shoulders and down his back. But all the while the Fox was careful not to look into his rival's face.

Herod turned from the passive Jesus, his head hanging, and in utter despair. "Cestas," he called. It was a weak call, barely audible.

I signalled my man at the door. He retrieved the bodyguard. By this time, the tetrarch had dropped to all fours and was sitting with his back to the king.

The bewildered Cestas approached.

"Bring the crown. The braided crown you're making. Put it…"

he sobbed piteously. "Put it on…put it on the king."

Cestas left hurriedly.

The messiah stood in silence. His gaze was steady. Still, he looked beyond this.

Herod pulled his legs up around him. He rocked from side to side for eternal moments.

Cestas returned with a braided crown— a crown of thorns in his hand. He was truly dumbfounded. He had no idea what he was to do with it.

Jonathon intervened. He gestured to Jesus.

Cestas stepped before the king and firmly pressed his hand-fashioned crown down upon the regal brow.

Here was a fitting crown for a donkey king.

Cestas sneered, and then he began the same cackling laugh I had heard earlier from Herod. As if on cue the tetrarch joined in the demented cackling.

"Now take him. Take him from me," Herod whimpered in a different voice from all the others I had heard from him. He did not even dare to look back following his rival's coronation.

Now on seeing their moment pass, the high priest's appointed delegates broke loose with a torrent of accusations against the messiah. Rebellion. Heresy. Sedition. Sabbath breaking. All manner of false teaching. Threatening to destroy the temple. Blasphemy! The litany poured out till it reached a rabid crescendo.[41]

The whimpering Fox showed no interest, no interest whatever. Still naked, seated and sobbing, with the back of his limp hand he waved for us to leave.

A drop of blood trickled down the messiah's thorn-pierced temple.

I put my hand to Jesus' elbow. Together we turned to the door. I was last to leave.

As I pulled the door shut, the naked Herod was on all fours.

He was over at the bed licking the hand of a doting Herodius. With her free hand she soothingly stroked his balding head.

25

Jesus had survived Herod. This was no small feat in my estimation. In reality he had totally dominated him. Without speaking a word he had thrown him into a state of raving lunacy. Without raising his voice above a whisper, he had stilled the raging voice of hell. Without moving a hand, he had reduced this pretentious monarch to a pathetic fool, grovelling and naked.

I was both impressed and confounded by what I had witnessed. His power baffled me. It was from another realm. Of that I was convinced.

He was the master of the events around him, not the victim. One could not help but feel that this was a drama of his own choosing and we—all of us—were somehow players in it. We were players moving at his discretion, and at any moment he could have stepped out of this drama, if he had seen fit. I am sure of it. Undoubtedly, the unfolding script for this play was written well in advance, and he was following it—following it to a destination he had chosen.

For the first time, I began to actively hope for his release. I wanted free of this.

As I helped him on the stairs, I took courage and glanced into his eyes. If eyes are the windows to the soul, then this was a very different soul. It appeared to me that the wellspring of eternity was in residence there.

I felt small, so very small.

Now for these twelve steps down, our roles were reversed; I felt I was the weaker brother.

The same pikemen who had escorted us into the fortress were waiting to escort us back out. As our party stepped into view, the expectant mob on the street erupted with the cry, "Crucify him! Crucify Him!" They were vociferous.

"Crucify him! Crucify Him!"

Leading the chant was an immaculately robed man. Unlike the masses, he faced the crowd and urged them on—the portly commander of his blood thirsty cohorts. "Crucify him! Crucify Him!" he bawled with his arms raised.

"Crucify him! Crucify Him!" the crowd echoed.

As he swung around, I caught sight of his face. It was Timaeus. There was bloody determination in his eye. This was a battle he and his fellow merchants intended to win. A human sea of hatred urged him on.

The pikemen's magic had lost some of its charm. The men on the street moved when confronted with the point of a spear, but there was a belligerence there that I had not noticed an hour ago.

"Crucify him! Crucify Him!" Some began to hurl dust in the air. I feared stones would come next.

We rounded the turret.

"Crucify him! Crucify Him!" They pressed in behind us as we advanced. Seething shouts lashed the air. "Crucify him! Crucify Him!"

I felt genuine relief when we reached the safety of our line of pikemen on the Praetorium steps. What a different response to this man from what I had seen on Sunday!

Jonathon and the guards with him rejoined Caiaphas and Annas on the third step. The high priest's appointed delegates were soon in animated conversation with their master. I moved past them with my purple-robed prisoner to where Flavio waited with three other centurions on the fourth step. They were standing to the right of the empty judgement seat.

"So, what is the verdict?" Flavio discreetly inquired.

"There is no verdict," I answered.

"No verdict?" Flavio sounded surprised. "Did Herod hear the case?"

"Yes, he heard it." There was a vagueness to my voice that betrayed the baffling nature of what I had witnessed. Quick pat answers said so little.

"Well, did he find him guilty?" Flavio persisted as though he had not heard my earlier answer.

"No." I paused in thought. "He just sent him back."

"Then he should be free to go." He gestured in the direction of the messiah.

Strangely, this had not occurred to me. I think I was so mesmerized by what had transpired in the guest apartment that I failed to link Herod's dismissal of the charges with Pilate's earlier acquittal of Jesus on the same charges. It logically followed that he should be freed.

"Go ahead and report to the governor." Flavio motioned in the direction of the Praetorium entrance. "Tell him what happened before Herod. Renaldo here can accompany you."

Putting my hand to the nail pouch on my belt, I responded, "I guess there will only be three men on Golgotha after all."

Flavio wrinkled his brow and then nodded in agreement with this assessment. But a quick glance out to the crowd hinted that he thought this was a verdict that would not go down well with the people.

I turned to the three soldiers accompanying me and gave them their new orders, "Report to Claudius. Have him get Barabbas and his two friends ready for execution. Have them brought out front here. We should be free to set out shortly."

Turning to Jesus, I motioned for him to follow me. Renaldo took over as prisoner escort.

166

Once again, I glanced up before passing through the Praetorium entrance. Once again, the first lady was watching from her window.

Pontius Pilate was seated with the province's chief revenue officer when we entered. He glanced up from his ledgers and beckoned us forward. Addressing me he inquired, "What word do you bring from the tetrarch?"

I bowed. "Your excellency, the tetrarch has heard the charges against this man—the charges prepared by the high priest. He has examined him, and, my lord, he has sent him back to you."

Pilate sighed. "Did he provide a written judgement?" His eyes flitted to the roll of parchment still in my hand.

"No, your excellency."

He frowned.

"He simply dismissed us," I added in an attempt to clarify.

Pilate put his hand to his chin and made a smacking sound with his lips. "Well, dismissed is dismissed," he said perfunctorily.

Then he fixed his attention on the messiah. For the first time he noticed the crown of thorns, and the robe. He arose. He came around the table where he sat and approached us. He examined the bloodied brow, the penetrating thorns.

"A fine bit of work!" He shook his head in disgust. Then he touched the fabric of the purple robe. His interest piqued. He stepped behind the messiah and immediately spotted the rust brown stains. He rubbed the crusted stain between his fingers. Recognizing its source, he snorted in revulsion. Here was the purple wrapping for Herod's small presentation at the banquet just three days ago. The governor grimaced and once more shook his head.

"A fine bit of work!" The words dropped heavy with sarcasm.

My eyes shifted to Renaldo. I could hear the unspoken questions churning through his mind. A flicker of his eye told me we would talk of this later.

"A fine bit of work!" Pilate again repeated his words. He paused in reflection, and then he seemed to shake himself back to the present reality.

"Well, dismissed is dismissed," he reiterated as he came back in front of the messiah. "We'll inform the high priest of your acquittal," he announced to Jesus.

Then he called for two of his attendants to take up their positions by the judgement seat on the steps out front. He intended to deliver this decision with the proper decorum warranted under Roman law. He moved to the window and surveyed the crowd on the street. The numbers had not grown. Marius and his pikemen had seen to that. But the assembled throng had grown more restive.

By closing off the street and hedging in this partisan crowd, the army had ensured that there would be no clash between the opposing camps—the messiah's followers, and the high priest's temple faction. But this same move also served to provoke a strident hostility in this confined faction. It was hostility which stiffened incrementally with the passage of time.

The Badger shrugged and then sighed deeply. Instinctively he knew this would be a challenge. He turned back to us and brusquely declared, "Gentlemen, follow me."

He strode to the large double doors, and then paused to see if all of us were ready to follow him at the moment he gave the signal to the doorkeepers. As he turned for this final check, a messenger called out.

"Your excellency, I have here a message for you from the first lady."

Clearly annoyed by this interruption, he threw up his hands and snapped, "Well, what is it?"

The young man unrolled a small parchment and read, *"Don't have anything to do with that innocent man, for I have suffered a great deal today in a dream because of him."*[42] Having accomplished his assignment, the messenger bowed and handed this brief missive to the governor.

Pilate took it, sniffed as though amused, and cast questioning eyes on the messiah.

I could not help but remember Renaldo's words from earlier in the week. "He has a certain way with women," he had said. But then if the harlots came to follow him, why not the governor's wife?

This time my eyes signalled my friend for a later conversation.

Pilate turned, readjusted the cuff on his sleeve, and nodded to the doormen. The eagle-emblazoned doors swung open. The sentinels snapped to attention. Once more, their right arms rose in salute. A hush fell upon the throng.

The governor strode out, head held high. We dutifully followed in his wake.

Upon taking his seat, he unrolled the note from his wife and read it for himself. I tried to read his face for a clue of what action he might take, but no clear course was written there.

We positioned ourselves before him just as before.

Jesus stood before me. His abused body was present, but I perceived his focus was elsewhere.

Pilate beckoned for Caiaphas and Annas to approach. He cleared his throat and with mustered authority he began. *"You brought me this man as one inciting the people to rebellion. I have examined him in your presences and have found no basis for your charges against him. Neither has Herod, for he sent him back to us; as you can see, he has done nothing to deserve death."*[43]

With these words, a murmur arose from the crowd.

As if taking this discontent as his cue Pilate added, *"Therefore, I will punish him and then release him."*[44]

I am not sure these were his intended words, or if they were the words thrust upon him by the hostile throng. They were words intended to appease. They had the opposite effect.

Caiaphas reacted. He put both hands to his face and clutched his greying beard. It seemed he would pull the whole mass of it out by its roots.

Annas stamped his foot and twisted his aged frame as though smitten with mortal agony.

A howl of protest erupted from beyond our line of pikemen on the first step. No, this pronouncement did not sit well. There was cold resistance. Had the prophet been released at that moment, this mob would have torn him to pieces.

Then fate seemed to intervene. I noticed Pilate's eyes move to a spot off to the far right, a spot near the turret. I glanced that way. It was Claudius and his contingent arriving with the three men destined for Golgotha.

Seeing Barabbas in chains, the Badger tried a new tack. Rising from his seat and stretching out an open hand to Jesus, he repeated, *"I find no basis for a charge against him."*[45] There was sincerity in his voice, but a conniving manipulation at work in his mind.

He continued, *"But it is your custom for me to release to you one prisoner at the time of the Passover. Do you want me to release 'the king of the Jews'?"*[46]

Again he gestured to the purple-robed figure.

The high priest's response was instant and vehement, *"No, not him!"* He raised his arm and pointed to the terrorist. *"We want Barabbas!"*[47]

"Barabbas! Barabbas!" the cry went up from the street.

The Badger smacked his lips. This was not the response he had wanted. But now, at this precise moment, he determined that he would play with this crowd. He would play them to reach his own desired end. He loved this sport. He had seen the Emperor Tiberius do the same with the crowds in Rome.

Jesus stood alone. He stood silent. He fixed his eyes beyond this. He had his own destination in mind.

Pilate strode over to me. His step was purposeful, resolute. "Have him flogged," he said with a decisive nod. "Then bring him back here."[48]

He turned from me and once more retreated to his inner sanctum behind the eagle emblazoned doors.

His wife's parchment note was left behind. It balanced precariously on the edge of the judgement seat. A sudden gust of cool wind caught it. It skittered and flew across the stone steps. Then it was caught up.

In an instant it was gone.

26

WEDGE FORMATION IS THE BEST WAY TO ADVANCE THROUGH A hostile crowd. Under Flavio's direct orders we formed up accordingly on the stairs, with added manpower assigned at his discretion. He viewed the mood of this mob with growing alarm.

Jesus was placed at the heart of this bristling wedge. He was there for his own protection. Renaldo and I accompanied him on either side.

Claudius and his contingent remained on the broad stairs with the three condemned men. The ultimate fate of Barabbas still hung in the balance, with the messiah as the counterweight.

As we set out I could not help but reflect on what a change this week had brought for my kingly prisoner. The Sunday before he had entered as the heroic saviour riding the crest of a human wave of unsullied joy. I had feared the very power of Rome would be trampled under the feet of his horde of followers. Now, five days later, he was leaning on my arm, under Rome's protection from a mob of his own people—a seething mob thirsting for his blood. He needed our protection on the way to the whipping post. There was a dreadful irony in all of this, an irony as cruel and twisted as the piercing thorns that crowned his head.

Once again, the shouts of "Crucify Him! Crucify Him!" went up. Once again, Timaeus raged against him. His puffy face was red with exertion. He kept just beyond the advancing spears of the pikemen—a huffing heckler bent on revenge.

Upon entering the fortress, I was thankful for the extra manpower. Flavio had exercised a rare bit of sober wisdom.

The whipping post stood at the very center of the fortress courtyard. This silent wooden sentinel reminded the errant or lazy soldier of the cruel consequence which might well await him. Insolence and insubordination found their remedy there.

The city's residents only rarely met such a fate. They had more to fear from the temple guards, and the ritual stonings that were routinely carried out to enforce the dictates of religious law. Only when the offence was aimed directly at Rome would the offender be brought here. Already that morning Barabbas and his cohorts had endured the lash in preparation for the cross. Now, so too would the messiah.

Oddly, the only bit of greenery within the fortress walls was to be found here at the whipping post. The courtyard itself was hard packed dun-coloured clay, but from a crevice at the base of the whipping post a dandelion sallied forth. Its gaudy yellow flowers spoke eloquently of spring. Here, it thrived while boldly mocking its drab surroundings.

I called for the men to administer the scourging. Every legion has its share of men who draw perverse pleasure in inflicting pain on others. Within our ranks were some of these. Today, two such men had been assigned to administer floggings. Wearing Herod's gaudy robe, and the crown of thorns fashioned by Cestas, Jesus stood before them. His attire served as a standing invitation for abuse.

"Ah, the king of the Jews!" Lucius exclaimed. The news about Jesus had spread fast. His clothing confirmed the rumours of kingly aspirations. Lucius seized a corner of the purple robe. "We have a royal treat for you." He bowed low and then as he straightened he let fly with a vicious backhand slap to the face.

The messiah reeled back with the force of it.

"We have far more for you, your highness!" Gaius smirked. He seized him by the beard and gave a twisting yank, forcing the messiah to his knees. Simultaneously, the soldier's knee smashed

173

into Jesus' chin. The snapping slam of teeth to teeth testified to the force of the blow.

I intervened, "Look, you two. I need a man I can take back to the governor, not a mutilated corpse."

"Ah, Marcus," Lucius answered with a broad grin, "we'll give you your man. We were just havin' some fun. Weren't we?" He laughed as he glanced to Gaius. "It's not every day we get to flog a king."

"Flog him, then. Don't kill him, or you'll be next on the post."

They nodded. A surly silence followed.

Gaius removed Herod's robe and handed it to me. Then they stripped him naked—naked except for his crown. They shoved his face to the post. Lucius shackled the king's up stretched arms to an iron ring near the top of the weathered cedar post. Meanwhile Gaius stooped to bind his feet to the base. Suddenly he raised his head and exclaimed, "He *smells* like a bloody king."

It was the scent of perfume I had noted earlier.

They stepped back to admire their work. They chuckled at his nakedness. "Looks the same as any beggar's butt," Lucius groused.

"Yes, but he smells like a bloody king!" Gaius shot back. He was quite astonished by this aromatic discovery. His nostrils flared as he inhaled several whiffs for the amusement of his fellow soldiers.

I examined both flagrums, the multi-thonged whips used to administer the scourging. I had pulled them from the large bucket of salt brine where they were temporarily stored. The lead balls and metal studs on the strips of leather determined the brutality of each blow. Forty lashes with the most vicious whip could shred a man's back. In Germania, I witnessed a young man's death by whipping. The flailing had exposed his kidneys. The messiah had already been brutalized during his night with Caiaphas and the temple guard. A measure of restraint was warranted. I consulted Renaldo. Then I drew my dagger and, to the dismay of Gaius and Lucius, I cut the lead stud from four of the multiple leather thongs. There were plenty left to do their damage.

"Kings and beggars need a break sometime," I said as I handed each man their implements.

I gave a quick nod and the flogging began.

"One."

"Two."

Lucius worked from one side, Gaius from the other.

"Three."

"Four."

They began at the shoulders.

"Five."

"Six."

Each thwack of the whip opened multiple wounds.

"Seven."

"Eight."

Their rhythm was established now. They were moving lower on his back. The pikemen cheered them on.

"Nine."

"Ten."

The blood began to flow freely.

"Eleven."

"Twelve."

Jesus' body quivered with the shock of each blow. But he was silent. Silent and gasping.

"Thirteen."

"Fourteen."

I moved to one side, trying to get a look at his face. His thorn-crowned brow was pressed to the post.

"Fifteen."

"Sixteen."

He was mouthing a word with each blow. What was it?

"Seventeen."

"Eighteen."

It came with a gasp. Barely audible.

"Father."

"Father."

At twenty, I called a halt. They had traversed the whole of his body, from shoulders to feet. It was a bloody path. I examined the wounds—more damage than I expected.

His breath came in huge gulps. His eyelids flickered. He remained conscious. At least he remained conscious.

I stepped over to Gaius. I cut another three studs from his whip. Then I did the same for Lucius.

"Harder! Harder!" came a shout from above and behind me. It was Cestas—Cestas going wild on the balcony of the guest chamber. He could not wait for the lashing to resume. Like a giddy child, he bounced up and down and hollered for more.

I gave an upward nod to Lucius, and then began calling out the stroke count again.

"Twenty-one."

"Twenty-two."

They started over at the shoulders.

"Twenty-three."

"Twenty-four."

Once more the frenzied cheers went up.

"Twenty-five."

"Twenty-six."

Each man aimed to outdo the other; each blow was more savage than the last.

"Twenty-seven."

"Twenty-eight."

He did not cry out, unlike many men I have seen. He was silent beneath the cracking whip, uncommonly silent.

"Twenty-nine."

"Thirty."

Stroke by flailing stroke they moved once more across his bloodied frame. A quivering, rutted mess. That is what was left by the time we reached forty. I stood near him—watched his breathing. It was fast but shallow, very shallow by the time we finished.

Lucius fell to his knees. Sweating. Gasping. Exhausted from exertion.

Gaius did the same. "That was floggin' good!" he exclaimed as he arose and clapped his partner on the back. "Floggin' good!"

Here they were laughing—laughing like two brothers in that tight but brittle fellowship that is formed by inflicting pain. The fellowship of the torturer.

I beckoned to a young soldier.

"Get me a bowl of figs." I motioned in the direction of the officer's mess. It was time for a bit of breakfast.

After that performance we were not going anywhere fast. Jesus needed time to recover. I watched his eyelids flicker, saw his bare ribs heave.

The dandelion at the base of the post was drenched in blood.

The young soldier returned with a heaping bowl of figs. I was hungry. And angry. More angry than hungry. Barabbas would walk free. I knew it. The Badger would bow to the crowd. I saw it in his eyes.

The messiah? Where was the power? It must have evaporated like a desert pond, left him like a harlot's lover. Stripped naked, he was a man after all. Just a man. Was he not?

Renaldo recognized my brooding. While I ate my figs, he made small talk. He knew better than to probe. I felt now was not the time to tell him that the robe folded over my arm was stained by the blood of the beggar boy staying at his house.

The men filled the air with coarse humour and ribald jabs aimed at the man on the whipping post. On another day with another man I might well have joined in. Why are men that way? Why do we wear cruelty like a second skin? Why do we revel in abusing others —draw comfort in it, like a pig in a wallow?

"Is there another one?" Gaius asked. He would cheerfully flog the morning away if we supplied the victims. When I shook my head, he grabbed the bucket of brine and dumped it over Jesus.[49]

He writhed and gasped—writhed and gasped.

Lucius freed the shackles from his wrist. Gaius untied his feet. Renaldo and I stood on either side of Jesus for support, expecting he would collapse. His hands fell to his side. His head dropped limp. But after a few moments he turned slowly, tentatively, on unsteady feet.

"Have some figs, my good man," I offered. "Have some water and some figs."

I motioned for a bucket of fresh water to be brought.

His clothes were returned to him. His hands trembled as he tied his bloodied loin cloth about him.

He drank deeply from the pewter ladle I handed to him. When he dipped the ladle in the bucket for a second drink, Lucius grabbed it from his hand. He rapped the messiah sharply across the side of the head with it.

"Your majesty," he bowed low in mock adoration, "I did the work here. I'll have a drink now!"

A fresh trickle of blood flowed down near Jesus' left ear from where the ladle hit the stabbing thorns.

Jesus needed strength, I reasoned, strength to walk back and face the Badger. It would not do to have him fainting on the way. As he struggled into his outer garment, I pressed a dried fig to his lips. He received it like some sacred gift. Through a fog of pain, his eyes smiled back at me.

He might just as well have shot me with an arrow. I was wounded. Wounded by a glance. Why did he bother me so? Strangely, there was power in his weakness, more power than I dared imagine.

Seeing the king back in his commoner's clothes, Gaius cried out, "The robe! Where's his purple robe?"

Suddenly, I was uncomfortable with the filthy purple article draped over my arm. I handed it to Renaldo. He made a grand show of flipping it fully open, then tying the sleeves once more around the messiah's neck. He stepped back and bowed courteously.

Not to be out done, Gaius fell to his knees in mock obeisance. *"Hail king of the Jews!"*[50] he called out.

Now the platoon of pikemen joined in. One by one they knelt before the thorn-crowned monarch and hailed him as the Jewish king.

I ordered his hands bound once more. Someone produced a hickory stick which they shoved between his tightly bound fingers. Here was the royal sceptre. A fresh round of bowing and hailing ensued. Lucius bowed deeply and then seized the crude hickory sceptre and delivered a sharp blow to Jesus' head. Several other soldiers followed suit. For these men, months of pent up frustration found a vent.[51]

Jesus was silent. Always silent.

Soon he grew unsteady on his feet.

When Cestas on his second level perch began to shout and bounce about once more, I came to my senses. I called a halt to the abuse. After all, why should we entertain Herod's bloody butcher?

I should have stopped that brutal mockery far sooner. I felt less than a man because of it. I had my own anger to blame for it. My brooding had permitted this to happen.

With a backhanded slap to Renaldo's forearm I snapped, "Have them form up!"

He began barking orders. In moments our pikemen were back in wedge formation. Once again, I flanked Jesus at the core of the wedge.

"Forward, ho!" Renaldo bawled. As we set out, he retook his position to the left of Jesus.

Once again, Timaeus was waiting for us when we hit the street.

While keeping just ahead of the lead pikeman in the wedge, he maintained a steady full-throated scream.

"Crucify him! Crucify him!"

Again his confreres took up the chant.

"Crucify him! Crucify him!"

How Timaeus managed to keep just beyond the point of the lead spear defied logic. While bellowing himself hoarse, he retreated backward in the crowd, glancing neither to the right nor left. It was a stunt few fools would dare to repeat.

A few paces from the steps leading up to the Praetorium, his luck ran out. One instant, I saw him clutching his chest. The next instant he was down, felled by a spear I presumed. The lead pikeman stepped on him. The second pikemen stepped by him. When finally we reached him, he was white-faced, gasping and twitching—a corpse in the making. There was not a mark on him, though. I presumed his heart had given way

Thus , I stepped slightly to the left so his body, lying prone on the cold cobblestones, would pass between me and my prisoner. The hem of Jesus' robe brushed lightly over his pallid face.

Timaeus emerged from beneath the messiah's purple robe transformed, like one awakened from a dream. Not knowing where he was, he shook himself. He arose and was silent. Arose and went home. At least that is what I presume he did. I never saw him again.

It was strange. Such a strange happening!

It happened so fast. But I saw it all. I saw the physical change —a miraculous transformation in the body of this fallen man. I saw it clearly.

I felt small once again, very small beside this man in the middle, very small helping him up the Praetorium steps, very small while waiting.

Waiting for Pontius Pilate.

27

FLAVIO QUICKLY BROUGHT ME BACK TO PRESENT REALITIES.

"It looks like our boys got the job done," he remarked as his eyes surveyed the brutalized messiah.

"Yes," I responded dryly. "Lucius and Gaius had a bit of fun."

"Well, I guess we better find out what the governor wants done with him now," Flavio offered.

The commotion that our arrival had created among the throng fronting the palace had not brought Pilate through the eagle-emblazoned doors, so some further action was warranted. Flavio turned and addressed Renaldo, "Report to the governor that you have returned with the prisoner." As Renaldo strode off, Flavio turned back to me and added, "You can wait at the door with your man till we know the governor's will."

Having accomplished their purpose, I dismissed the pikemen from our wedge formation. They rejoined their comrades on the first step while I assisted Jesus to the top of the broad steps. We positioned ourselves near the door and waited for Renaldo to return with further instructions.

From this higher elevation I had a commanding view of the confined and seething masses on the street. Their patience was wearing thin. They had assembled for one purpose: to spill the blood of this man, the man beside me. His life hung in the balance, but he seemed somehow distant from this circumstance, as though he was standing on an entirely different plane.

Perhaps he was.

Claudius and the soldiers with him waited off to the right on the second step. With them stood an anxious Barabbas and the other two condemned men. His fellow terrorists had a rather wilted appearance. Their heads hung low. Only Barabbas had a reason for hope. After all, it was he who was the favorite of the crowd on the street.

Annas, Caiaphas, and Jonathon fretfully consulted on the third step.

Flavio stood on the fourth step, conferring with another centurion he had pressed into service. Next to the tribune stood the empty judgement seat. From thence the Badger would speak. One man would die, the other walk free.

The Badger! I tilted my head back in thought. I once saw a dog attack a cornered badger. It was a battle royal. The dog barked and yapped. But the moment the canine would lower his head to sink his fangs into the smaller beast, the badger would lunge forward, hissing, his sharp claws flailing. The dog would retreat, and the same process would again be set in motion. Eventually the dog was distracted for an instant. In that moment the badger started digging. He disappeared in a hail of flying dirt.

This, too, was a royal battle. We would soon see how this Badger would respond.

Momentarily, one of the double palace doors opened and Renaldo emerged. He beckoned for me to enter with my purple-clad prisoner. Upon entering, we moved to the same position we had assumed during the earlier interrogation. Pilate stepped back from the window where he had been scanning the street scene. Seeing me first, he inquired, "Ah, Marcus, how is our man—our man of truth?"

"See for yourself, your excellency," I answered with a courteous bow and an openhanded gesture in the direction of my prisoner.

Once again, Pilate made a full circuit around the messiah. He examined the spot where the ladle hit, saw the fresh welts inflicted by the hickory scepter, and took note of an open gash on the side of his neck.

Not satisfied with merely a facial view, the Badger barked, "Strip him."

I stepped forward and untied the purple robe. I handed it to Renaldo and then loosened Jesus' own garment. The blood from the flogging had begun to soak through the fabric on his back. Some of it had congealed. Tearing it loose brought a sudden gasp from the people's king, and this was followed by a fresh crimson flow. I dropped his bloodstained white robe on the floor.

"Hmm!" Pilate grimaced and moved around for a better view. He smacked his lips and then looked away like one caught up in thought. "Tie Herod's robe back on him." He gestured to Renaldo, who quickly obliged.

The thorn-crowned messiah now stood in only his bloodied breechcloth with the purple robe draped cape-like over his shoulders.

The Badger looked him over as though Jesus were a courtier trying on the latest Roman fashion. Again, he circled him for a full view to catch the full effect. Satisfied with what he saw, he nodded approvingly and then grandly announced, "Our king! Our Jewish King!" Pilate gestured to Jesus and bowed. He followed that up with a clever smirk. But throughout this time I noted that he did not dare look Jesus in the eye, not even once. I suppose he knew, even as I knew, that looking truth in the face can bring a jolt of soul-searing distress.

Having settled the issue of the prisoner's attire, with a quick beckoning motion, the Badger called for us to follow him out to the judgement seat. When we reached the doors once again, he paused. "Just as before I will go first," he perfunctorily announced.

The doors swung open again. Sentinels saluted. As we stepped out this time there was a surprising chill in the air. The brilliant morning sun had been replaced by a bank of low hanging cloud along the western horizon. Rain seemed possible.

The hushed crowd watched as the governor descended to the

183

fourth step, but before he took his seat, he motioned toward me as I advanced with my limping prisoner. Referring to Jesus the governor announced, *"See, I am bringing him out to you, so that you may know that I do not find him guilty."*[52]

Then, as Jesus took his position in full view before this partisan crowd, Pilate stepped over to this bruised and bleeding captive and declared, *"Behold the man!"*[53]

Jesus was indeed a sight to behold. Spittle drenched. Face swollen. The skin on his back and legs shredded and oozing blood. The mocking filthy robe. The agonizing crown. Here was royal splendor, stripped naked and standing on its head. Splendor enough for a donkey king.

If the Badger's intended response was pity for this man, none was forthcoming.

"Crucify him! Crucify him!" Caiaphas rasped.

His temple guards took up the chant, *"Crucify Him! Crucify Him!"*

Soon the entire crowd joined the chorus, *"Crucify Him! Crucify Him!"*[54]

Their voices echoed off the palace, the fortress, and the rock hewn temple beyond.

"Crucify Him!"

After a few moments, silence returned, and Pilate defiantly hissed, *"You take him and do the crucifying."* There was a flash of anger in his voice. *"For I find no guilt in him."*[55]

Here was the nub of the issue. In the heat of the moment the truth was blurted out. The Badger was unwilling to act as the high priest's butcher. Let the Weasel slaughter his own Passover lamb.

Caiaphas shrugged his stooped shoulders and scowled. His exasperation seemed complete.

The wily Annas intervened. *"We have a law,"* he explained as he eyed the messiah. *"And according to that law he must die, because he claimed to be the Son of God.* "[56]

The superstitious governor reacted to this statement with alarm. He shot a glance heavenward, then over to the tortured king. Perhaps there was something to his wife's discarded warning? Perhaps there was something to the rumors that had circulated? The rumors of miracles. Maybe he was more than an ordinary man? At the very least his curiosity was piqued.

The Badger let out an audible sigh. He was clearly frustrated by this delay, but nevertheless he would investigate the matter. His pity-arousing tactic had fallen flat. Perhaps another approach was warranted. He turned and motioned for me to bring the prisoner back in for a further round of interrogation.

We had barely reached the spot where the king's outer garment still lay on the floor of the judgement hall, when Pilate abruptly wheeled around and demanded, *"Where are you from?"* [57]
No answer came.

When the pause grew beyond enduring, Pilate snapped, *"Do you refuse to speak to me?"* [58]

In that moment I drew some consolation from knowing that even the governor found this man baffling. The interrogator was flabbergasted.

Pilate went on, *"Do you not know that I have power to crucify you?"* He paused to let the gravity of his words sink in. *"And power to release you?"* [59]

"You would have no power over me," Jesus answered, *"if it were not given to you from above. Therefore the one who handed me over to you is guilty of a greater sin."* [60]

Pilate carefully considered these words. In an odd way, he drew comfort from them. He fancied the notion that his own authority ultimately came from the God of heaven. Better from there, he reasoned, than from that prancing, self-proclaimed Roman god, the Emperor Tiberius Caesar.

Then there was the second part of Jesus' statement—the part about the greater sin. The greater sin rested with Caiaphas, after all, it was he who had Jesus arrested. It was he who brought him before the judgment seat of Rome. Was he not the guilty party in this brutal travesty? Of course he was. If guilt did not rest in the accused, it must rest in the accuser, and the Weasel was the accuser. His was the greater sin. As for his own responsibility, Pilate would rather not think about that.

Jesus' words provided the feint and dodge the Badger was looking for. The greater sin lay with the temple authorities. Let them carry the weight of it. If they would not accept the messiah's release, then by the gods he would insist they carry the guilt for his death.

Still, I could see that Pilate would fight to have Jesus released. He admired the man. This Galilean prophet had the courage, the guts, to stand up to the high priest—the common enemy in the governor's realm. At the very least, the prophet deserved a modicum of support.

Pilate knew it was out of jealousy that Caiaphas had acted. He was jealous that the whole Jewish world was racing after this prophet. Caiaphas, the man of position, could not bear to watch the success of Jesus, the people's choice as leader. His entry on Sunday had left no doubt as to who was the most popular. Caiaphas was determined that Jesus would pay for his audacity.

Suddenly the decision was reached.

"I will have you released," Pilate summarily announced. "You will wait here," he said, addressing the Jewish king. "Why provoke that crowd out there?"

Then, turning to Renaldo he said, "Put his own clothes back on him." The governor signaled his intent by giving a light kick to the bloody garment on the floor.

"Marcus, follow me," Pilate called as he headed for the door.

I was relieved, genuinely relieved! The ordeal was over. The decision was made. Barabbas would die. The innocent man would walk free.

Once more we trooped out to The Stone Pavement, the local term for the six steps on which these proceedings occurred. With Jesus safely inside, there was no jeering to greet my ears. He could walk free after the high priest's hostile followers dispersed.

As we approached, the Weasel lifted his head from conferring with Jonathon. A thin smile crossed the corners of his grizzled mustache.

Without taking his seat, the governor cleared his throat to begin his address to this belligerent assembly. "As I stated earlier, I do not find the prisoner guilty of anything deserving death, neither has Herod. I have questioned him repeatedly. I have had him scourged. Even now I find no fault in him. Therefore, I will have him released."

The Weasel's shrill response was instant, *"If you let this man go, you are no friend of Caesar. Anyone who claims to be a king opposes Caesar."*[61]

The words pierced like a double-edged sword. The Badger had a choice. He could fall on it, or retreat.

He retreated. In that instant he knew the game was up. Here was the high priest's final squeeze. The governor's head dropped. Having dressed and paraded Jesus about like a king, he would now need to judge him as a king.

After a moment he turned to me. With grim forbearance in his voice he said, "Bring out the prisoner."

With those words I knew Jesus' fate was sealed.

The Jewish king greeted me with an expression of sublime resignation, as though he were expecting me. Yes, he appeared to be expecting this outcome. He had preached of a kingdom. And for the folly of this kingdom message, he would die.

One last time I helped him as he hobbled down the steps.

Pilate was already seated, ready to pronounce judgement. A thin smile was now on his face. The cunning Badger would make the most of his final moves. When Jesus was in position, he began. Once more he motioned in the direction of Jesus, and to all assembled he announced, *"Behold your king!"*[62]

"Away with him!" came the instant response. *"Away with him! Crucify him!"*[63]

There was vehement insistence coming from the crowd. Some began to hurl dust in the air. This was verging on a riot, a point that was surely obvious to the governor, yet he played them on.

"Shall I crucify your king?"[64] Pilate called back to the throng.

"We have no king but Caesar,"[65] the Weasel spat back.

The Badger's eyebrows shot up.

Then the governor smiled and nodded. It was a smile of triumphant satisfaction. *We have no king but Caesar.* The Badger mulled over these words. He had waited years for these words. After all he had endured in this place, was it not well worth hearing this confession from the high priest's mouth?

Ironically, the governor had Jesus to thank for the high priest's sudden conversion and submission to imperial Rome. This declaration would never have come forth from the Weasel's lips, except to secure the conviction of the good Galilean. Caiaphas was willing to stoop before Rome in order to spill the blood of this prophet. Here was the true measure of his hatred for the northern messiah.

Pilate knew all this and he drew a good measure of perverse satisfaction from it. He understood his foe.

He called for his personal attendant to bring a basin of water. Now he would lay the blame where the bloody blame belonged. With the attendant holding the basin before him, Pilate made a great show of washing his hands before the crowd, and with insistence in his voice he declared, *"I am innocent of the blood of this man."*[66]

Here was the feint, the great pretend.

Next came the dodge.

With water still dripping from his hands he looked out over the crowd and declared, *"See to it yourselves."*[67]

He spoke as though he had abdicated—bore no responsibility for the blood that now trickled down Jesus back. He absolved himself of that, and of all that would soon flow on Golgotha.

This Badger could throw a bit of dirt.

It was fitting for Annas the aged priest to respond. It was he who answered for the people. With his finger pointed at Jesus, and his gaze fixed on him, he replied, *"His blood be on us."* Then he paused as though looking down through the generations of time. *"And on our children,"*[68] he added with a cold sardonic stare.

Out on the street the people answered, "Yes!"

They nodded their agreement.

28

Friday 8:50 a.m. April 7th, 30 AD

"SEE TO IT YOURSELVES."

Pilate's words still reverberated in my ears, setting them on fire.

"See to it yourselves."

They were fine words for him to say.

"Take him yourselves and crucify him."

I heard him say that earlier to the high priest. Fine words indeed!

Pontius Pilate was not the executioner. He could wash his hands and walk off into the palace. The provincial ledger books awaited his attention.

Joseph Caiaphas was not the executioner. He could crow over his victory, and crow he did, as he returned triumphant to preside over his resplendent temple domain.

Herod? Herod Antipas could get back to what Herod did best, chasing and bedding women.

No, the mighty could blithely pronounce judgement, and then walk off. It fell to me and my men to execute this, their rendering of profane justice.

Justice? What justice was this?

I walked over to where Claudius stood with the beaming, exultant Barabbas. "You're a free man, Barabbas," I announced, stating the obvious.

"God be praised!" he shouted with hands uplifted. "God be praised!"

Why a just God would want this leprous dog roaming free defied all earthly logic. This filthy dog's joy made my blood boil!

Then the completely unexpected happened. Barabbas turned to his comrades and suddenly his head dropped. He had led them to this fate. Now he would walk away while they bore the burden of the cross. I saw the weight of it all suddenly come crashing down on him. In an instant he caught the despair etched on Thaddaeus' face.

It staggered him.

Barabbas, the free man, pinched his eyes shut and then began to tremble uncontrollably. He sank to his knees and turned away from his brothers, his two fellow terrorists.

The weight of his responsibility was too much for him. He was free. But now it was guilt that seized him—unbearable guilt.

"Get out of here," I yelled to the kneeling figure. "Get out before I run you through."

He was a sack of wheat rooted to the stone pavement. I let fly with a kick to his fat rump to add force to my words. My hand rested on the pommel of my sword. It took real effort to keep it there. If he had not moved, I would have made good my threat.

"Move!"

Slowly he picked himself up and lumbered off—a sobbing, blubbering idiot, suddenly seized with remorse.

Surely I thought, for such a man, an accident could be arranged in the dark of the night. The common Roman soldier knows a few things about justice, even if the Roman governor does not. At a later date we could see to him—to this bit of unfinished business. But now we had another bloody job to do.

Flavio, caught my eye, then beckoned me over. "I'm heading back to the fortress now," he announced. "I'll have a dozen cavalrymen meet you at the Fish Gate. There may be a big crowd out for this one," he commented, referring to the public crucifixion. "If you need help send a dispatch." Without waiting for a reply he walked off.

In the meantime, Claudius had three crossbeams brought out of the fortress, one for each man. The condemned would carry these to their death. In length, the *patibulum,* or horizontal cross-beams, were the span of a man's arms fully extended. I inspected these roughhewn, squared timbers. They were notched in the center so as to fit into the similarly notched uprights now standing at the ready on Golgotha. Since crucifixions were quite common, why go to the trouble of removing the upright poles from their secure position on the hill? Besides, their public display, even in the singular empty state, served our purpose well. They acted as a deterrent for the hostile, the tempted, and the wayward. On more than one occasion, I have heard Jewish mothers warn their young sons, "Bad men end up there."

The crossbeams were reused time after time, until rot set in or the wood became hopelessly splintered due to repeated nailing; hence the need for this inspection. The first two cedar beams were showing signs of long service.

"I think these will do for today," Claudius commented. "But we should get these two replaced for the next trip to the Skull."

I nodded absentmindedly in response, and then motioned for Thaddaeus to pick up his beam. The man we called Animal spewed curses as he shouldered his cross. The third beam was heavier and more recently put into service. It went to Jesus, the messiah king.

As Jesus stepped over to receive it, a messenger arrived. He was clutching the crumpled purple robe in his left hand. He addressed me, "Sir, the governor sent this garment. He said it belongs to the prisoner."

With a reluctant grimace, I took the filthy thing from him, and then flung it over to Claudius. "Tie it on him," I said in disgust.

Jesus seemed to receive it willingly. But it came on him like a weight—the weight of the world. It was his now, and every stain on it. And now royally dressed, the patibulum was placed upon him. The notch in the beam fit neatly over his bloodied shoulder. He staggered and swayed under it.

THE OTHER PERSPECTIVE

The condemned were ready to set off.

Setting this death procession in array took only a few brief moments. I had an ample supply of men to call on. With the final sentencing of the Jewish messiah, a more relaxed atmosphere prevailed. Part of the angry crowd began to disperse. I was now free to call on my men who had been used for crowd control. I reassigned the same pikemen who had served us earlier. They would advance in wedge formation before us. Then twenty foot soldiers were arrayed on either flank of the procession, and finally an additional half dozen pikemen brought up the rear.

I specifically assigned two soldiers to guard each criminal. At the back, Claudius oversaw two soldiers with his prisoner, Thaddaeus. Then came the two guards with the Animal. Jesus lead the way with two more guards escorting him on either side. I walked directly behind him. If there would be any trouble from the public, I knew it would erupt around him.

"Forward!" I shouted.

The column lurched into motion. Jesus moved on unsteady feet. Each step was summoned with effort.

We were heading north, out through the Fish Gate. We were retracing the same route that Herod had followed on his gloriously ignoble entry on Tuesday. The very thought of him brought a scowl to my face and I reflexively clenched my fist in rage.

Bloody Fox! He had brought this on. In my mind, he was the reason I was leading the Healer out to the Skull.

I reached down for my nail pouch. The worn leather held its grim treasure. They were there. Five inch spikes. Hard steel. Ready for use. Ready to pierce bone and flesh.

And before me the victim struggled beneath his burden. Wrong victim. Dead wrong victim. Hell's choice for a victim.

But then, where is heaven's justice in this world?

I caught sight of Renaldo as we marched past the Antonia

193

Fortress. Strangely, it was seeing him that served to remind me that the notices had not been picked up. The notices were to be posted over the head of each crucified man. Each flat wooden board announced to the world what crime had been committed—what brought the malefactor to this wretched state.

I hastily beckoned for Renaldo to approach. "I forgot the damn notices." I gestured my frustration with the upraised palm of my hand. "They're with the jailer in the southeast turret. You'll need to get Pilate to rewrite the notice that was meant for Barabbas."

Then with a shake of my head and a huff I added, "I don't know what he'll write for this man." I motioned in the direction of the stumbling messiah. Then with a shrug I added, "I guess it's Pilate's problem."

"Don't worry, Marcus. I'll look after it," Renaldo confirmed. "I'll have one of my men deliver the two notices that are ready. When the other one is ready, I'll bring it out myself."

He shot a glance at my thorn-crowned prisoner. Then he pressed his lips tightly together, shook his head, and turned from me. It was his way of signalling his displeasure with this turn of events. He, too, would have preferred seeing the backside of Barabbas heading off to the Skull.

Barabbas! He was the reason I was on this assignment. I detest crucifixions, but for him I had made an exception. I needed to be here, to oversee this bloody ending. I owed it to the dead, to Andreas and Hermes. Hell, I owed it to the living, the men along-side me now. But the murdering dog walked free! Free! I was left fuming—in a killing mood.

The wrong man trudged slowly, each step conceived and born in pain. He was mocked continually by the angry mob surging along both sides of the street. But why had the free man buckled? Why had Barabbas folded? His fall before Thaddaeus, just minutes earlier, reminded me of the siege of a wood pole stockade back in

Germania. I and twenty men pushed forward, straining every muscle. Suddenly the wall gave way, and we all pitched forward and collapsed right along with it. Then the arrows showered down.

That is how he fell, how Barabbas came down. He resisted Rome, pushed against Rome, until Rome backed off. Then he fell flat on his face. Only the arrows were missing.

Or were they?

The response that a pardon can bring is well beyond understanding. But then bloodguilt has a way of fashioning its own sharp arrows.

We were advancing slowly, far too slowly. The guard to the left of Jesus barked at him, "Move your feet, Jewish dog!" He followed this up with a slap to the shoulder. It was a light enough slap, but it caught the king off balance, sending him sprawling in the dirt.

Chest heaving, Jesus struggled to get to his feet, but the crossbeam was clearly too heavy for him. After an initial attempt to rise, he sank down again.

"Halt!" I shouted up the column to the advancing pikemen. Then, with a backhanded jab to the guard's shoulder, I demanded, "Pick up the beam."

He obeyed with a reluctant scowl aimed at Jesus.

Jesus rose.

I silently motioned with a jerk of my head for the beam to be passed back to the king. He shouldered it once more, and advanced again on struggling feet. I could tell the effort was valiant, but from the labored breathing I knew he had very little left to give. I was beginning to wonder if he would make it to the hill.

"Forward!"

We were soon in the market section where the evicted temple merchants had set up shop. Many of them were still there. It seemed that none missed this opportunity to jeer and heap abuse upon the man they viewed as their nemesis. I half-expected Timaeus to appear among them and lead the verbal assault. But he was nowhere to be seen.

Timaeus had disappeared. Disappeared like Barabbas. Timaeus, too, had fallen. His vitriol had been silenced. Silenced by a pardon...a healing pardon.

Jesus stumbled again. He spilled forward like the tipping of a stone water jar.

"Halt!" I shouted once more.

Both guards shouted obscenities at him. But then they glanced my way, and moved to lift the crushing beam from off his bleeding back.

He rose slowly. Street dust stuck to his sweat-drenched face and beard. A bit of yellow straw had been speared by one of the thorns in his crown. He sucked in each breath as though he were drowning. With effort he straightened and then slumped forward again, unable to hold himself erect, or assume his burden. He drew in three more gulps of air and straightened once more. Now he was ready and the beam was shifted back to him.

"Forward!"

The Fish Gate was now within sight. Jesus pressed onward with whatever vigour he could summon.

The crowd changed now. Here, for the first time, we encountered his supporters. Women. Wailing women in full anguished lament over his fate. They fell to their knees on either side of the narrow street. Pleading! Hands outstretched. Dishevelled. Begging for his release. A pathetic sight. Not a few were kicked or pushed aside by the soldiers on either flank. And they were incessantly heckled by the high priest's mob.

Now we were near the spot where Cestas had sliced off the beggar boy's hand. Lucas, young Lucas!

The images rolled in. They were relentless. There was no blocking them. I found myself clutching tight my wrist, just as he had done.

Suddenly, Jesus fell again. He had reached his limit. His collapse was complete.

I stood over him, the fallen wreck. It was clear that further progress at a reasonable pace would require a change in tactics.

"Halt!" I bellowed above the wailing voices.

Off to the right, behind the weeping women, I spotted a tall young man. He appeared to be making his way into the city. Here he was, a fish swimming against the current. I stepped in his way, aimed my index finger at his dark-skinned face and demanded, "You! Carry his cross." With my other hand, I stabbed my thumb in the direction of the fallen king.

Startled by my approach, the man took a half step back. His eyes darted to the two boys half hidden behind him.[69] His sons.

I dropped my right hand. It came to rest on the pommel of my sword, a gesture well noted by my opposite. His eyes took in the whole scene. I pumped my thumb once more in the direction of the fallen cross carrier.

The tall man stepped forward, but the boys desperately clung to the backside of his robe. Terror marked their faces. Surely, they dreaded the worst.

"Papa! Papa!"

He nodded his willingness to comply, but then stooped before his sons to whisper some words of assurance.

The youngest boy would have none of it. "Papa!" he bawled as tears streamed freely down his face.

A twitch of my eyebrow signalled the soldier next to me to intervene. He drew his sword, and then put a hand to my conscript's shoulder. Seeing the situation take on a deadly urgency, the conscript turned from his children to assume his service. My soldiers became a wall between him and his sons.

He was a fine choice, tall, broad-shouldered, muscular. He shouldered the crossbeam with ease.

The boys were another matter. They reminded me of my sons. They trailed along the whole way to Golgotha, crying piteously, gnawing an ever deepening hole in my conscience.

"I'll be fine, Alexander," he shouted across to them. "I'll be fine, Rufus! I'll be fine." They clung to one another, but seemed little comforted by their father's words.

With his burden lifted, Jesus rose to his knees. Then with gasping breaths he addressed the kneeling women just beyond the military cordon. *"Daughters of Jerusalem, do not weep for me; weep for yourselves and for your children."*[70]

In fact the two boys were weeping. The women sobbed as he spoke.

But his words grew dark. *"The time will come when you will say, 'Blessed are the barren women, the wombs that never bore and the breasts that never nursed.'"*[71]

Slowly struggling to his feet, he continued in ominous tones, *"Then they will say to the mountains, 'Fall on us!' and to the hills, 'Cover us!' For if men do these things when the tree is green, what will happen when it is dry?"*[72]

Having spoken his piece, I motioned him on.

"Forward!"

Soon we were through the Fish Gate, and were joined by the promised escorts on horseback. It was a very mixed throng that surged around us in the more open space. Mostly it was made up of his enemies, the men who endured his trial. Now they would gloat over his demise. They would see this through to the bitter end.

His disciples, the men I had seen around him earlier in the week, were strangely absent. All the better, from my perspective. No hostile confrontation. No need for reinforcements. Perhaps they knew better than to mess with the Roman army.

Only the women were there, vainly pleading his case.

He limped on. Jesus slowly limped on. He was free of the burden of the crossbeam, but not the burden of the robe.

On his own power he limped right up the round stone hill.

29

THERE WERE THREE UPRIGHT TIMBERS ON THE BARREN HILL. My tall conscript lowered his burden before the middle timber. His job was done.

"Papa! Papa!" The youngest boy, Alexander, cried once more. Then he rushed to where his dad stood within the military columns inner circle. This time my soldiers did nothing to restrain him. The father caught the young boy up in his strong arms. Then he dropped down to hug his older son, Rufus.

Their ordeal was over. This tall man would walk off the barren hill. The other man would not.

A party of five young soldiers stepped forward, the crucifixion detail, lead by the head jailor. They had been patiently waiting on the Skull for our arrival. They saluted. Their leader swaggered forward with one hand planted firmly on his hip.

"Greetings, Marcus," Octavia began. "We brought a ladder and the props." He motioned to these with a toss of his head. "Oh, and we brought the drink." He gestured to a wooden bucket containing a crude copper dipper. It stood off to his right in the shadow of the central cross. "The notices," he hesitated. "There's only two of them?"

"Yes, I know that," I snapped. "I looked after it already." Gruff irritation leaped from my throat. "It should be here soon."

Then a quizzical look came on the jailor's face. He took a step forward and inspected the thorn-crowned prisoner. He had never seen this man. "Where's Barabbas?"

"Free," I spat out the word. "Free as a summer sparrow."

Octavia caught the extent of my frustration. He gestured with upraised hands, wanting some explanation.

"A governor's pardon. A stinkin' Passover pardon," I answered with bitter anger dripping from my lips.

My eyes dropped, dropped to the foot of the central cross, "Instead of him, we have the king of the Jews, here." And with that I kicked at a bit of loose rock and sent it skittering down the backside of the knoll.

"King of the Jews?" Octavia responded. Once more he eyed the purple-robed prisoner, and then gave a derisive snort.

With a quick turn from the jailor's reception party, I barked and waved my orders to my own men. With a sweeping motion I signalled for the cavalrymen to take up their positions surrounding the hill. "Thaddaeus to the right," I indicated with a wave of my arm. "Animal to the left."

Jesus was where he needed to be. His central position needed no comment.

A crowd of a few hundred men gathered just off the knoll. Kneeling women gathered in tight little knots a good distance off. They were on what we call the Mother's Hill. Knowing their role, the pikemen instinctively moved to secure the perimeter of the Skull.

The religious men, the merchants, and the riffraff had come for a bloody spectacle, and a bloody spectacle they would get.

Let the show begin.

The guards moved their victims to the appropriate upright. Only now did the two other unfortunates drop their crossbeams. Thaddaeus immediately fell to his knees. He began to quiver and shake—a strong man reduced to a grovelling, whimpering mess.

Jesus stood silent.

"No! ... Noo!" The fear-filled Thaddaeus began a low desperate wailing, panting between each utterance. "No! ... Noo!"

The guard to his left began to kick at him viciously.

"Shut up, dog! Shut up!" he shouted at the bent figure.

A few quick strides brought me to his side.

"Soldier!" I yelled in his ear, "Get the notice up there." I signalled with a jerk of my thumb. It was my way of getting him out of the immediate situation. When he stepped aside, I turned to Thaddaeus.

"Thaddaeus!" my voice cut through the swarm of activity that engulfed the hill. "Stand to your feet."

Whether he recognized my voice from our previous meeting, last evening, or he simply recognized the authority behind my voice, I could not tell, but it brought the desired response. He stopped his mournful wailing and slowly brought himself to an upright position.

"I brought the myrrh. As I promised." I looked into his despairing eyes. "I brought the myrrh."

Relief spread across his tortured face. Here was a straw of hope to distract the hapless while he drowned in a sea of doom.

"Bring the drink!" I said with a summoning wave of my cupped hand.

One of Octavia's men saw to it. I took the bucket from him. It was just over half full. The dark liquid beckoned. I retrieved a copper dipperful. The acrid smell of wine vinegar punched holes in my brain. I took a sip. The myrrh was in there all right. The bitter afterkick numbed my throat.

"It's good. A good strong batch," I said with a backhanded wipe of my mouth.

I passed the half-filled dipper to Thaddaeus. He downed it all in three voracious gulps. I took it back from him and turned to refill it once more. Behind me the ladder went up. Soon the condemned man's notice would be nailed in place.

As Thaddaeus again reached for the dipper, I pulled it back. "First," I said, cocking my head to one side, "take off your clothes."

His face dropped. He knew full well what this meant. Would

he comply? He sucked in a breath and then plunged ahead pulling off his outer garment.

I handed him the swill. He downed the second dipperful with the same raw enthusiasm.

As he drank, I motioned with a jerk of my head and a twitch of my eyebrow for the crucifixion crew to stand ready. The cross-beam was laid behind him. Then four men gathered behind the prisoner on either side.

"Another?" I asked as he lowered the dipper.

He nodded and just a hint of a smile crossed his handsome face.

I stooped once more to fill the dipper, to supply his need for another drink of this potent brew. As I handed it to him, three hammer blows rang out. The notice was now pinned to the top of the cross.

He drank more slowly now, his movements were more deter-mined, as if some great effort was required. Perhaps he sensed what was coming, and the dread of it made him slow. Perhaps the effects of the drug were hitting home.

I could not see his eyes. They were hidden by the uptilted dipper. But my eyes signalled to the men on his right and left. They were fully prepared.

After a long pause he brought the dipper down. I took it from his hand. He had a far off look.

I smiled at him. Then gave a sharp signalling nod with my head.

In that instant eight men seize him.

"Aaaaaahh!"

Two men on each limb.

He is dragged back.

Slammed down onto the crossbeam.

"Aaaaaahh!"

His scream pierces through my hollow soul.

Octavia swoops down. Hammer in hand.

Spike is pressed into base of palm.

"Xchuuuung!"

Hammer to spike.

"Aaaaaaaaahhh!"

His scream sears the morning air.

His back arches upward until I think it will snap.

"Xchuuuung!"

"Xchuuuung!"

"Xchuuuung!"

Three strong blows drive it home.

One nail in.

Two huge strides bring Octavia around to the other pinned arm. Two men are kneeling on the condemned man's forearm, pressing it to the rough beam.

His arched spine collapses.

The victim's breath comes in enormous gasps.

The point of the spike is jabbed into the base of his second palm.

Hammer rises.

"Xchuuuung!"

"Aaaaaaaaahhh!"

Fresh scream.

Arched back.

"Xchuuuung!"

"Xchuuuung!"

"Xchuuuung!"

Two nails in.

Arched back collapses.

His breath comes in monstrous gulps, then changes to short quick bursts. His face is ashen. Beaded sweat runs in rivers down his brow.

Octavia smiles my way.

"Well done," is my response. I stoop down and pull the breechcloth, the last shred of clothing, off Thaddaeus. Then I toss it over the shoulder of the nearest soldier.

He will die naked—naked and despised, like all the victims of the Roman cross.[73]

"Hoist him up!" I yell.

Instantly, four men respond by lifting the beam and dragging the nail-pinned victim to a point directly below the upright.

His face is contorted. Weak, agonized, groans escape from his lips. He can do no more. Pain overwhelms.

Two forked wooden props are shoved beneath either arm of the crossbeam. Two of Octavia's men are on each prop. At this point Octavia takes full charge of this rather difficult manoeuvre.

The ladder is moved to the back of the upright. One man hastily climbs it to a point just above the notch in the upright that will receive the crossbeam. He has a short but sturdy length of rope draped over his shoulder.

At this point, Thaddaeus is held in a standing position. The crossbeam is supported equally from the front by the men on the forked pole props, and from the back by the four men holding the beam in place.

Octavia motions with a raised hand. The men behind the beam respond by lifting it above their heads.

Thaddaeus gasps as his arms are now forced above his head. His heels leave the ground. With hands pinned and bleeding profusely, he is forced onto his toes.

The prop men adjust their implements to this new higher position.

At just the right moment, Octavia calls out, "Ready…
One… two… three… now!"

The pole props are pushed upward. The pinned victim is launched skyward. A fresh scream erupts. His back slams against the upright and he is dragged higher by the upward thrust of the pole props.

The notch in the crossbeam finds its mate in the upright.

With lightning hands the ladder man secures the crossbeam by means of the rope. He wraps it around the point where the two beams cross and then draws it tight.

The victim dangles. Dangles naked. Naked before the crowd. Naked between heaven and earth.

Blood pours from the pierced, ripping wounds. Two men grab his loose hanging legs. Octavia steps forward, hammer in one hand, a six inch, foot spike in the other. Soldiers' hands press the victim's feet together, press them firm against the upright. Octavia checks the spot, the contact point between flesh and wood.

"Xchuuuung!"

Steel hammer on to steel spike.

"Xchuuuung!"

Steel spike into flesh.

"Xchuuuung!"

Steel spike into bone.

"Xchuuuung!"

Steel spike into wood.

"Xchuuuung!"

Human scream reaches heaven.

Then silence. Hushed silence envelops the crowd.

Three spikes in.

Two men left to do.

I aim a grim nod at Octavia, and then add a slap to the shoulder for a job well done.

But Jesus stands silent—silent through all this.

Beyond him, near the far upright, a scuffle breaks out. The man we call Animal has sensed his own fate. He lashes out in abhorrent panic.

I walk by the quiet messiah. The crucifixion crew follows. The guards have pinned Animal to the ground. The swill bucket stands nearby.

"Has he had his drink?" I call out.

"The bastard drank most of it."

"Then, let's do him."

Animal is dragged screaming onto the crossbeam. Strong hands do the rest. Blow for blow, scream for scream, arching back for arching back, the same thing happens.

One in.

Two in.

"Hoist him up."

Naked scream.

"Xchuuuung!"

"Xchuuuung!"

"Xchuuuung!"

"Xchuuuung!"

Three in.

One man left to do.

A smattering of applause breaks out among the spectators. But they have come for more than just this. The main attraction is up next.

With Animal crucified, Octavia steps back from his handiwork, hammer in hand, blood dripping from his fingers. "Now, that's how it's done!" he grandly announces. "That's how it's done! Now the next man's yours, Marcus," with an upraised hammer he gestures in the direction of Jesus. "He's all yours."

I fall strangely silent. I spent the whole week waiting for this moment. But this is not Barabbas. This is Jesus of Nazareth—the guilty man's substitute. Jesus.... Close encounters with him have always filled me with apprehension. But surely his powers, whatever their source, are diminished. Why else would he be in this vulnerable, weakened, state?

The notice board has still not arrived, nor can I see any sign that Renaldo is on his way. The work has gone well. Quick. We have established a certain rhythm. Why stop now?

I pick up the nearly empty bucket and walk over to Jesus, uncertain yet what course I will take. "It's your turn, good man," I announce while extending the bucket his way.

He makes no response, shows no interest.

The crew gathers round.

I tip the bucket to one side to get enough swill to fill the dipper. I offer it to him.

He takes a sip, works the liquid around in his mouth, discerns the true nature of this bitter potion, and then spits it out. It leaves a dark stain on the dull grey rock near his feet.[74]

"It will dull the pain," I state emphatically.

He raises his eyes. They lock with mine. I see in him the same look, the same determination, I saw on the first day I set eyes on him, the day he rode the donkey into this city. I can still see he has a destination in mind. Some mystical purpose, a purpose, he somehow feels compelled to fulfill.

I drop my gaze. He must be a fool. In his condition, in this situation, he must be a fool. A fool who unnerves me, but a fool nonetheless.

Once more I offer the drink.

With lips pressed tight, he shakes his head.

He is a fool. An arrogant fool! A fool who thinks he is tough— who can handle this—who can take it straight.

Well, we will see who is tough. I will show him who is tough!

Let the big show begin. "Now boys!" I call out to the crew.

Still wearing the purple robe, he is snatched like a young child and slammed down onto the crossbeam.

A cheer goes up.

My right hand seizes the hammer from Octavia, my left fumbles, then dives into the nail pouch.

I drop my knee onto his fingers.

Stab the sharpened point of the spike into the base of the palm.

Raise hammer.

"Xchuuuung!"

An enormous cheer goes up from the crowd.

Blood spurts across my thigh.

"Xchuuuung!"

"Xchuuuung!"

"Xchuuuung!"

One in.

The messiah is silent. Still...

Octavia urges me on, "That's it, Marcus!"

I spring to my feet, remembering the full rush of battle. Then scramble to the other arm.

From just off the hill, in the throng, a chant begins. Gets established. "More! More! More! More!"

Knee on fingers.

"More!"

Spike jabbed in.

"More!"

Hammer raised.

"More!"

"Xchuuuung!"

"More!"

"Xchuuuung!"

"More!"

"Xchuuuung!"

"More!"

"Xchuuuung!"

Two in.

THE SOLDIER, THE TERRORIST AND THE DONKEY KING

Jesus is silent.

Still... He is still beneath the piercing blows.

I rise panting. Heart pounding. Bloodied hand dripping. On seeing a stain-free area farther up my arm, I wipe it across my sweat-drenched brow.

Octavia salutes me with a smile and a thumbs up signal.

The crowd roars their approval.

This time it is Octavia who yells, "Hoist him up."

The messiah is dragged gasping—desperately gasping—to an upright position before the death mast.

Now they can see him, and the crowd goes wild with frenzied excitement. Cheering. Clapping. Hooting. Bloodlust takes hold.

The props are applied to the arms of the crossbeam.

A new chant goes up.

"Raise him up!"

"Raise him up!"

"Raise him up!"

Octavia signals, and the men in back lift the beam on which Jesus is pinned above their heads.

Then we all see it—see the obvious. He is still clothed. The purple robe billows out as it is caught by a sudden cold gust of wind. The sight of it brings all my frenzied demons to the fore.

I step before him, look into his agonized face, and say, "You won't be needing this... King of the Jews."

Then to the cheers of my men, I spit into his face. I add my spittle to all the rest that has dried and is clinging to his beard.

I untie the royal robe and drop it in a heap to my right. Using the dagger from my belt I slash and rip his seamless tunic along each shoulder, and across the length of each sleeve. It drops down around his ankles. Finally, with a wicked smile, and to cheers all around, I snatch his breechcloth from off his loins.

I toss it to Octavia. He holds it up. A trophy!

We laugh. We all laugh. It is a laugh not our own. I recognize it. It is Herod's demonic laugh. His spirit is with us now.

When he has regained some composure, the head jailor starts the final count.

"Ready… one… two… three… now!"

To chants of, "Raise him up! Raise him up!" Jesus, the messiah, the king, is lifted up—up before the world.[75]

His head twists from side to side in writhing agony. His whip-sliced back slams against the upright as he is dragged higher.

With a flesh tearing lurch, the notch in the horizontal beam finds its match in the vertical. The rope is flung around, then drawn tight, securing the two cross members as one.

The silent messiah hangs. He hangs naked and bleeding before a jeering world.

Only the last spike remains. Awkwardly, I fumble for it.

A creeping unease overshadows me. I glance over my shoulder. Claudius stands alone, off to the side. Silent…. He is ghastly pale and silent, transfixed by the sight before him. I hand the last nail, and the hammer, back to Octavia and say, "You do it." He snorts his surprise, but then sets quickly to his task.

The blows ring out. They echo off the distant city wall… off the temple pinnacle… off the Mother's Hill… off the cavernous abyss within me.

Then silence.

A great collective gasp is heard from below the hill.

The trophy has been mounted. The high priest's trophy has been mounted. Now his victory is assured.

30

WITHIN ME I KNEW THERE WAS SOMETHING PRIMEVAL ABOUT this position, the position on the cross. It is a man's first nightmare, his worst nightmare. There he hangs, naked, ripped open, nailed open, unable to cover himself. He is unprotected. He cannot hide; he cannot run. In shame and nakedness his tormentors lift him up. His sin is posted above his head. Body and soul are pried open, and he hangs fully exposed. He is exposed before heaven and the world—the world that has rejected him—the heaven that he has offended.

Nothing can be worse. It breaks the strongest men.

But he was silent. The messiah was silent. He was still—quiet—beneath the flesh piercing blows. I had never seen, or heard the like of it.[76]

It troubled me.

Now that he was pinned and mounted, he summoned his strength, and raised his voice for all to hear.

"Father," he gasped, *"forgive them... They do not know... what... they are doing."*[77]

Then silence, troubling silence.

I dismissed his words. I knew what I was doing.

Claudius doubled over, as though punched in the stomach. He staggered off the back of the Skull and began vomiting.

He was green, I suppose, green and soft, yet to be hardened by the sights and sounds of the battlefield. He reminded me of how I was when I first arrived in Germania. A few more of those trips up the Skull, and the toughness would come.

A squabble broke out over the messiah's clothes. Who got what? I intervened and said, "The purple robe goes to Octavia's crew." I wanted nothing to do with the abominable thing.

"Yes," Octavia answered. "I got my stinkin' reward!" he said with a laugh as he looped the king's breechcloth around an open spot on his belt. "Your men can have the other clothes."

One of my crucifixion crew, a young fellow named Philip, piped up, *"Let's not rip it apart. We will gamble to see who gets it."*[78] With that he produced a pair of dice, and after a few tosses, it was decided. In fact, the messiah's clothes changed hands several times that day, as bored soldiers in small huddled groups entertained themselves with the roll of the dice. After a few moments, Octavia's crucifixion workers borrowed the dice, and used the same method to determine the ownership of the accursed purple robe.

"I think I'll take my crew, and we'll be off now," Octavia announced above a howling wind. "You can handle the rest?"

"Yes, we'll be fine." Checking the sky, I added, "Maybe a little wet, but we'll be fine."

As Octavia's men walked off the hill, a low, rumbling, thunder pursued them. The sky was ominous. But it was the wind that toyed with us. It clawed at our clothes, reaching down from dark swirling clouds. It picked up sand and grit, then spit it in our faces. It chased away the spectators. It seemed to come at us from every angle, buffeting us until it made the crosses creak and sway.

Then came the rain, big dark splotches of it, dark as the messiah's own vinegar spit. But that is all there were, dark splotches exploding on the rock surface of the Skull. There were not enough drops to darken the whole of the rock, just enough to spot it, to stain it.

Then it stopped. The sun came out to tease us, and Jesus' hecklers returned.

One of the more audacious, well-clad men approached. He aimed his finger up at Jesus and yelled, *"Aha!"* He wagged his head.

213

"You who would destroy the temple and build it in three days, save yourself."[79] Venomous sarcasm dripped from his lips. *"If you are the Son of God, come down from the cross."*[80]

"Yes," another chimed in, "come on down, Son of God!"

A frocked man from the high priest's coterie gave a snort of contempt, and then started in at him, *"He saved others, but he cannot save himself!"* Then he puffed himself up, and with his hand raised in gesture to this, the high priest's Passover lamb, he called out, *"He's the King of Israel! Let him come down now from the cross, and we will believe in him."*[81] He laughed, but he was not finished.

"He trusts in God; let God rescue him now, if he wants him." He snickered again and went on, *"For he said, 'I am the Son of God.'"*[82]

These words troubled me. The Son of God? Who was his father, anyway?

Then my men took up the taunt.

"Hey, this dog thinks he's the Son of God. The Son of God? Di' ja hear that?" Philip motioned to his comrades. "They called him the Son of God!"

"Well, his daddy ain't treatin' him too good."

"Hey, Jewish dog," Philip addressed the messiah. "Maybe ya otta get a new papa. He must be some mad at you." He shook his head in mock dismay, "He ain't treatin' ya right. No." He shook his head again. "I'd walk right out on him."

"'Cept you can't walk."

They all laughed, thought this was great fun, a fine bit of grim humor. They went on in the same vein for quite some time until Renaldo finally arrived with the notice board.

"Sorry I'm late. It took longer than I thought," he said as he dismounted. "First Pilate was busy, and then it took a while to find someone to do the Hebrew inscription."

He handed it to me. It read, *JESUS OF NAZARETH, KING OF THE JEWS.* The top line was in Latin, and clearly had the marks of the governor's own writing style. This was followed by the Greek translation, and then finally by the Hebrew.[83]

"King of the Jews," I remarked. "I was wondering what he would write."

"He wrote the truth," Renaldo commented dryly and nodded in Jesus' direction. "He'd make a far better king than Herod."

I sniffed and nodded my amen to that. I turned from him and called out to Claudius, "Are you well enough to nail up this notice?"

"Sure," he instantly responded. He rose from where he sat on a small boulder. But he did not look all that sure. The ladder was erected once more at the back of the cross, and with two men holding it, Claudius ascended with the sign tucked under his arm. He fumbled awkwardly for a nail. I could see fear on his face, and it was more than just the fear of falling. He feared what he saw on the front of the cross. But then the hammer rang out once more, and the job was done.

The notice set off a new round of mocking from the soldiers. One man fell in obeisance before the monarch on the cross. He was the first of many; others followed in his steps. Mock supplication followed for all manner of asinine trivia. It was a pathetic sight that went on for hours until it wearied me, and I called an end to this sham.

I motioned for Renaldo to follow me off the back of the hill. There we could have a more private conversation. He led his horse past the ring of encircling cavalrymen.

"That was some storm," I commented with a look skyward at the bank of retreating cloud.

"What storm?" he asked.

"The storm that nearly blew us off the Skull. It nearly blew the crosses down."

He seemed genuinely surprised at this. "I didn't notice it," he responded, and then changed the subject. "So you've had no trouble from his followers?"

"Not a single dog has barked, not one." I motioned with my head toward the Mother's Hill. "Of course, there are the women, but they'll keep their distance."

"Where did they all go? Where did his cheering thousands go?" Renaldo shrugged recalling the splendid entry on the first day of the week.

"I guess they went home. Don't you know? They're hiding under their beds. They know better than to mess with us. We're the bloody Roman army," I chided.

He gave a grim smile, but then added, "Well, if there is any trouble, signal the watchman at the Fish Gate, and we'll have more cavalry out here at double speed."

"I'm sure we'll be fine," I commented. "But all the same, I'll make sure everyone here keeps their eyes open."

"So, what do you make of this, Marcus?" But before I could answer, he went on. "I guess you were right about the high priest. You said he would go after the prophet, and he did."

"Yes, and he got him." There was bitterness on my tongue. "Got him exactly where he wants him," I pointed to the cross. "The pompous Weasel wins again! And Barabbas, the killer, Barabbas the terrorist, walks free!" I was livid. I was ready to start in on the dark-eyed Badger, but thought better of it.

Renaldo sighed. I could tell he was not sure how to respond. For my part, I was just glad he was there, so I could let out some of my frustration with the authorities. I did not want to explode in front of my own men.

"Look, Marcus. We are the middle men. We do what we're told. And plenty of times, we do it with one hand over our nose, and the other hand over our mouth. You told me that once. And by Mother's breasts I swear, you're right. Marcus, you're right! We know too much, but can do too little. The big boys always decide. But they don't know which end of the mule they're lookin' at. And they're too fat-headed proud to ask." He paused and looked off in the distance. "And for us, I suppose life will always be that way."

"Yes, it will always be like that," I echoed. "But it doesn't make doing the wrong thing on their bloody behalf any easier."

I kicked a loose bit of rock and sent it skittering off into the weeds. Suddenly, I remembered how I had ripped off the messiah's clothes, spat in his face. Drove the hammer down.

"So this is the wrong thing?" Renaldo made a sweeping motion up the hill to encompass the crosses.

"Is it the right thing? Is it right to strip a good man, a healer, a miracle worker, and nail him to a cross?" I paused for his response but when none came I pressed on. "And you! You should know the answer. You've got the proof living at your house. That boy is proof we've got the wrong man up there," I fumed. "Hell is laughing—laughing all the way to heaven's heights." After a long and surly pause I added, "Hell! Stinkin' Barabbas is proof enough we got the wrong man up there."

He was quiet for a time. He knew I was right. But then my argument was not with him. It was with those higher up. They produced this situation, rendered this judgement, sent me on this mission. I was just the dutiful soldier obeying their bloody filth-covered orders.

"Look, Marcus," he began. "You're right, absolutely right. But that isn't going to change anything now."

"I know," I sighed. It was a sigh of grim resignation. "I know. I'm just tired of this. Tired of living in this messed up world."

After a moment spent staring at the ground I began again, "You know, Renaldo, when it comes to leaders, political leaders in this world, it's not the cream that rises to the top. It's the crud. The stinkin' scummy crud!"

"You're right again, Marcus. You're right again."

I slowly shook my head. I said my piece; I changed the topic.

I looked up at him and asked, "How is the boy? How's Lucas?"

"Better. Much better. He'll pull through all right."

"Good. Maybe there is one good thing in all this," I commented, while taking another kick at some loose rock. He moved toward his horse and said, "I should go. Tomorrow is the Sabbath. We can talk then."

I nodded, and he was off. I walked back up the hill and into a storm of trouble. Angry voices were all around.

"What do you mean by pinning that up there?" It was Jonathon, the head of the temple guard. He, along with some high priestly official, had pushed past the pikemen at the base of the hill, and they were castigating one of my men.

"We were following orders," the soldier answered, holding his ground.

"Well, this is a travesty. A total travesty!" Jonathon stormed. "It will have to be changed." His voice rang out with authoritative insistence.

Then, my arch rival caught sight of me. "I should have known you were behind this, Marcus." He pointed an accusing finger.

"Behind what?"

"Don't play innocent with me," he shot back. "The sign. The notice!" he gesticulated angrily. "You had it nailed up there."

"Yes, I had it nailed up there," I acknowledged.

"Well, have you read it? Or can't you read?"

"Yes, I read it. And yes, I can read." And to prove my point, I faced the cross and read it out to him. "*JESUS OF NAZARETH, KING OF THE JEWS,*" I read it out in Latin, and then in Greek. I followed this up with some guttural grunts and snorts in mock imitation of Hebrew. This set my men off in hoots of laughter, while the two temple officers glowered in a state of red-faced agitation.

After a long, self-calming pause, Jonathon responded, "It isn't funny. None of this is funny." He waved a finger in my face.

"Hundreds of people come down this road," he stretched out a long arm to trace the path, "the imperial road, and they walk right past this." He thrust his hand skyward. "This declaration that—that fool—that naked fool is the king of the Jews. It's an affront to the whole Jewish nation." He was shaking with rage.

"What nation?" I shot back. My voice rose. "I didn't write that notice. The governor wrote that notice. If you want it changed, see him." I looked him square in the eye. "I don't take orders from temple scum. Now. You're standing on my hill." I jabbed a finger in a downward gesture. "Get off my hill!" I yelled in his face.

Behind me I heard swords being drawn. My men would back me up.

He huffed mightily. "I will see Pilate," he declared. And with that, he and his fancy-robed friend turned and walked off.

"You just do that, big man!" I called after him.

I waited all day for some new, revised, notice board to arrive, but none came. I knew it would not come. The Badger had already bowed once to the Weasel, and a man hung dying because of it. Pilate would never bow twice in one day, not over some words on a board.[84]

This defense of the public notice set off a new round of ridicule. One of my men walked over to the dying messiah and yelled up at him, "Did you see that, Jesus? We stood up for you. You're still king of the Jews. We believe in you, Jesus." He raised his fist in a show of mock support. "You're king of the hill, king of the whole bloody hill!"

Now another soldier joined in the game. "He's a funny king, though," he commented with a glance to his friend. "A very funny king! I've never seen a king on a cross. Have you seen a king on a cross?" he asked with a slap to his partner's arm. Then looking up at Jesus, he hollered, *"If you are king of the Jews, save yourself!"*[85]

"Save yourself, Jesus," Thaddaeus called out.

219

Then Animal called to him, *"Aren't you the Messiah?"* There was cold derision in his voice. *"Save yourself and us!"*[86]

But Thaddaeus, to his credit, would not let this lie. Yelling past Jesus to his partner in crime, he said, *"Don't you fear God?"* He paused to breathe. *"Aren't you getting the same punishment as this man?* He pushed down on his pinned feet so he could pull in a gulp of air. *"We got what was coming to us."* Fresh push for air. *"But he didn't do anything wrong."*[87]

Then he turned his face to the messiah. *"Jesus,"* he gulped. *"Remember me,"* he pushed up on spiked feet, *"when you come into your kingdom."*[88]

He dropped back with the effort of his words. His lungs were filling with fluid. The characteristic pattern of launch, gulp, collapse, wheeze, was now established. It was the rhythmic pattern of a man on a cross. They would each die, one by one, when they were too weak to launch up and forward to catch their dying breath.[89]

Jesus responded. Each phrase was marked by chest-heaving gulps for air after a painful upward thrust on spike-pinned feet. He turned to the repentant thief.

"I tell you...
the truth...
today you will be...
with me...
in paradise."[90]

I turned away, and looked skyward. The wind had shifted. Now it was coming from the north. A fresh bank of cloud was moving in from that direction. In just a few moments it had covered the noonday sun. It was strange weather, more than a little unusual. It chilled me.

A large clay jar was brought out from the fortress. A skin of wine was emptied into it. Here was a small reward for my men, a reward for an abominable job done well. Some flat bread and a few pressed dates were distributed.

Now there was movement on the Mother's Hill. A middle-aged couple came down. Their heads were hanging. They clung to one another, supported one another, every step an anguish. They made their way before the encircling pikemen.

I knew who they were—knew why they had come. Here were the broken parents, broken beyond this world's repair. I met them at the base of the hill, told them they had some time.

They advanced up the Skull. She fell, fell whimpering before her son. Thaddaeus.

Boisterous soldiers fell silent, and then walked off, right off the hill. The family was alone with their grief.

Having witnessed this grim, but welcoming reception, another party stepped off the Mother's Hill, and advanced to Golgotha. This was a group of five. The women clung to each other in couples. They were shepherded by a tall young man. He truly was a young man. His fresh face and scant beard bore witness to that. I recognized him. He had been with Jesus, had stood closest to him.

He introduced himself. He said his name was John. I received his party—ushered them by the outer ring of soldiers.

They were bowed by the sight. They clung to one another afresh, repulsed by the horror of what met their eyes.

After a few moments, the young man came before two of the huddled older women. He stooped to speak with one of the women—Jesus' mother, I assumed. With his arm about her shoulder, John advanced up the rock mound.

Jesus saw them. He struggled.

"Woman... Behold your son!"[91]

There was a double-edged meaning here, almost too painful for words. At first, I thought he was simply referring to himself—to his own wretched state. And perhaps on one level he was.

His body sagged. But then he thrust himself up and forward

for another breath, and with his next words his meaning became clear. To the young man, to his disciple, he said, *"Behold your mother!"*[92] He had committed his mother into this disciple's care.

She fell to her knees. She trembled, unable to speak. Only wretched sobbing was heard from within the circle of the hill.

In due time, I led them off. I led both families off. They left willingly. This was too much to bear, too much to watch.

From his cross, Animal watched the Mother's Hill. But no one came. That is when he broke—broke like a clay pot dropped onto the hard rock of the Skull. He sobbed. He moaned. His tears flowed like rivers into his dark young beard. But no one came. No mother came. No one came at all.

The wind picked up. The sky grew dark; grew darker yet. The horses began to neigh and paw the ground. In the distance a dog barked. It was a bark that changed to a howl, and ended in a whimper. I looked about. I could see it on every face. It was fear. Raw fear. This was not the dark of cloud or storm. This was the sun covering, hiding its face from what it saw upon the earth.

A total darkness descended, as black as any night.[93]

There was a discord here—a discord utter and complete. If heaven and earth had come into some perfect union, some perfect harmony, on the day Jesus arrived in this city, it was in blaring dissonance now. Blaring dissonance echoed off the empty chambers of my soul.

It was a deafening darkness. The mocking crowds fell silent. The highway traffic stopped. All was still. Only the three men were heard. Heard in the darkness. Three men working to maintain this perverted thing called life.

Working.

Pushing up to catch a breath.

Retreating.

Exhaling.

Mounting up.

Ever-heightening pain.

Catching a breath.

Retreating.

Here is the very antithesis of sex—love-imparting, life-giving sex. Naked men, unwillingly mated to two beams. Thrusting upward. Thrusting the whole of their bodies upward in excruciating pain, ever-increasing pain to reach the ultimate climax: a climax not bringing life but, rather, death.

This is the shame of the cross. Here is the depravity—a profane sacrilege inflicted upon the human body. The ghastly rhythm of it was driving me mad.

Then in soul-wrenching anguish his voice erupted, *"Eli, Eli, lama sabachthani?"*[94]

"What does that mean?" I cried out in the darkness.

From beyond the military cordon came the answer. *"My God, my God, why have you forsaken me?"*[95]

He had broken. The messiah hung broken. The cross had broken him. He, too, was human.

We were all together now, a great crowd caught up in this drama. There was no us and them. We were together. We were caught between heaven and hell in this dark, surreal, atmosphere.

It was dreadful!

Someone frantically yelled, "It's Elijah! *He's calling Elijah!*"[96]

Exhaling.

Mounting up.

Ever-heightening pain.

Catching a breath.

Retreating.

From on the Mother's Hill a wail went up. It was steady, constant, a wave of woe flowing over the dark scene.

Exhaling.

Mounting up.

Ever-heightening pain.

Catching a breath.

Retreating.

"Will Elijah come?" someone entreated. "Will he come?" Many of the hostile were even now on bended knees. The cavalrymen dismounted.

Exhaling.

Mounting up.

Ever-heightening pain.

Catching a breath.

Retreating.

"*I thirst,*" the king called out.[97]

Claudius leaped to his feet. There was a jar of wine off to one side. The soldiers had been drinking freely from this. He ran over to it, and got a sponge. He dropped the sponge into the jar of wine, and then skewered it with a long reed. This, he held up to dampen the lips of the donkey king.

But some yelled out, "*Wait! Let's see if Elijah will come and save him.*"[98]

Exhaling.

Mounting up.

Ever-heightening pain.

Catching a breath.

Retreating.

The rarified air crackled with anticipation.

Exhaling.

Mounting up.

Ever-heightening pain.

Catching a breath.

Retreating.

The sin of Eden—the transgression—is now thrown into reverse.

Exhaling.
Mounting up.
Ever-heightening pain.
Catching a breath.
Retreating.
"It is finished!" he cried.[99]

But there was no anguish in his voice. There was the ring of victory to it, as if he had caught with that last breath—a glimpse— a glimpse of his kingdom. A glorious kingdom! He had gained the summit. Now with vigor renewed, he pushed up and forward one last time.

Exhaling.
Mounting up.
Ever-heightening pain.
Catching a breath.
Retreating.
"Father…
Into your hands…
I commend…
My Spirit."[100]

His head dropped. It was over.

As his chin hit his chest, the earth began to rumble. Low thrumming. Building. Building! The rock Skull began to move beneath my feet. And with it my soul.

I fell to the ground.

The crosses began to vibrate and rock with the power of the quake. His head bobbed from side to side.[101]

But he was dead. He was dead!

Everyone was with me on their knees.

Heaven had rendered its dark judgement. The sun had hidden its face. The very earth had answered back. The verdict was in.

I caught two huge breaths of air, and then, for the whole world to hear, I cried out, *"He really was the Son of God!"*[102]

He was the Son of God.

The sun broke through.

A rooster crowed.

31

I ROSE TO MY FEET—WE ALL ROSE TO OUR FEET—LIKE MEN aroused from a nightmare. But the nightmare was not over. It hung before us, a cruel reminder of what our hands had done.

The light had come, but what it showed left me in desolate misery. Strangely, it was I who felt naked. It was I who was exposed. I stood exposed before his bloodied naked corpse. His brutalized body was a mirror erected before my very soul. And what I saw of myself there brought no comfort, no comfort at all.

I felt that the weight of his patibulum, now rested on my shoulders. And what a crushing weight it was! I had brought him here, and now that he was dead, the full weight of who he was, and what he bore, came down upon my own head. It was no wonder that I bowed. An oppressive heaviness settled over me.

A good portion of the crowd that had assembled below Golgotha now disappeared. They went slinking off. Even in death the Christ had managed to silence his enemies, and rattle his critics to the core.

With most of the crowd dispersed, my troop requirements were also reduced. I sent twenty of my foot soldiers back to their regular assignments on the wall. Six of the cavalrymen were ordered back to the stables, but I also asked that my own horse be brought to me. I sensed that I needed the lift my mount would bring. I still retained ample manpower to finish this job on the Skull.

Now on the hill, only Animal and Thaddaeus remained. They hung in perpetual motion, fighting for each breath on pierced limbs. There was a good deal of strength left in them. Unlike the Christ, they had suffered only the whip, but not the brutality of the multi-thonged and studded flagrum, nor had they been beaten and abused by the temple guards. Their ordeal could go on long into the night, perhaps even for days.

Quite unexpectedly, Marius arrived. There were six soldiers with him.

He saluted. "I've just been sent by Pilate," he informed me. "A Jewish delegation requested that the bodies be removed before the Sabbath. That's why I'm here," he pursed his lips, "to finish the job."

I looked to his men, then to the crosses. "Go ahead," I responded with a grim jerk of my head.

The lead man among them, a heavyset fellow, pulled a hefty sledgehammer from the holster on his hip. He strode over to the quivering Animal. With one hand, he gripped a position just below the dying man's knee, with the other, he raised the hammer, and delivered a smashing blow directly to the shin bone.[103]

A piercing scream followed.

Then he handed the sledge to his comrade, and held firm the other knee while his friend delivered the next tibia-shattering blow.

Animal moaned. His body slumped. Now he could only rise for air by drawing himself up on spike-pinned hands, a near impossible task. Death would come to visit soon.

They moved over to the Christ. He hung motionless.

"He's dead!" I called out. "He's already dead."

The lead man gave a shrug and a snort and then moved on to Thaddaeus.

I turned my back to them. I stared off to the city, to Jerusalem. But my ears heard the thudding crack. The rending screams.

"O Jerusalem!" I whispered to myself.

Another thudding crack.

"Jerusalem!"

The final whimper.

My mind flew back to when we left the city, when Jesus spoke to the wailing women. He said something about the wood being green. Now what was it?

"Hey, centurion. Are you sure he's dead?" the lead man called out to me. His words cut right through my sound-blocking thoughts.

I turned. They were back before the Jewish king. "Yes, I'm sure!" I called back with irritation ringing clearly in my voice.

"Let's *make* sure," he responded, addressing no one in particular.

"Pikeman!" he called out to a fellow standing idle at the base of the Skull. "Lend me your spear."

The man promptly complied.

The lead man took this, but he did not use it as I had expected. Rather than delivering a decisive quick thrust, he used it like a probe. He placed the tip just below the left side of the messiah's rib cage. Then he began a slow push angled upward. He pierced the skin. A trickle of blood. Probed higher. A sudden burst of water splashed down upon the rocks at the base of the cross.

"The lungs!" he called out.

They were water-filled all right.

"Now for the heart," he said. He thrust higher. More water trickled out. It ran down the full length of the spear shaft. Then suddenly, a second flood. This one thick and red.[104]

"He's dead," he stated the obvious, as he withdrew the gore-covered head of the spear.

I turned to Marius, "You've got quite the crew," I remarked.

"Yes. They're old hands at this."

"Look, Marius," I began slowly. "I've been thinking that I should report what I have seen here today to Pilate."

"You've had some trouble?"

"I guess you could call it that," I answered, not wishing to go into the details of all that I had witnessed.

He gave a nonchalant shrug. "Sure, go ahead. You have been here all day," he said with a sigh. "Take a break. We'll stay."

"I'll be back before sundown," I promised.

"Oh, don't forget, Marcus. You need to complete the execution registry. It's with Flavio. You may as well do it on your way in."

"Oh, yes," I answered. "I'll do that first."

I turned from him and walked off the hill. At the base of it, I looked back, saw the crosses etched against the sky. My head dropped.

That's when I saw it. There was still blood on my hands. Dried blood.

It was the blood of the Son of God!

32

Friday 5:00 p.m. April 7th, 30 AD

A BRISK RUBBING OF MY HANDS REMOVED THE DRIED BLOOD, the visible stains.

The shadows were already getting long. But then, the very fact that there were shadows bothered me. It was as though normal had returned. After storm and cloud, and black of night in mid-afternoon, we were back to a typical sunny spring day.

But the ground had shifted within. There had been a double quake. Within me, normal could not be found. Crucifying him had completely overturned my inner world. What troubled me most was that I now knew who he was—who he really was. But I knew it too late.

I was nearly halfway to the city gate when I was met by my groomsman coming out with my horse. It was convenient timing. I rode the rest of the way back in. But it was a different ride. I rode lower in the saddle. It seemed that I had to look up to find ground level. I could not help but think that a donkey might provide a better view.

There was activity to the left of the Fish Gate. A long narrow fissure had opened up. It traced a jagged course from the base of the wall right to the top of the parapet. Earthquake damage. Several men were out inspecting this. Renaldo was among them, but I did not stop.

In the city itself I saw only one instance of damage. Some roof tiles had slid off an old building. They lay in a broken heap to one side of the street.

I went directly to the fortress and, after hitching my horse to a post, I took the stairs up to Flavio's briefing room. I brushed by the sentinels at the door.

There was something different. I did not see anyone; the room looked empty. Then I noticed it. It was the god shelf; it had collapsed.

Something stirred. It was Flavio. He was on the floor behind the great cedar table picking up the pieces of the magnificent Apollo. He looked as shattered as his bronze god.

"He's broken!" he lamented as he heard me approach. "Broken beyond repair."

And it was true. The cast bronze idol lay smashed like an old clay pot. He had gathered the pieces together, but assembling them was beyond anyone's skill.

"Help me up, Marcus."

He reached up a hand to me. I fidgeted nervously before extending both of my recently bloodied hands.

His head wove from side to side. Clearly he was drunk. With what seemed like a great effort on his part, I managed to get him to his feet.

"You're a good man, Marcus," he slurred his words. "A good man."

I helped him to a seat.

He looked back at the broken heap, and then he repeated himself, "He's broken! Broken beyond repair." He shook his greying head. Then he put his elbows on the table, and with his head in his hands he began to cry. "I'm broken too, Marcus. I'm broken too." The tears streamed down his face. "Broken," he sobbed. "Broken beyond repair."

I sighed. I did not know what to make of this drunken confession. "You need some sleep, sir. You need a good night's sleep." Then noting the slanting rays coming through the window, I added, "It's getting late."

He sniffled a few times as he seemed to consider this. When he made no response, I called out, "Servant!"

He arrived promptly.

"The general here needs some help to his sleeping quarters," I stated.

He gave a knowing smile, and nod.

"Shall we go, sir?" He held out an arm to the broken man.

We both worked to get him to his feet, and Flavio tottered off clutching his servant's arm. At the door he stopped and turned. He called back. "Did I tell you Marcus? You're a good man." He raised his free hand, and waving an uplifted index finger he repeated, "You're a damn good man."

He left. But I was unconvinced. I was damned! But good? After the events of the day, and my involvement in them, I did not fit that description.

Fortunately, I was able to find the execution registry without any difficulty. I entered the date, and three names, Thaddaeus Crispus, 22, Jesus of Nazareth, 33, and Animal, 28. He never gave us his proper name, and I only guessed at his age.

There was also a spot to enter who claimed the body. I completed this for Thaddaeus. His parents expressed great concern about this matter. As I escorted them off the hill, they told me over and over that they would wait as long as needed to collect his remains.

Jesus was another matter. John, the young man who accompanied the Messiah's mother, told me arrangements were being made. But he did not know the details. They were all far from home. Undoubtedly, finding a burial plot in a strange city on a few hours notice presented its own set of challenges.

I left that spot empty. I could complete that section tomorrow when I had the information. Animal was the big question mark. But then if no one came, we did have our own solution for him.

I left my horse standing where it was, and rounded the turret of the imposing fortress, then walked on through the great eagle doors. I hoped to give the governor some account of what had transpired on Golgotha. I entered the same large room where the Christ had been interrogated that very morning.

The governor was seated behind his great oak desk. He was discussing some point of law with someone from Herod's delegation. His voice grew impatient. Finally, after some perfunctory remarks, he looked beyond the man before him and called out, "Next!"

But I was not next.

A tall tassel-robed man had entered before me. His religious garb, and overall deportment bespoke money and position. He stepped forward, bowed, and then began. "Your excellency, I have come to request the body of Jesus of Nazareth."

"And you are?" Pilate inquired.

"My apology, your excellency." He bowed once more. "My name is Joseph of Arimathea, a member of the Sanhedrin."[105]

"Hm!" the governor snorted. "You had him put to death. And now you want his body?" The Badger obviously found this to be a strange turn of events. He looked at his hands and then nervously rubbed them together.

"I did not consent to his death, sir." Joseph swallowed. "I stood opposed."

"You opposed Caiaphas?" Pilate responded with surprise. "I suggest you watch your back, holy man."

Joseph appeared to take note of this remark, then added, "We were not all of the same mind concerning the prophet."

Pilate paused to consider this, but when he made no response, Joseph continued, "I have just come from the hill of execution. The prophet is dead. His brother, James, asked me to request the body from you."

"He's dead!" Pilate feigned surprise. "Dead already?" He rubbed his hands once more.

"So I have been told," Joseph reported.

Then Pilate looked my way, and with a beckoning motion he called me forward. "Is the Christ, the Jewish king, dead?" he inquired.

I found his choice of words most interesting, revealing.

"Yes, your excellency," I nodded. "It is as you say."

"Hmm!" He rubbed a hand across his chin, then furrowed his brow. He glanced at his hands again. He looked pensive, perhaps even worried. Then, with a deep sigh, he addressed the holy man. "Follow the centurion here. He will give you the body."[106]

That said, the governor motioned for us to leave, and even as we did, he too got up and left the judgement hall.

33

Friday 6:00 p.m. April 7th, 30 AD

"My name is Marcus Aureolus," I said with a slight nod of my head.

"Joseph," he answered. "Joseph of Arimathea." Then he signalled to another well dressed tassel-robed man waiting outside the eagle emblazoned doors. "This is Nicodemus, a fellow member of the Jewish high council, the Sanhedrin."

This man had an anxious look. I gave another nod to my head, and then I addressed them both. "Look. I'm sure you want this done before sunset," I gestured skyward. "That gives us less than an hour. My horse is just inside the fortress. I will ride ahead, and get things ready."

"That would be wonderful," Nicodemus responded as though a great weight had been lifted from off his stooped shoulders.

"The tomb where we will lay him is just a stone's throw from Golgotha," Joseph added.

"Good. I'll be off then," I answered.

It was the Sabbath that had them worried. "Of course this would have to happen before a Sabbath," I fumed to myself as I headed to the fortress. No work could be done after sundown and they wanted him buried by then.

I soon had my horse moving at a light trot.

I was angry. The whole of this day made me angry. I had no opportunity to say anything to Pilate. Everything was out of my hands. Everything seemed to conspire to place me in a role I did not want to play. I hated this drama—this nightmare. I hated my part in it. I was as much pinned to my role as those agonized men were pinned to their crosses. And it was a role that was making me sick—sick at heart, sick at soul.

I arrived at Golgotha only to find it in a state of disarray. No. It was more like a scene of primaeval chaos—a small outpost of hell on the face of the earth.

The clusters of distraught women had abandoned their spot on the Mother's Hill. They had come closer and were wailing mournfully as sunset drew near. Their high-pitched discordant voices floated over the scene.

Not a single soldier was to be found on the hill itself. They were dispersed around the base in raucous groups. Some were clearly drunk, and the rest appeared to be well on their way. Marius must have sent for another skin of wine, or maybe two or three. The only exception to this was Claudius. He sat like a stoic off by himself.

A shaggy mongrel had slipped through these less than vigilant ranks, and was now lapping up the blood at the foot of the central cross. Three or four more dogs were skulking around the back of the hill, waiting for their chance to come on board.

Swarms of flies had settled in for a macabre feast. The pierced wounds of the dead were black with them.

"Claudius!" I called out, barely controlling my fury. "Where's Marius?"

He got to his feet and sheepishly answered, "He said he was going off to relieve himself, and he hasn't come back."

"Pfff!" A fierce puff of air exploded from my lips. "He relieved himself all right, relieved himself of all responsibility."

I slipped off my horse's back, grabbed a loose pebble and fired it at the shaggy stray. It caught the mongrel on the rear haunches. He spun around, let out several sharp yelps, and then vanished from the hill.

This action caught the attention of most of the clustered soldiers. They rose to their feet, as two or three men among them alerted the others of my arrival. But one particular group was totally oblivious. They were squatted in a circle, engrossed in a game of chance. Philip was the most boisterous among them. The young fool would gamble away his brain, if he had one.

A quick sharp lesson was in order. I stepped over to them. I seized the squatted soldier by the back of his armoured collar, yanked him full force onto his back, dropped my knee onto his chest, put my dagger to his exposed throat, and then screamed in his face, "You're dead! Dead, soldier! Three times dead!"

I rose from off him. "Where's your battle readiness?" I yelled at him once more, and then glared at the other stunned men. "Get to your feet," I delivered a kick to the fallen man's ribs. "We've got work to do." My voice crackled with anger. I scanned their stunned faces. "Get those rotting corpses off the crosses," I gestured with both arms raised.

They leaped into motion.

But as Philip turned to follow the others, I caught my example by the arm. I pushed my finger into his face. "You'll see me on Sunday," I snarled. "Sunday morning." A flogging might well be in order, I thought, or perhaps the latrines could be emptied.

My actions achieved the desired result. They began with Thaddaeus. Using a heavy pry bar, and a block of wood as a fulcrum, they pulled out the six-inch spike embedded in his feet. The ladder was thrown up once more at the rear of the cross. The rope, which bound the two members together, was removed. The pole props were again applied to the horizontal crossbeam. The man on the ladder pushed the patibulum free of the notch in the upright. Then the corpse was lowered.

The condemned man's father laid out a linen burial sheet. The body, patibulum and all, was placed upon it. Then the pry bar was used again to remove the five inch nails that pinned the hands.

Once this was done, the crossbeam was rolled off the sheet.

The weeping father lovingly wrapped the burial sheet around his son, then aided by what appeared to be his three younger sons, Thaddaeus was carried away.

In the interim, Nicodemus and Joseph arrived. They worked with feverish haste below the central cross. They spread out a similar linen sheet and then sprinkled it with myrrh and aloes.[107]

The removal of the Christ began. His mother drew near with a clutch of weeping women. The bottom edge of the sun touched the horizon.

Nicodemus straightened his back, and thus seeing the sun, he raised both hands to heaven in supplication, "May the great Name forgive us!" He shook his head mournfully. He knew they could not possibly make it to the tomb before the sun set. But having come this far, they were determined to press on. They would throw themselves upon the mercies of God.

I knew this was no small concession for a religious Jew of his rank and station. It was, in fact, a measure of his high esteem for the crucified Christ. Being of the priestly class, Joseph was prohibited from touching the body of the dead. But here he was on the hill of execution, hovering near Jesus' lifeless corpse.

Jesus was laid upon the burial cloth. His once healing hands were pried free from the cruel clutch of the cross.

Joseph stood on one side of the body, Nicodemus on the other. Then Joseph instructed two of the young men in their party, "Now, bring down his arms."

One of the young men, possibly John, picked up one of the Christ's death-stiffened arms and laid it by his side. From the opposite side a young man did the same to the other.

Now his mother knelt over him. She wrestled the thorn crown off of his bruised head. One last time she kissed his face.

She turned away and wept as only a mother can weep. Are

not a mother's deepest sobs saved for her sons?

The young men wrapped his face with a white linen cloth, and then enfolded his entire body in the death shroud.

The sun sank below the horizon.

"It's over here," Joseph directed, and with that the young men picked up the body and followed him off the back of the hill.

"Move on to the next one," I called out to the whole troop. Only Animal remained. Then with an aside to Claudius I said, "I'll be right back."

I wanted to confirm the location of this tomb. Something inside me hinted that I would be questioned about this matter. I tagged along behind the burial party, and it was just as Joseph of Arimathea had said. It was a stone's throw away, on the backside of the next rock hill.

And quite the tomb it was. It was newly constructed. In fact, I had seen excavation going on in that location for as long as I can remember, but now this rather grand project was completed, and ready for its first occupant. It contained a large chamber, cut into the white dolomite. A huge circular stone, as tall as a man had been chiselled and shaped to cover the entrance.[108] It was a tomb for the wealthy, fit for a king, at least for a donkey king.[109]

I did not dare linger. I was not about to relieve myself as Marius had done. Even so, by the time I returned, the third corpse was down, and darkness was closing in on us like a great shroud.

When I returned, Claudius approached me and gesturing to the corpse he said, "There's no family. What do we do with him?"

Of course, there probably was a family, but the young rebel had been disowned by his parents, by all his relatives. Quite likely, this was something that had happened a good long while before this day. Now this was the ultimate outcome, the final fate.

"That's not our problem," came my curt reply. "He and Barabbas dumped Andreas on the street. We'll dump him in the bushes." There was a measure of grim satisfaction in my voice. "Pull him off the hill, down to those bushes over there," I motioned with my left hand. "The dogs will do the rest. And what the dogs don't get will be left for the birds. The birds and the worms."

I rode back into the city alone, downcast and alone, into the gathering darkness. I returned my horse to the stables at the hippodrome, and then walked home in solemn gloom. Just before I reached the villa gate, my foot brushed against something soft. I stopped, and then stooped.

It was the sparrows' nest.

The purple-skinned hatchlings lay dead on the cobblestones.

34

Saturday 7:00 a.m. April 8th, 30 AD

IT WAS A HORRIBLE NIGHT. HORRIBLE!

I could not sleep. The events of the day flooded my mind—a constant bloody torrent. During the daylight hours, you can steel yourself against other men's suffering. But at night your hard shell dissolves from around you, and you are left in just your own skin again. Then their suffering soaks into your flesh; it becomes your own.

There seemed to be no end to it—no end to the torment. I willed myself to sleep. But I could not find that door of escape. It eluded me. Instead I was pursued relentlessly by the dreadful events of the day. The hammer blows rang in my head. Their pain was mine.

All night my mind was on Golgotha. Why me? Why Jesus? Why, by some cruel twist of heaven's fate, did I find myself with him upon the hill of excution?

When I closed my eyes, his face appeared before me. His gentle eyes stared down at me, boring a hole into my very soul. Blood oozed down from the stabbing crown of thorns. It pooled and dried along his eyebrows. And his pain? His pain was my own.

Once in the night Zelda put her arm around me, and drew herself close. I pulled away. I could not be comforted. I could not be loved; neither could I give love. She could not reach me. I was well beyond all this.

Why did I spit in Jesus' face? Why did all hell erupt from within me? I hated being forced into this role, the role of the killer, the executioner. Just as in Germania, I was compelled—forced by circumstances into a role I despised. But when my moment came, with my men gathered around, I played it to the hilt. The brute lurking at the bottom of the chasm within me took full control. Today, on Golgotha, the horror and rage of Germania had found a fresh vent.

But this was no Barbarian village. This was no blond-haired girl; this was the Son of God.

The Son of God…. The words of my confession reverberated through my throbbing mind, over and over, until I thought my head would split.

Finally, toward dawn a dream came—a dream as horrid as the state of my own soul.

Now, I was on the cross. Flies buzzed and droned around my naked, heaving frame. They licked the sweat from my face, drank my trickling blood, mated on my flesh, laid their eggs in my piercing wounds.

And I? I could do nothing. Nothing!

My nail-pinned hands could not brush them away. I had no puff of air in reserve to blow them from my face, no means whatever to resist their fickle buzzing dance of torture. I was helpless, and beyond all help.

Three times I dozed. Three times I fell into this unfathomable hell. Each episode was more vivid than the last, until finally my will to sleep crumbled. I fought against the very notion of sleep. I got up more weary than when I had laid my head upon the pillow.

It was late, much later than I usually rise. But then it was Saturday, the Sabbath. This day had no urgency to it. The day of rest. Here was a Jewish custom that in normal times I quite enjoyed. May it come to the whole of our world.

Technically, it was not a day of rest for the Roman military, but practically it was, since all commerce in the city was shut down. We reduced our operations proportionately. We maintained a mere skeleton crew on the city walls. The gates were closed. Quiet reigned.

But while Zelda and the boys still slept, I resolved to visit Pilate and speak my mind. I pulled on my multi-layered linen cuirass, strapped on my sword, and slipped out of the bedroom door.

Noisy sparrows chattered about the villa courtyard. I placed my hands on the familiar handrail and looked over all that was my home. I could see no earthquake damage. Yet, there was damage. There was no peace here. This damage, this problem, was not in my home. It was in my heart, in my soul, and on my mind, so oppressively heavy on my mind. It was the prophet, the Galilean, the Jewish king, the Son of God! The man with a thousand titles. It was he who had upset my world. He turned it upside down, threw all of it into chaos. I blamed him.

Or should I blame Pilate? The Badger knew more than he let on. He knew the Christ was innocent. But he caved in like a brick-roofed hovel. Why did this man have no spine? Why did he let Caiaphas lead him around like a bull on a nose ring?

For the second time, I would try to talk to him. I would tell him what I saw. How I saw the prophet heal. How he brought the dead Timaeus back to life. How the very sun refused to shine, refused to see what we had done to him. How the earth quaked and the cross shook when he died. I would tell him. I would tell it all to him. I would tell him who he was. The Son of God! Maybe that would bring me some peace.

I suspect Pilate already knew—knew in his heart that Jesus was no ordinary man. He had heard all the miraculous stories, then read the warning message from his wife. He had seen the same darkness, and been shaken by the same quake which rattled me.

Still, I would go. Let the Badger rage. Let him hang me on a cross if he so desired. In my tortured mind, I was there already. The real thing might not be so much worse than this, this hellish torment.

I went down the stairs. I ate some of the cook's thick porridge. I ate it with a few of the early rising men. I savoured it like a last meal. And then I set out not knowing what response might await me at the other end of my journey.

The streets were largely quiet. A few men sat out in the morning sun. Not a child was to be seen.

For the second consecutive morning, I walked up the six broad steps of the stone pavement. I stood before the carved eagle doors. But to my great surprise, there was someone already there. Three clerics were waiting in their gold-ornamented garb. One of them I recognized. It was Annas. The other men were high-ranking Pharisees, members of the Sanhedrin.

What could possibly bring them to the governor's palace door on the Sabbath, the Passover Sabbath nonetheless?

On hearing me approach Annas turned, and greeted me. "Ah, a centurion! What a pleasant surprise." He nodded, and then, as if in thought, he raised a finger my way and said, "We may have need of you." There was a curious twinkle in the old man's eye.

"I am here to see the governor," I responded.

"As are we," one of the Pharisees confirmed, stating what was patently obvious.

"Have you spoken to anyone?" I inquired.

"His chamberlain," Annas replied. "He said he would be right back, but we have waited here for quite some time now." He heaved a weary sigh.

To this I made no reply. Stony silence descended. No natural link existed between us, nor was one desired by either party.

In due course the governor's chamberlain arrived. He showed a measure of surprise at seeing me with this group. Then he bowed courteously to Annas and said, "His excellency will see you now."

Annas beckoned that I follow, so I entered. The chamberlain undoubtedly thought I was a late-arriving addition to this delegation.

Pilate was seated even as I saw him yesterday. He looked

haggard, as though he had slept on the bloodstained rocks of Golgotha. He motioned for the temple delegation to step forward. I waited at the back of the room.

Annas bowed and began, *"Sir, we remember that while he was still alive that deceiver said, 'After three days I will rise again.'"*[110] A strange tingle ran through me as he said this.

Pilate rubbed his hands.

Annas continued, *"So give the order that the tomb be made secure until the third day. Otherwise his disciples may come and steal the body and tell the people that he has been raised from the dead."* Then he concluded by lifting a bony finger and saying, *"This last deception will be worse than the first."*[111]

On hearing this, Pilate sighed deeply, then beckoned me forward. There was worry in his eyes. "The centurion here, Marcus Aureolus, is fully acquainted with the case of the Galilean prophet. He oversaw his crucifixion." Then he addressed me directly, "Is that not so?"

I nodded, "Yes, sir. It is as you say."

With that, he raised his hands and motioned both parties together. Speaking directly to all of us, he said, *"Take a guard. Go, make the tomb as secure as you know how."*[112] Then, rubbing his guilt-stained hands once more, the Badger got up and skulked off.

Annas was jubilant. With eagerness in his voice he turned to address me. "How soon can you have your troops at the tomb?"

"We should be there in about an hour."

"Excellent!" he enthused. "These two gentlemen will meet you there. They will ensure that all is in order. Understood?"

"Yes. Understood," I answered. Then I addressed the Pharisees, "Do you know which tomb? Do you know where it is?"

Annas answered for them, "Ah, they know it well." He gave a contemptuous snort. "The traitor's tomb, Joseph of Arimathea!"

"I will bring my men and meet you there, then," I said and gave a slight bow to my head.

The chamberlain saw us to the door, and I set off, back to my home.

I shook my head several times in disbelief as I trudged back. Every time I tried to extricate myself from this messiah pit, this kingdom of God affair, this abysmal hole, I would find myself sucked in even deeper. And now it had happened again. Was there no escape?

Would I ever be allowed to speak my mind before Pilate?

I decided to see Renaldo first, so rather than turn into my gate, I went directly to his. There was no sign of him, or Brutus, his big, friendly dog, but there were a dozen soldiers in the courtyard. Some of them were about to leave for the fortress. Competitive games had been planned for today—races and feats of strength between Flavio's hometown team, and Caius and his men.

"I may have some work for you men," I called out to these soldiers. "So don't leave just yet."

Upon hearing my voice, Renaldo emerged from a side room where he and his wife had been tending to Lucas. "What is it, Marcus?" he inquired.

"Oh, I need some men to guard the prophet's tomb." It was impossible to hide my frustration.

"Why?" Renaldo reacted with a shake of his head. He found this quite perplexing.

"Well," I responded, "It seems that the high priest and his crew are worried that either Jesus will arise from the dead, or his disciples will come and steal his body."

"That's bizarre." Renaldo shook his head again. "Just bizarre. Where did they get that notion?"

"From Jesus. From the prophet himself. Apparently he predicted it," I answered.

He smacked his lips and shook his head again. He bowed his head slightly, and brought his hand to his forehead in what appeared to be a desperate attempt to mentally digest all this.

"Look, Renaldo. I don't have time to try and explain this." My exasperation clearly showed. "And I don't really know if I even can. Right now, I need sixteen men to take to the tomb for the first shift. I need them there within the hour. I thought if we combined your men here with my men next door, we could make up this first contingent."

"First contingent?"

"First contingent, first shift. They want it guarded day and night for the next three days," I explained.

He shook his head again, and threw up his hands in exasperation. " Fine. We'll prance around and do the Weasel's bidding." He was angry. "Did Pilate approve this?"

"Yes, sir," I said as I bowed low in a show of mock subservience. "He's back licking the holy man's stinking feet—once again! He started yesterday during the messiah's trial," I said bitterly, "and now, who knows when he'll stop."

"I can only shake my head," Renaldo answered as he did just that. After a pause, with grim resignation in his voice, he said, "Well, let's get on with it. I suppose we have to do it." He turned and bellowed at the twelve waiting men. "All of you head over next door."

After a bit of haggling and to and fro banter we settled on eight men from each troop who would accompany me to the tomb. The rest of the soldiers were released to go to the fortress in preparation for the games which were to begin at noon.

I lined up my men four abreast and we marched out to the tomb in rhythmic military style. We would do this right. On the surface, I protested being drawn into this, the high priest's plan of preemptive precaution, but within me, I was filled with dark apprehension. These measures had merit. This guarding of the tomb might well be warranted. I did not fear his disciples. There had been no sign of them, no sign of armed uprising. No, it was the prophet himself that I feared.

This notion of him rising from the dead did not strike me as all that farfetched. On the surface the Christ's prediction seemed impossible—utterly impossible—totally preposterous. But then, in life he had been a total master of the impossible. The example of the blind Bartimaeus sprang to mind. This messiah had tossed off miracles like he was tossing off the covers from his bed. Could he now toss off the shroud of death?

There was something far larger at work here. This was more than the raving of a lunatic. Why else would the sun refuse to shine as he hung dying? Why else would the earth shudder with his last breath? No, he was the Son of God. My very own words came back to haunt me. Anything was possible; nothing could be ruled out!

Then I remembered the worried look I had seen on Pilate's face just this morning, when Annas had raised the matter. Without saying a word I knew we both were of the same mind. He, too, thought a resurrection could occur. Why else his prompt response?

Oh yes, and then there was the rubbing of the hands. Guilt stains are not so easily removed. I should know. After all these years, the blond-haired girl still visits me quite regularly on those soul tormenting nights.

Only the high priest's men seemed sure of themselves, cocky in their victory, but not cocky enough to throw all caution to the wind. Why else post a guard? Winds can change, and all this could yet blow up in their faces.

They were there. The two pompous Pharisees were already there at the tomb. There was a change of garb though. They were no longer in their Sabbath Day finery, not for a visit to this king's tomb. They would burn these clothes when they returned to the city.

"Greetings," I said stiffly.

They ignored my remark. One of them began, "This is all your men?"

"All that I'll be bringing," I responded.

"Hmm!" He sniffed, obviously disappointed with the number. "Well. This tomb will need to be sealed," he said as he put his hand to the huge rock door.

"Why sealed?" I questioned.

"Because I don't trust your men," he shot back.

Now it was my turn to say, "Hmm!"

"If a bit of silver crosses their palms, they'll remove that body," he motioned toward the tomb's contents lying behind the rock door. "No. It will have to be sealed. We will have it no other way."

I frowned, but by way of defence I said, "I trust my men. Nevertheless," I conceded, "for your sake we'll seal it."

"Now let's see if he's there," the other Pharisee said as he motioned again to the round rock door.

"He's there. I saw them put him in here last night," I spoke with growing impatience.

"We will see if he is there," he repeated with marked insistence in his voice.

I sighed, then called two of my larger, more muscular men by name. "Roll back the stone," I commanded.

They responded eagerly enough. The whole platoon had listened intently to our conversation. Now they were being drawn into the action. One man crouched low and applied his back and shoulder to the polished rim of the boulder. He would push up and forward with the full strength of his legs. The second man placed his hands above the first man's head and braced himself for a tremendous push in a straight forward direction.

I counted out the numbers, "One, two, three. Push!"

To cheers of encouragement from the other soldiers, the huge rock slowly ground into motion. It rolled ever so slowly in its cut rock track. After a herculean effort, the opening lay fully exposed. The light shone in. My two men collapsed in a jubilant heap.

"Well done," I called out to them.

The Pharisees stepped inside, and I followed. There were several rock shelves cut in the sidewalls. All of them were empty. It was, after all, a new tomb. In a central position near the back was a raised rock platform, the place of honour. On this, the Christ lay. The Pharisees cautiously drew near. One of them turned and beckoned me to approach.

"Unwrap him," he instructed.

I stiffened. "I will not unwrap him." I glared defiantly.

"Then have your men unwrap him," he demanded.

"I will not have my men unwrap him," I answered with growing anger. "If you want him unwrapped, do it yourselves!"

This produced an impasse. For a moment no one moved. I was bothered by this whole scenario. We crossed an invisible line when we rolled back the stone. We crossed another line when we entered. I was not about to cross the third line. We were now verging on the desecration of the dead. I would not yield on this point. I found it shocking that these men, these holy men, who abhorred the presence of the dead, insisted on carrying this matter so far. Without question, they were acting on the explicit instruction of the hoary-headed Weasel. Some holy man!

"Look," I argued. "This is Jesus of Nazareth. If that's your concern. I saw him taken off the cross," I motioned in the vague direction of Golgotha, "wrapped in that shroud," I pointed to it, "and carried into this tomb," I raised both hands to encompass the rock room in which we stood. "This body is his body." I emphasized each word.

"Will you swear to that?"

I raised my right hand. "By the Emperor's throne, by the sacred temple, by all that is holy, I will swear," I spoke with mounting anger.

This assertion appeared to satisfy them. We walked out of the tomb, and I chose two fresh men to roll the stone back.

Once more, I addressed the high priest's men, "I didn't bring any wax, or a pot to melt it, or the governor's seal. I will need to return to get these."

This news was greeted with a disdainful sigh, but they insisted that they would wait by the tomb until the job was done.

I took two men with me and in due course we returned. We built a small charcoal fire, melted the wax in the pot, and then ladled it over the crevice that separated the rock door from the rock face of the hill. We cleverly used some broken rock shards to help with containment, and the poured wax formed an airtight seal around the upper half of the circular rock. At two points, one on either side, I affixed the governor's own stamp into a thickened layer of the pliable wax. Any tampering would break this seal and obliterate the imperial stamp.

At last they were satisfied. Caiaphas himself would have approved of this seal. But then, why was I working for him?

It was mid-afternoon when we were finally finished. I posted my men on guard and headed back to the city.

Some Sabbath! Some day of rest!

But I was done sealing the dead.

35

THE BOYS BOUNCED AROUND ME LIKE PLAYFUL PUPPIES AS AT last I walked through the gates of home.

"We made a kite," Julius said, and with that he rushed off to retrieve it.

"You were gone all day," my youngest boy complained as he grabbed my hand and began to swing from it.

"Yes, I was gone. I had work to do." I sighed and rubbed my free hand across the back of my neck.

"Look at this!" Julius trumpeted and he went careening about the courtyard with the kite tail streaming out behind him. "Let's go fly it, Papa!"

"I think it's too late," I slowly answered. I found the nearest bench off to the side and collapsed onto it. My words took the wind from both their sails.

"Can't we go, Papa? We waited all day."

"I just can't do it today," I answered with genuine regret in my voice. Then, to soften the blow, I said, "Let me see that kite. It looks great."

He handed it to me with some reluctance.

"So you did this?"

"Well, Mama helped," Julius admitted.

"She helped a lot," Andrew corrected him.

"Well, your mother is really good at this kind of thing."

"You're better," Andrew answered, "but you weren't here."

With that mild rebuke, my depleted patience ran out. "Boys,

go away! Just go away!" My voice rose and I motioned them out of my sight. "I just need some time to myself."

They retreated in crushed despondence.

It was not very long before Zelda came. She was wearing one of her best dresses. Her long hair was freshly brushed and I quickly caught the scent of her perfume.

"You look exhausted, Marcus," she observed.

"I am."

"Let me get you some wine," she offered.

"Have the servant girl get it. Come and sit down." I slid over. "Come sit by me for a while."

"She's not here, Marcus. Remember. It's the Sabbath."

"Hah! The Sabbath," I muttered. "Some Sabbath!"

"So, where were you all day?" She sat down and then continued, "I kept telling the boys you would be home soon, but you never came."

"Pfff!" I glowered. "I was working for the Weasel. The bloody Weasel!"

She was taken aback, unfamiliar with this derogatory term.

"The high priest! Caiaphas! The holy stone thrower," I erupted. "That butcher has the morals of a graverobber!" I threw my head back and rubbed my fingers over my hair. A week's worth of exasperation gripped me.

"How come you're working for him?" Zelda asked. She was truly confused by all this. I usually said very little about my work.

"It's a long story." I felt myself tensing up. "I—I don't even want to go into it." I hesitated. "Just get me the wine." I motioned with a backhanded wave. I slumped forward with my elbows on my knees and my chin cradled in my hands.

She got up and touched her hand to my hair, as though in blessing, and then was off. In a few minutes, she was back with a wine-filled chalice cradled in her hand.

I took a few sips.

Zelda stood awkwardly before me. Without speaking a word, I knew she had something to say.

"What is it?" I said.

"Junia and Renaldo invited all of us over for supper." She paused before adding, "I said we would come."

"Hmm," I snorted from within my ongoing state of dejection.

Normally, this would be welcome news, but nothing could shake me from the dark foreboding that had settled around me like a death shroud. Besides, I felt my whole life was being planned for me. Everything was out of my hands, whether at work or at home.

"If you have a nice bath, I'm sure you'll feel better."

I made no response.

"She made *shlemkins*. The boys are looking forward to it."

"Fine," I snapped. "We'll go." It was a reluctant concession. "But I'm not sure that I'm fit company for anyone."

She left me. I sat in bleak silence, then I drained the chalice and headed for the bathhouse.

Within about an hour we were ready to head over to our neighbors. Zelda was right. I did feel better after a bath and a change of clothes, and the boys had gotten over their earlier disappointment. I told them to bring their kite because Renaldo was a kite-building expert, or so I said.

We walked over together. I told Julius to call out at the gate. Soon Rana greeted us with a graceful curtsy, and ushered us in. She is the oldest of Renaldo's four daughters. In contrast to all the other days this week, the courtyard was deserted. By common consent our uninvited military guests were spending the night at the hippodrome.

The boys rushed over to the corner where Brutus usually sleeps, but the dog was not there. Renaldo called out to them, "He's gone. I let him out this morning, and he's still not back." As an aside to me, he said, "He probably found a lady friend."

Young Andrew heard this comment and asked, "Do dogs get married, Papa?"

This brought a good bit of adult laughter. Renaldo motioned to me for an answer.

"Not exactly, but they like each other a lot."

More laughter.

"We can talk about it another time. Now, boys, why don't you show Renaldo your kite?"

The kite was presented, and duly admired. In the meantime, Zelda went off with Junia to help with the meal.

"I know who would like a look at this," Renaldo told the boys. He returned the kite to Julius and with a beckoning motion said, "Come, follow me."

We mounted the stairs to the sleeping quarters, and there on the balcony sat the harlot's son on an old wooden chair. He had been watching us with eager eyes from the moment we arrived.

"This is Lucas," Renaldo began the introduction.

The boy smiled.

"He has had an accident," Renaldo spoke the words more slowly, by way of explanation. "But he's getting back his strength." He turned to him. "Aren't you, Lucas?"

"Yes," he said. The boy turned and as he did, he brought the bandaged stump into view.

I saw my sons' eyes widen. Julius stepped back. Andrew took my hand.

"It's getting better," the older boy said. "It doesn't hurt as much today."

But I could see marks of strain in the beggar boy's eyes.

"I'm getting a new hand," he announced. "Jesus of Nazareth said he would give me a new one." He spoke the words with a matter of fact confidence.

Renaldo shot a glance my way.

"Ah, Lucas," I began slowly, "when ah… when did Jesus say this to you?"

"Last night. He told me last night. He came to my room."

"It was a dream?" I inquired.

"No." He was emphatic. "I don't think so. He was real." Then he extended his formerly crippled leg, glanced down at it, and with conviction asserted, "He fixed my leg. He'll fix my hand."

"It was a dream," I said with a shake of my head. "You can't put your trust in a dream."

He turned away from me. His lips tightened. I thought he might start to cry. He did not want to hear this. But neither had I wanted to say it. Yet why let some false hope linger? Why let the poison of disappointment take root? This was one dream that needed to be shattered before it had time to fully form. The boy had suffered enough. Why let false hope add to his torment?

The whole topic—the visit from Jesus—brought an eerie discomfort, a startling disconnect with what I knew to be reality.

Renaldo gave me one of his instant eye signals. The signal spoke of his approval of my words. He probably had told Lucas something similar. I did not want to tell the boy that the northern prophet was dead. At times like this, such things are better left unsaid.

I gave Julius a nudge.

He held up the kite and said, "We brought this for you. We made it today."

Suddenly, the kite had turned into a gift.

Lucas took it. His whole face changed. He held it with his one hand. He moved it in a swooping fashion as though it were in flight. But then a tear from his eager eyes trickled down. He tried to wipe it on the sleeve of his upper arm while he still held the kite in his hand.

"I've never had a kite. I couldn't run," he choked on the words. They were spoken with bitter-sweet joy. "But now I can run."

"Yes," Renaldo put in, "in a few days you'll be running."

Rana called up from the courtyard below us, "Supper! Supper is ready!"

Renaldo helped Lucas to his feet, and except for the stairs, Lucas walked the whole way to the dining hall on his own.

"I thought Claudius might come with you for supper," Renaldo ventured.

"Ah, I've got him out guarding the tomb tonight," I answered.

"So, how did it go today with the Weasel's men?" Renaldo asked.

"Puhhh!" the breath exploded from my lips. I shook my head. "Let's just say they're happy. I'm dead. But they're happy."

There was enough bitterness in my voice to ruin my meal. And it did.

We all sat down together. I ate only a little, and drank a little too much. Voices, conversation, children's laughter buzzed all around me. In my overtired state, it had a lulling effect. But all too soon it reminded me of flies, lazy Sabbath Day flies, buzzing, buzzing over a corpse.

I seemed to awake from this half stupor as Zelda put her arm to my shoulder. "Marcus, you're so quiet. Are you falling asleep?"

"I guess I am," I admitted.

"You poor man! They're working you too hard," she said with a quick kiss to my brow.

Then she turned to Junia and said, "I guess we should go. I hate to leave so soon after supper, but I don't want Marcus falling asleep on your table."

"Oh, he can sleep on our table—just not in our bed," Renaldo quipped.

Junia rose from beside me and she called the boys from the next room where they had gone to play. The mandatory compliments and thank you's were exchanged as we all made our way out to the courtyard.

The night watchman had arrived, and he opened the gate for us. As he did, a large dark beast surged by us. It was Brutus. Something white protruded from either side of his jaws. Even in the dim light I saw it.

Recognition was instant. It was the well-gnawed bones of a forearm. The hand with fingers intact dangled from one end.

"It's Brutus!" Andrew called out eagerly as the dog retreated to his corner with his ghoulish trophy.

The dog was so quick, and the light so poor, that no one had seen what I saw.

"Stop!" I screamed as the boy began to run to greet Renaldo's family pet. I lunged for Andrew, caught him by the shoulder, screamed at him, "Stop! Stop when I say stop!" My voice was breaking. I shook as I gripped him tight.

He started to cry.

"Why don't you listen!" I yelled. I shook him so that his teeth rattled.

The poor boy was terrified. He had never seen me in such an agitated state. My chest heaved with each breath. I was visibly shaking with ragged-edged rage.

When my hands released him, he ran bawling to his mother.

I rose off my knees. "He's got a bone!" I snapped. "Don't bother a dog with a bone."

It was a feeble attempt to explain what appeared to be a bizarre overreaction to an innocent situation. No one knew why I had lost control, and I was not about to tell them. Both families stood in stunned silence, unsure of how to respond to what they saw as an irrational outburst.

"Take the boys home, Zelda. Just take the boys home." I motioned.

They left with Andrew still crying, "I didn't mean to, Papa. I didn't mean to." His body convulsed with huge aching sobs.

"Let's go back in, girls," Junia said. "There's clean up to do."

Only Renaldo, the gatekeeper and I remained in the courtyard. I stood with my head down.

"Are you all right?" Renaldo asked as he approached.

"No. I'm not all right," I confessed in a voice just above a whisper. Then I threw up my hands in exasperation. I bit down on my lip, shook my head. I walked over to the gate. With a jerk of my head I called Renaldo to follow. When we were out on the empty street, I leaned my forehead against a brick in the outside wall. As Renaldo drew near, I began to whisper, a hoarse whisper, with my face into the wall, "I'm going crazy! I'm going crazy!"

He put a hand to my shoulder.

"That messiah—that crucifixion! It's driving me crazy!" The words hissed out from me. They were more breathed than spoken. I clenched my fists and rolled my forehead over the jagged surface of the brick. Long pause. Breath catching, throat stinging, pause.

"Your dog, your filthy dog came home with a dead man's arm tonight. Hand and all. Ugh!" I whimpered. I rolled my forehead over the brick again. "It's from Golgotha! The bloody Skull!"

I sank to the ground, turned my back to the wall, hung my heavy head between my knees.

Renaldo stooped before me. He was speechless.

Time passed.

"It's Animal. It's Animal," I whispered. I do not know if he knew what I meant by this.

More time passed. More aching silence.

Then he spoke, "I'll kill him."

Pause.

"I'll kill the dog!" he resolved.

"No," I sighed. "No…. Just clean it up." I rolled my head from side to side. "It's your dog. Just clean up after your dog," I looked up into his face. "Don't let your girls see it."

My head dropped like a stone again. I said my piece, but there was no peace. I braced myself against the wall, put my hand to Renaldo's shoulder, and pulled myself up. I walked home.

I collapsed onto the courtyard bench. For about an hour I lay there alone, rolled up in the chilly night air. Then, from the yard next door, I heard a yelp.

A singular, sharp yelp.

Then silence. Just cold silence.

36

THE SAME COLD SNOW. THE SAME WOODED VALLEY IN Germania. The same stealthy, encircling, approach. The same signal for attack.

In unison we rushed forward, swords drawn, bucklers held at the ready, swift but silent. Surprise was our sharpest weapon.

I rounded the corner of the first hut, and all but collided with a child—a girl.

Thhuuck!

My sweeping blade caught her just below the ribs, slicing three quarters through her slim torso.

Her blond head snapped back in shock.

Questioning blue eyes shot upward looking me full in the face.

She spoke. For the first time in a hundred nights she spoke.

"There is a solution," the words tumbled from her lips even as her body fell severed from this life.

I felt a hot red gush cover my sword hand.

I leaped from the bed, sweat-drenched, chest heaving, once more filled with dread and dark foreboding.

I rubbed my guilty hands in the moonlight. Collapsed by the window. Rocked back and forth in the darkness.

Here I was again, caught in another round of torment, with each nightmare more hideous than the last.

I wondered what she meant. I wondered why she spoke. Why did she speak tonight? She had never spoken before. What solution could there be? What cleansing for the constant dripping stain within my hollow soul? What cleansing for my bloodied hands?

What solution?

After a time, Zelda hauled herself out of bed. She knelt beside me. I made no response. She wrapped her arm around my shoulder. Why did she still care? Why did she even care?

I scared her. My outbursts scared her. My nightmares left their own cut marks inside her gentle heart. Why come close to me again?

I hurt the boys. Today, I hurt the boys. Would I lash out at her next?

Suddenly, my life was careening out of control like an arrow glancing off the rock-hard surface of the Skull. Next, it would go slamming into hell. In the last week the demons long held in check had all been let out. Now they were laughing. Laughing! I could hear them laughing in the night. Their maniacal laugh echoed off the gaping chasm deep within me.

Zelda kissed the side of my head. Then she sighed deeply.

After a long while she spoke. "I'm pregnant."

Long pause.

"We're going to have another baby," she said as she rubbed her hand across her tummy. "It's three months, Marcus."

I was silent. I sighed. My head dropped lower.

"What's wrong? What's wrong, Marcus? Whatever has come over you?" Her tone was not accusatory. These were words born out of concern, loving concern.

At last I lifted my head and spoke, "I'm scared, Zelda. I'm scared… I'm scared that I'll never see that baby. I'm scared that it will be stolen from us, just like Tara."

"I'm scared too," she admitted.

"I'm scared of what I'm turning into," I confessed with a slow and mournful shake of my head.

My head dropped again between my legs. I wrapped my arms

around my knees and squeezed them together. My head, my skull, was caught in this vicelike grip. My posture, my physical form, reflected my spiritual reality.

Somehow, she wrapped her arms around me. She kissed the top of my fallen head. "I love you, Marcus. Don't ever leave me."

I sighed a sigh from so deep that it rattled round the very roots of the chasm.

After a time I got up and dropped myself into bed. I lay flat on my stomach, my head turned aside.

She put her arm over my shoulder and whispered in my ear, "You're a good man, Marcus. A very good man."

But then, she did not really know.

She did not know what my hands had done... She did not know me.

37

THE EARTHQUAKE JOLTED BOTH OF US AWAKE.

It was a different kind of quake. Friday's quake was of the slow, rumbling, grinding type that rolls to a crescendo. This one was short and sharp. It felt as though for an instant the earth had disappeared from beneath us, and we were allowed to fall into the lurch left by this pocket of empty space.

The foundations shuddered; the walls shook. My helmet fell off the peg on which it hung. It clattered to the floor, bounced once, and made a crazy half roll over the floorboards.

It was sunrise. The first shafts of light streamed through our open window.

It was late, again later than I usually rise. But then, I had desperately needed that bit of sleep. I scrambled to my feet. I could hear voices on the street. The city was awake, and this seismic tremor was giving them plenty to talk about. Fortunately, for the moment, there were no aftershocks, and I could see no obvious damage when I emerged onto the balcony in only a breechcloth.

The sparrows resumed their flitting here and there, but their chatter had been stilled. I moved quickly and pushed open the door to the boys' room. Both of them were sitting up in their beds. They too had been jolted out of sleep.

"Something happened, Papa!" Andrew said with fear in his small voice. Simultaneously, he held out his arms to me for a hug.

I pulled him right out of bed and into my arms.

"Yes, something happened. It was an earthquake," I explained as I moved over to Julius. I put an arm around him too and said, "Let's go downstairs, boys."

By this time Zelda was clothed and at the door. "We'll go down to the courtyard," I motioned with my head. "There might be another one."

We walked down together. I pulled two benches to the middle of the courtyard for us to sit on. Then I felt the morning cold.

"I forgot my clothes!" and with that said, I turned to go back upstairs.

"Be careful!" Zelda called after me.

I pulled my linen cuirass, my helmet, tunic, belt and sword out onto the balcony. I felt safer dressing there, and my family was within view.

It was the strangest quake, singularly sharp and potent. But nothing preceded; nothing followed. Urgency was replaced by an uneasy calm.

As I strapped on my sword, the cook called up to me asking if he should proceed with breakfast. I answered in the affirmative. With some apprehension, I followed him back in the house, and since the porridge had already been prepared, we simply scooped it into four bowls. Then he helped me carry these out to my family in the courtyard. We felt safer out there.

It was a strange way to start the day. I had downed three big spoonfuls when someone started banging at the gate. There was clearly a commotion out there. There was an urgency to the pounding. I set my bowl down on the bench and covered the ground to the gate with large, quick strides.

Where was that gatekeeper, anyway?

But the bar would not release. The gateposts must have shifted in the quake, and now the bar was jammed. Finally I jarred it free with a painful upward thrust with my open palms. A dozen men surged in. The guards from the tomb! They were breathless. Sweat dripped from them. Some collapsed on the ground. Others were doubled over and gasping for air.

They must have run the whole way from the tomb. Yet it was more than exhaustion I saw written on their faces. I saw fear.

"What's happened?" I called out to no one in particular.

Philip caught his breath, "There was a light. It came down." He shook his head violently, then grabbed some more air, but he could not go on.

I moved to another man who was stooped over, hands on his knees. I motioned for him to speak with quick desperate jerks of my hands. But he shook his head.

I spotted Claudius. I grabbed him by the front collar of his cuirass and forced him upright. "What happened?" I demanded as I yelled in his face. "What happened?" My words were forced out through clenched teeth.

"The light... the light became a man," he swallowed. "When it touched the ground... the earth shook. It dropped out from under us."

His head slumped down again.

I shook him. "What then?" I demanded again.

From behind me Philip resumed the account, "We all fell down. Fell flat."

I stepped toward him again.

He caught another gulp of air. "It was so bright—like lightning. I closed my eyes. I couldn't see. We couldn't look." He held up his hand up as though he was shielding his eyes. "We lay there shaking."

He still was shaking. I looked about. Others were nodding their heads.

"What else? Was there more?"

A third man came to his aid. "When I opened my eyes, the angel was on the stone. He was sitting on the stone."

"The tomb was open," Philip continued, but then he fell to the ground. "A man walked out of it. The dead man walked out!" he wailed out these last words, as though he had seen a spirit—a ghost.

"You all saw this?"

They nodded their ascent.

"We all saw it," Claudius confirmed.

I brought my hand to my forehead, and then expelled a huge breath of air. This was beyond understanding. It was clearly from beyond the realm of the normal. How do you handle heaven's messenger? How do you deal with the supernatural?

I looked over them again. "Some of you are missing. Where are the other men?"

"I don't know," Claudius admitted. "Some just ran off. I guess they were too scared." He shook his head as though he was waking from some dreaded nightmare.

I did a head count, confirmed that there were twelve there, then told them to sit still. With a few quick questions, I determined who was missing.

The men before me were in shock. They were as traumatized as any troops routed in battle. You could see it on their faces. This was no fabrication. Whatever they had witnessed had nearly scared the life right out of them.

I had no idea what to do. My family had watched all this—this double quake. They would have questions for me later. I turned to them now. Then I turned back to my men. I never felt more caught between two worlds.

I turned again to Zelda. I walked to my little two-bench island in the middle of the courtyard. "I'm leaving," I announced. "I have some work to do."

After a round of hugs, I said to Zelda, "Have the cook serve these men some breakfast. I should be back in about an hour or two."

"Be careful, Marcus."

I returned to my tomb-guarding platoon, and singled out

Claudius, "You're coming with me." He slowly got to his feet. "We're going back to the tomb. We'll see exactly what happened."

As I spoke the word *tomb*, he fell to his knees. "Don't take me back there!" he cried out as he slowly shook his head. "Don't take me back, sir!" Fear rippled through his voice.

I considered this for a moment and then responded, "You are a man. Not a dog. Now stand to your feet."

He hesitated.

"Stand now, or I'll have you flogged tomorrow."

He obeyed.

"Philip. On your feet," I barked. "You are coming too. Here's your Sunday morning appointment. As for the rest of you, wait right here," I pointed to the ground on which they sat. "If our missing four show up, have them wait here with you. I should be back before too long."

Then the three of us set out. I walked at a brisk pace, and as I did, I listened for the two men's footsteps right behind me. They were keeping up.

Unlike Friday, the signs of earthquake damage were everywhere, cracked mortar, shifted stonework, broken tiles. Everywhere people were out of their homes. They were out on the streets, drawn out by fear, inspecting damage, talking in loud excited voices.

Although I tried my best to hide it, I was terrified. I learned long ago that the best way to hide fear is with action. Sitting and thinking brings deadly paralysis, but moving, doing, advancing on your fear, brings relief. It is the only way I know to overcome it. But it was not the earthquake that unsettled me. That was only a minor concern. It was the cause of the quake that rattled me to the core.

The timing of the quake was uncanny. On Friday it had been at the point of death that the earth shuddered. This morning, did it jump at the start of life? Was that what jolted us out of bed? Had the prophet's last prophecy come true?

269

I stopped suddenly. Both Philip and Claudius nearly collided with me. I swung around, "Tell me about this light."

"It was like lightning."

"It came down from the sky."

"It was like it turned into a man."

"What sort of man?" I asked.

They both turned their eyes away and squinted as though they were shielding themselves from the memory.

"Like a warrior," Claudius spoke and then he started to slowly shake his head, just as he had done earlier. It was as though his mind could not handle what his eyes had taken in.

"Yes," Philip concurred. "An almighty warrior!"

"When did the earthquake hit?"

"When he touched the ground," they both answered.

"When his feet touched the ground," Claudius clarified.

"You weren't dreaming this? You weren't asleep?"

"No!" There was annoyance in his voice. "No, sir! We weren't dreaming. We all saw this." His face was red with the intensity of his words. His voice was raw with emotion. "Flog me if I'm lying, sir! Flog us both!" His eyes were pleading to be believed. Then his head dropped and he began to roll it from side to side. Claudius was clearly at the breaking point.[113]

"Come then," I said more gently. I put my hand to his arm. "I want to see what you saw."

We resumed our trek. We passed the steps of the governor's palace and the Antonia Fortress. The soldiers were scurrying about like ants who have had their anthill kicked in. Damage to the fortress gate was clearly visible; undoubtedly, there was more destruction that we could not see.

If the day had gone as planned, I would have been arriving at the fortress about this time to pick up another platoon of guards to replace the men who were now sequestered at my villa. I had already drawn up the list of soldiers the afternoon before. But if I correctly understood this morning's hair-raising report, the very purpose for the next shift of guards had gotten up out of his tomb and walked away.

It was unbelievable! Though my men's words appeared credible, though their physical response appeared credible, I had to see it to believe it! It was too fantastic, too otherworldly, too far beyond the natural realm!

Yet, in life, Jesus seemed to be that way. At times, he appeared totally natural, even ordinary, but at other times there was nothing natural about him. The supernatural moved through him; the power of God appeared.

Did it show up this morning? Did it move upon his corpse?

At the Fish Gate, the cracks which had appeared due to Friday's quake had grown exponentially. In fact, the wooden members of the gate were in a mangled and twisted state. Some heavy stone blocks had fallen from the gate house. I feared for my life as I passed under it.

As we headed north, I thought of the other king, Herod Antipas. He had come this way, been carried through this gate, and passed by the cross uprights that were coming into view on Golgotha. On Friday, he had his rival nailed there. I could not help but wonder, who was the real pretender, the pretender to the throne? In my heart I knew the answer. This morning did heaven pronounce its own verdict on the matter? In moments I would know the answer.

The uprights were there, just as we had left them on the Skull. They looked somehow different in the morning light, perhaps less threatening, less ominous, more at peace with their surroundings. What a strange thought this was!

We were drawing very near now. I made a short detour around the Skull. As I stepped off the road, I turned to my two companions. "You changed nothing? You left everything as is?" I asked.

"We did nothing," Philip answered. "We dropped everything. All we did was flee after the angel came." They were clearly apprehensive.

"I just don't want to see that angel again," Claudius shuddered as he spoke.

"Stay behind me," I responded. "If he's there and he's as scary as you say, we all have legs. You can use them again." These words brought only a small measure of assurance.

We resumed walking. We had gone only a short distance when two men came running from the tomb. They ran right by, ignoring us completely. One of them I recognized. It was John, the messiah's young disciple.[114]

This did little to staunch our fears. My two followers were now on the verge of becoming panic-stricken.

"We will advance more slowly," I said. "But we will advance."

And we did. It would be fair to say I crept around the corner of the last hill. The tomb came into view, but my two soldiers were well back. Seeing no one there, I beckoned them forward, and then advanced a few more steps.

It was as they said. The stone was rolled away. But it was not merely rolled to the side as I had expected. It had been pushed right up and out of its stone track, and it had toppled over a good distance from the tomb entrance.

I edged my way toward it. About two paces from the end of the stone track, there was a gouge in the shallow soil, where the round cover stone had landed and then rolled. This was a real head shaker. How had this happened? It must have been rolled back with such force that when it reached the end of the track it had bounced up and out.

No wonder the men were scared! It was awesome. Forty men could not do this! Suddenly I felt very small, small and afraid. This was the very stone we had sealed just a day earlier. A close examination showed that in a few spots there were still remnants of wax on it.

I exhaled a huge puff of air. This discovery in itself was beyond all expectation. The force of the quake could not have done this. A quake of such a magnitude would have collapsed the tomb itself; not a building in the city would have been left standing. No, a direct force had hurled this boulder away from the tomb's entrance. An almighty warrior from heaven's realm?

I rejoined my two men. Suddenly, they gained a new level of respect in my eyes. Their fears had become my own. I found I was rolling my head from side to side just as I had seen Claudius do.

"You saw this happen?" I gestured to the fallen round rock, and then put a finger to my lips. I was astounded.

"Actually," Philip admitted, "I didn't see him roll the stone. We all fell like dead men when the earthquake hit. But after, after when I opened my eyes the angel was sitting on it, and… and Jesus was walking out of the tomb…" he fell to his knees and began to beat the ground as he said this last part. He was gripped afresh by the memory.

"Where were you when this happened?"

He raised his head and pointed to a spot a few paces away, "Right there."

"And you?" I looked at Claudius.

He pointed to another spot. "Just over here," he answered. "That's my cloak. I left it when I ran."

There was, in fact, a good bit of flotsam scattered about: a few cloaks, a water jug, Philip's precious dice, even a helmet. Here were all the signs of panicked flight. They had left all and fled for their lives.

For me, only one question remained. Was the open tomb truly empty?

"Get to your feet, Philip," I directed. "Now, you two stay here and watch, while I go take a look inside."

I took three deep breaths and set out on my little journey. It was only about twenty paces to the tomb entrance, a distance made much longer by my fear. The whole scene was bathed in the warmth of morning sunlight. I started slowly. About halfway to the entrance, a songbird broke forth in glorious melody. The sun's rays streamed into the rock tomb, lighting my way.

It was empty! The stone slab lay empty. Actually, it was not entirely so. The death shroud had been rolled up, and the face covering was neatly folded and lay off to one side. It appeared as though the awakened corpse had taken a moment to make his bed after getting up.

The Galilean prophet, the true king had arisen and gone forth!

38

WHEN I RETURNED, BOTH PHILIP AND CLAUDIUS WERE ON their knees. It seemed fitting. They might well be overwhelmed with awe, but they might just as well pray for their lives. Whether they knew it or not, at that moment, their lives hung in the balance. The consequences for deserting one's post, whatever the circumstances, can be severe indeed.

I motioned them to their feet. "We will have to report this to Caiaphas," I stated.

"To Caiaphas?" Claudius expressed surprise.

"Yes, Caiaphas," I answered. "We were doing this job for him." I brushed my index finger over the coarse stubble on my chin. "He could insist that you be put to death for desertion, dereliction of duty."

They were white-faced.

"But I'll back you," I reassured them. "By God—by the God of heaven—I'll back every one of you!" I let out a deep sigh, then said, "Let's go."

Claudius took a few quick steps over to his cloak and then scooped it up.

"No!" I called out to him. "Drop it! Drop it right where it was. I want those religious bloodsuckers to see exactly what happened. We will leave everything as it is." I beckoned them. "Let's just go."

As we walked, my mind raced. This was serious. Deadly serious. I knew that, without a doubt, the temple authorities would shift the blame for this event onto the backs of my men. After all, they had been there when it happened. And they had let the dead man get away! I was sure the high priest would insist that they pay the ultimate price.

The evidence, the evidence as I saw it, all pointed to divine intervention. Their account of the events was convincing in and of itself, but the evidence at the tomb was even more compelling. Raw panic is hard to fake; material evidence even more so. The fallen position of the round cover stone spoke volumes to me. It did not get there by human hands. This fact would be patently evident to even a casual observer.

Then there was the body itself. It was gone. It had gotten up and left, according to the witnesses. An absurd proposition to any thinking person. It was absurd unless you saw this man Jesus in action, unless you saw him heal the sick, give sight to the blind, transform the crippled, restore the dead. It was all absurd! This was only the last absurdity in a long list of absurdities.

Then I thought, maybe his disciples did come and steal the body. There was ample time between the quake and my arrival at the tomb. After all, we had seen John and his friend leave from there. But body snatchers would do just that. They would snatch the body. They would grab it and go. They would not take off the death shroud and roll it up neatly. They would not fold up the face covering like a fine tablecloth and lay it to one side. No. John looked as shocked as I now was. He looked as perplexed and awed as any man from my tomb-guarding platoon.[115]

Then there were the prophet's own words, his own outlandish claim. I had not heard it, but his enemies had. He had predicted this. He had declared that after his death, he would arise. He even put a time limit on it. And today was the third day after his death.

I shook my head in amazement. "He is the Son of God," I muttered.

"Did you say something, sir?" Philip asked.

"Yes," I answered. I did not even realize I had been overheard. "I said, 'He is the Son of God.' Jesus is the Son of God."

"I heard you say that on Friday, sir," he observed. "You said it when he died."

"Yes," I responded. "I believed it on Friday, but I know it today."

"I believe it too," Philip confessed. "I believe it too."

"I know it," Claudius joined in now. "I knew it the moment the angel came." He shuddered with the remembrance of that instant. Then he nodded his head as though he were reflecting back over the week, and he slowly repeated, "I knew it. I knew it... In my heart, I knew it all along."

I had no cause to doubt his words.

We walked on in silence. Every sign of earthquake damage took on new meaning. The earth beneath us had jumped at the start of life!

As we approached the fortress, Claudius asked, "Sir, where are we going?"

"Well, we need to report this to the authorities. First, I'm going to see the tribune, and he will pass the news onto the governor. Then we'll go back and pick up the other men. Then we will go and see Jonathon. He will relay the news onto the high priest. Then, who knows?" I shrugged. "We'll see where they take it from there."

My attempt to see Flavio ended in failure. The door to the briefing room was closed. The two sentinels on duty had yet to set eyes on the man. He was probably still broken, broken beyond repair.

As the three of us came down the stairs, Marius spotted me. He called out my name and beckoned me over. He had a rather confused look about him.

"Marcus, just a short while ago four of your men showed up here. They were looking for you." He gave himself a light blow to the forehead with the flat of his hand. "They were a mess. Crazy! They said something about a bright light, a stone, and a man

277

coming out of a tomb?" He gestured wildly as he said all this. "They were terrified! Like they had seen a spirit! I—I ah, didn't know what to make of it. I sent them on to the Golden Gate." He gave a questioning shrug. "I thought you might be there."

"Jesus of Nazareth has risen from the dead," I said plainly. "That's what this is all about. Flavio needs to know. The governor needs to know. My men saw this. That's why they're a wreck." I gave my head a quick shake as I absorbed the images of this account. "Now, Marius," I asked, "Can you send a messenger to Pilate with the news?"

"What news?"

"Jesus of Nazareth has risen from the dead!" I repeated with some annoyance. "Just have the messenger tell Pilate that Jesus of Nazareth has risen from the dead. The governor will understand," I insisted. I felt as though I was speaking to the deaf and dumb.

Marius looked bewildered.

"Just tell him," I insisted again.

As I turned from him, I heard him call a man over and he began to give him my instructions verbatim. At least this time, he did not relieve himself of his responsibility. One job was done.

We hurried to my home. Arius responded to our pounding at the gate. The ten remaining men were pretty much where I left them. They stood to their feet as I walked in. They were expecting me to speak, to report on what I found, and so I did.

"The stone was rolled away—violently thrown away," I corrected myself. "The tomb is empty. I found everything just as you men reported. The prophet rose from the dead. He left his grave clothes and walked out."

This news was greeted with a measure of relief. It was vindication. They had not imagined this terrifying nightmare at dawn. This was no group hallucination. It really happened to them. The proof was at the site itself. Their commanding officer had just confirmed what they knew to be true all along.

Yet, it was only a measure of relief. The full implications of this rising from the dead could not be absorbed, not in two hours, maybe not in a lifetime. But it was plain to see that these men needed no convincing with regard to the veracity of this event. It had been indelibly etched upon their psyches with a stylus of supernatural power.

"Now, a message has been relayed to the governor," I continued, "so he has some idea of what took place. I will try and give him a full account later. In reality, we were guarding that tomb on behalf of the high priest. We have to report this to him."

This news was greeted with a fitting measure of chagrin.

"Oh, yes. The other four men showed up at the fortress, and they were sent on to the Golden Gate. So, we'll try to meet them there." This was good news. It brought smiles and nods to several faces.

"Fall in behind me," I instructed. "We're heading over there now."

Within a short time, we were at the Golden Gate, the Messiah Gate. The gatekeeper was relieved to see me.

"Sir, four of our men arrived about an hour ago. They were completely distraught. They kept mumbling something about seeing a dead man walking, and an angel. I couldn't make sense of it—couldn't understand a thing." He threw up his hands in frustration.

"So where are they now?" I asked.

"They went with Jonathon. He came by looking for you, all huffy like he usually is. Anyway, when he saw these men, he started asking them questions. Whatever they said seemed to make sense to him. Then all of a sudden, he said to me, 'I'm taking these men to Caiaphas.'" The gatekeeper threw up his hands again in a questioning manner and then concluded by saying, "So Jonathon took them and went."

"Puhhh!" The breath exploded from my lips.

"Did I do something wrong?" the gatekeeper earnestly inquired.

"Well, they should have stayed. You should have told them to stay. They're not Jonathon's men. What right does he have to boss them around?"

"I see," he meekly answered in response to this rebuke.

"Oh, well," I said with some frustration, "I need to see Jonathon anyway. I'll work it out with him."

I turned to the twelve who had followed me and said, "Just wait here. I should be right back."

I descended the stairs from the gate two at a time, gave a quick wave of greeting to Jonas at the tax booth, and then walked directly to the entrance proper of the temple compound. I knew I could always find a temple guard at this main entrance. There were, in fact, two on hand. I hailed one of them and said, "I have an urgent message for Jonathon and the high priest."

"Ah, yes," came his response, "Jonathon has been expecting you. I will tell him you are here."

He disappeared for only a brief time, and when he returned, Jonathon, the head of the temple guard, was marching briskly before him.

"You son of a harlot! You Gentile jackass!" Jonathon waved his finger in my face. "You let them steal that body, didn't you? Now what do you mean by sending those four yellow dogs over here?"

"I didn't send those men here," I shot back. "And you have no business hustling them off. They're under my command, not yours."

"Well, come and get them, big man. You're on my hill now!" He pointed to the temple grounds and sneered.

"You touch so much as a hair on their heads, and I just might do that! I'm not scared of you."

Our eyes locked and I stared him down.

"So where are the other dogs? The four I've got said there were sixteen of them in all."

"They're up there." I turned and pointed to the top of the Messiah Gate. Some of the men were watching this highly animated discussion.

"Well, bring them down here. The high priest wants to have a word with them."

"He can have a word with them, after he has a look at that tomb. And not until then. Those men aren't liars. The rocks don't lie. Take a look at that cover stone and you won't talk so smart." I waved my finger in his face. "Something happened there that's bigger than sixteen men. It's bigger than you and your fancy temple," I bristled. "So the high priest can have his word when he has a look, but not until then."

"Hhumm!" he snorted in reaction.

I stared back and held my ground. We were at an impasse.

After a moment he responded. "Well, I will report to the high priest on our little discussion," he brimmed with sarcasm, "and I'll get back to you."

"I will be right over there at the gate with my men," I said, nodding.

He turned and left, and I climbed the stairs back up to my soldiers above the gate. When they questioned me about what they should do, I simply said, "Wait. Wait and see."

The time dragged on. To fill it, with the help of the gatekeeper, I did a thorough inspection of the gate from top to bottom. There appeared to be no damage at all. I was surprised after the damage I had seen firsthand at the Fish Gate. I dispatched a messenger to report on the state of this gate to Flavio. Maybe he was on duty now.

There was still no sign of Jonathon.

I sauntered over to Jonas at the tax booth. He motioned to his son and then stepped aside to join me. I propped myself up against a stone section of the wall and began. "We didn't nail your man," I said referring to Barabbas. "He was pardoned."

"I heard." He shook his head in disgust.

"Free the terrorists! Hang the healers!" I snorted. "It's a sad world we live in."

"We do what we can, Marcus. We do what we can." He glanced my way and added, "You did all you could."

"Yes. You do it, and then you have those strutting idiots crap all over it!" My bitterness overflowed as I looked away.

"They'll have their day. This will all come back on them, Marcus. You'll see." With a nod of his head he added, "Some of it already has."

I knew a story would follow. He drew me farther aside as we stepped just outside the gate. He continued in a hushed tone, "The Almighty has answered back."

"What do you mean?" I looked at him quizzically.

"The temple veil has been torn in two," he said with a quick glance back to the Holy Place. "When the earthquake hit on Friday, the veil tore from top to bottom—like it was ripped by invisible hands."[116]

I wrinkled my brow. "How do you know this?"

"My uncle."

"The temple guard?"

"The temple guard," he confirmed. "It's got them in a panic. They're all in a holy panic. They thought they were playing religious pretend games. But now reality has hit. The LORD has answered back!"

"I don't understand," I confessed. "What do you mean He has answered back?"

"They have committed blasphemy—the ultimate blasphemy. And they know it. He has told them," he glanced heavenward as he said this. "He has shown them."

"I don't understand," I repeated.

"It's a sign from God," he said with some impatience. "It's a sign that they have committed blasphemy. It's God ripping His clothes over what they have done—what they have done to His own Son."

I wrinkled my brow again as I tried to grasp this.

"Now listen," he went on. "When this prophet, Jesus, was brought before the Sanhedrin on Thursday night, Caiaphas asked him if he was the Son of God. And Jesus confessed that he was. My uncle was there. He saw all this. Then Caiaphas," he nudged me on the shoulder to make his point, "Caiaphas rips his robe from top to bottom, and yells out that this was blasphemy.[117] Well, on Friday," he repeated himself for emphasis, "on Friday when Jesus died, God ripped His robe from top to bottom. Don't you get it?" He nudged me again. "Ripping the veil in front of the Holy of Holies was God's way of answering back. It was His way of saying, 'You got it wrong! You got it all wrong! He was my Son!'"

"Ohh! Now I see."

"They are scared spitless," he spoke each word slowly and distinctly for emphasis. "Nothing like this has ever happened before." He slashed the air to make his point. "Nothing!"

"Well, then, I've got a story for you!" I countered. "This morning when the earthquake hit, something else happened."

"What?" he asked brimming with curiosity.

I raised my hand to my head in a sudden gesture of frustration. "I can't tell you now. I have to go off with Jonathon."

The head of the temple guard strutted toward me. He was accompanied by the same two Pharisees who had overseen the sealing of Jesus' tomb on the Sabbath.

39

Sunday 12:00 p.m. April 9th, 30 AD

"WE'RE COMING FOR A LOOK AT THE JOB YOUR MEN BOTCHED," Jonathon huffed.

I chose to ignore this provocation. I looked past the two Pharisees and asked, "Where's the high priest?"

"Marcus," Jonathon shook his head, "you surely don't expect the high priest to come out to inspect the tomb of a common criminal?"

"A common criminal? I didn't know that the high priest was in the habit of sealing the tombs of common criminals. Oh, yes, and does he usually post sixteen men to guard the graves of these common criminals? I think not!"

This brought a moment of tense silence.

One of the Pharisees ventured into this heated environment. "We have been sent by the high priest. Both of us have just come from meeting with him," he explained.

"Fine, then," I conceded. "I'll get two of my men who were on duty at the time, and we'll set out. They're just up there." I motioned to the top of the gate, and walked off to retrieve them.

Most of the twelve soldiers, my resurrection witnesses, were seated in a row in the shrinking shade of the parapet.

"Claudius, Philip," I called out, "you two are going off with me for another inspection of the tomb. The rest of you are free to go for a stroll along the wall, or head back to the fortress. But be back here within an hour." I pointed to the sun. "Watch the time."

I rejoined the temple delegation with my two men in tow, and we set out. It was a speechless journey. We had nothing in common

284

except a loathing for one another. We kept our thoughts to ourselves.

The previous day still bothered me. I found it hard to believe that these strict fundamentalist Pharisees thought nothing of putting me to work all day on the Sabbath. They invaded a tomb, wanted me to disturb the dead, and treated me like a rebel for not obeying their unholy wishes. The incongruence was stunning to say the least. I suppose doing right, and being seen doing it, was what really mattered in their minds. Public display mattered. What was done on the sly, and more particularly, what was done on the sly with a Gentile, was of no consequence at all. Their holiness rang hollow. It was only decorative, even as their bulging phylacteries were only decorative.

By this time, some of the fallen debris at the Fish Gate had been cleared away. When we left the imperial highway, we followed the same path Claudius, Philip, and I had taken earlier that morning. We skirted past Golgotha, and came around to the front of the tomb.

But there were people here now. The news of these strange events had spread like wildfire. Family members, followers, and the curious had come. They trooped out, took a timid look inside the tomb, and then returned to the city. They would tell someone else, and, of course, the hearers of this tale had to come out to confirm that what they heard was really so. A cycle had been set in motion.

But this was no joyous throng. The curious stood in small huddled groups. They were a frightened and perplexed lot. Clearly, they did not know what to make of it. It had caught them by surprise, too.

I overheard one of the women suddenly exclaim, "He's alive. He is alive!" The man beside her just shook his head. Whether it was in unbelief or bewilderment, I could not tell.

This was the scene into which we stepped. Our presence changed it. Officialdom had arrived; the common folk drew back.

Fortunately, almost everything had been left exactly as we

found it in the early morning. I imagine the curious visitors found the random scattered debris as interesting as I did, and for the sake of the next visitors they left it just as it was.

"Take a look at this stone," I suggested. "Now see where it hit the ground." I pointed to the dark gash it had caused.

"Centurion," one of the Pharisees addressed me brusquely. "We have our own eyes. We can see. We don't need you to interpret these events for us. Just stand aside."

I did. Murderous thoughts sprang quickly to mind, but I did stand aside. Eventually, I had a seat with my two men on a nearby rock. The three temple officials moved rather quickly about the site. I interpreted their haste as a mark of their unease with their findings.

Finally they peered into the tomb. But they did not enter, not today. Others would see them. Fortunately, the death shroud and face covering were still in plain view—exactly where the risen corpse had left them.

I stepped toward them again. "Did you want to speak to my men?" I offered. "They can tell you what they saw."

"No," came the quick reply. "We can speak to them later."

The inspection was over. The verdict and the conclusions reached were unknown. I dared not ask.

"Now, you can pick up what you left behind when you fled." I signaled to Philip and Claudius.

They quickly scurried about doing just that. Soon they were overburdened, and I took a cloak and a water jug from them to ease the load. Only Philip's dice were missing. I showed no disappointment in this.

We trudged back to the city in the same divergent silence. The temple men were grimfaced, more grimfaced and joyless than usual. Their gloom put a certain spring into my step, although I tried my best to hide it.

When we reached the Golden Gate, the grey-bearded Pharisee

turned to face me. "We will report to Joseph Caiaphas, the high priest. He may wish to hear the testimony of your men. Will they be ready to appear before him?"

"I will make sure they are ready," I answered.

"Good. In due time we may call on you."

"But my other four men?" I quickly interjected.

"They are being well treated," he answered. "They have been questioned. We will return them to you for punishment, after the other twelve appear."

I sighed. This was not an arrangement to my liking. Yet, these men had abandoned their post, and run off on their own. A taste of temple hospitality might be in order. I wanted to say that a day spent with glum-faced Pharisees should be punishment enough, but by this time the temple officials had turned and walked off.

The afternoon wore on, and as it did, a distinct unease set in. My twelve men were reassembled. They were ready to testify as to what they saw. They asked me for advice, but all I said was, "Just tell them what you saw. Tell them exactly what happened. No more and no less."

Some of the men were still clearly distressed, and this interminable wait heightened the sense of tension. Lack of communication only exacerbated the situation. By this time some response from Flavio or Pilate certainly should have been forthcoming. I felt cut off, as if I had no support. Why were they not getting back to me?

Renaldo, who usually shows up for some conversation during the day, was also absent. Undoubtedly, he was overseeing repairs to the Fish Gate. The earthquake certainly could have accounted for a good deal of this silence, but at this juncture, some sign of life from higher up would have been most welcome.

Finally, I could wait no longer. I called for a scribe and a messenger. I dictated the following message to the scribe:

Greetings Flavio:

Four of my men are being held by the temple guard. Twelve more are about to be questioned by the high priest regarding the appearance of an angel or spirit, and the sudden rising of Jesus of Nazareth from the dead early this morning. I await any instructions you may have.

Your servant,
Marcus Aureolus

The messenger was dispatched with the message in hand, but before he set out, I said, "If Flavio is not available, for whatever reason, proceed directly to the Praetorium and present this message personally to the governor. Understood?"

"Understood, sir."

"Off with you, then."

No response came.

Finally, at mid-afternoon Jonathon and three of his men arrived at the Messiah Gate.

"The high priest will see your men now," he summarily announced.

I called my men to attention and they descended the stairs of the gate as though they were entering the gloom of hell. Jonathon and the same two Pharisees took the lead. The twelve dutifully followed and I and a temple guard brought up the rear.

As soon as we entered the temple compound, thirteen additional temple guards met us—one of their men for each one of ours. We were ordered to turn over our swords. When I protested, I was told that they would be returned to us later. We were then lead off. We skirted the edges of the Gentile Court for some distance, and then were escorted into a rather dark and musty anteroom.

"You will wait here," Jonathon announced as more armed guards entered.

What transpired in the next number of hours I found to be both frightening and bizarre.

First, we were not permitted to speak to each other. Our personal armed escorts saw to this. I expected that we would all be led together before the high priest for questioning. But that was not what happened. Jonathon came into the room. He selected one of my men, starting with the youngest, and then walked out with this hapless witness. After what seemed like eternity, he returned with this same man, and then chose someone else. So on it went through all twelve men. By the time the tenth man was led away, darkness had descended and three oil lamps were brought in to provide a flicker of light. The unsteady flames did an eerie shadow dance across the walls.

Finally, my time came. I was led down a long corridor and into a sizeable chamber. There may have been fully seventy long-robed priestly officials present—the Sanhedrin. The hoary-headed high priest sat on an elaborate throne at the front. After giving my name and position, the questioning began. The interrogation was pointed, detailed, and thorough. Questions were permitted from anyone in the assembly. I kept my answers brief and to the point.

After a time, the worried Weasel spoke. "We may call you again," he said, then he dismissed me with a backhanded wave.

Jonathon led me back to the antechamber, where we all continued to wait.

In due course, two of my men were taken out for a second interrogation. Everyone's patience was now wearing thin. Time dragged by in gloomy silence. Evening hunger pangs added their own edge to the mood within this holding cell. Possibly another full hour passed, and at last we were all ushered down to the same large council chamber.

It was a very different scene when we arrived. The room was mostly empty. There was no sign of the high priest. We were shown to our seats, and my four missing men were brought in. Despite the temple guards' best efforts, cheers, waves and smiles erupted. They all appeared to be in good health, and among us a general sense of camaraderie pervaded.

Surely our ordeal would soon be over.

And it was. A table was brought in and two long-beards seated themselves behind it. A hefty brown jute sack was placed onto it. Jonathon and the two tomb-sealing Pharisees stood before us. Jonathon cleared his throat to get our attention, but it was the grey-beard who spoke.

"A decision has been reached in this matter. You will each be paid a full year's wages. The table is set up as you can see." He made a sweeping motion toward it. "You will line up before it."[118]

Everyone sat in stunned silence. He certainly had our attention.

Then with the same hand he made a sweeping motion over all of us. *"You are to say, 'His disciples came during the night and stole him away while we were asleep.' If this report gets to the governor, we will satisfy him and keep you out of trouble."*[119]

Then he gave us all a sly nod and the devil's very own smile.

The lineup formed quickly. The money was dispensed promptly, but with ample judicious prudence.

Our swords were returned.

And we went out into the night.

40

Sunday 9:00 p.m. April 9th, 30 AD

THE MONEY BOTHERED ME. THEY PAID ME FIVE TIMES THE amount given to the common soldier. At first, it was not the money itself that bothered me, or the amount. If they were stupid enough to offer it, we were all smart enough to take it.

What bothered me was the bold-faced lie. Here was the classic bribe. We were being asked to spread this lie and, to make it worse, we were being asked to do this by religious men, by these teachers of the law, these Pharisees. That is what really bothered me.

The day before, the haughty greybeard had made the claim that my men would yield to a bribe from the Christ's disciples. Yet a day later, it was he who was handing out the bribe money. It was an astounding reversal. Their hypocrisy knew no bounds. It never failed to surprise. They were blind to their own faults, their own stinking corruption. They were insulated by a layer of conspicuous fat, a hoard of wealth, and the robes of power. They loved racing off to point out the faults of others, while they wallowed freely in their own moral filth.

How effective this money would be stood as an open question. My soldiers all knew the truth. For that matter, so did the high priest and the whole Sanhedrin. Why else offer the bribe? Jesus did rise from the dead. In a day or two, every soldier in the barracks would know the real story. These things always get out. There would be an official line, which would be conveniently trotted out to appease the right sort of people, and an informal, unofficial line which of course is where the real truth lay. Most thinking people can sort these things out, and in the end, I have confidence that the truth will prevail. It always does.

I neatly stacked the silver coins into the same pouch that only two days earlier contained the crucifixion spikes. The coins were heavy. The bribery money hung like a lead weight on the belt about my waist—a lead weight tied to a drowning man.

Dark, oppressive thoughts pulled down on me as I climbed the moonlit stairs to the top of the Golden Gate. It really was the Messiah Gate. Now I realized that truth afresh. The Messiah rode through it, triumphant, just a week ago today.

"Who goes there?" a nervous night watchman called out.

"Marcus Aureolus."

"Oh!" he expressed his surprise. "Sir, I didn't know it was you."

"You're awake," I answered wearily. "And you're doing your job. That's good enough for me."

I took a few strides along the wall and then cast my gaze over the parapet and down toward the Kidron Valley. The familiar view was bathed in moonlight. The path Jesus had taken was clearly visible. The light-colored roadway stones took on the soft glow of the moon.

Then, in my troubled mind, the scene played back. The donkey king was riding again. The cheering thousands sang his praises.

"Hosanna in the highest!
Hosanna to the Son of David!
Blessed is he who comes in the name of the Lord!"

The palm branches waved. The Messiah advanced. At the proper moment our eyes met, and I heard the words afresh. "I have a future for you."

"I have a future for you?" I breathed out the words in a whisper. What did he mean by that?

Why did I hear him speak?

I slowly shook my head. It was a mystery to me. It was all a mystery to me. Why did he speak in mysteries? Why did he haunt me so? Was I stupid? Why did I not understand?

I shook my head again. I thought about going back home—the logical thing to do. But there was no peace there. No peace at all. I had turned inward and cold toward Zelda. I did not even have the peace that comes with sleep. The blond-haired girl would surely come again. Or worse yet, the flies, the crucifixion flies, the torturing flies of hell!

No, for me there was no peace; there was no rest.

But she spoke. Last night, the blond-haired girl spoke. While her warm blood flooded over my hands, she said, "There is a solution."

Here was another mystery. What solution? Death was the only solution I knew. Is that what she meant?

I surveyed the valley again. It was quiet down there, quiet and dark. The silence beckoned. I ambled back to the watchman. "I'm going down." I motioned in the direction of the stairs. "Raise the gate and let me out."

"I'll watch for you when you come back," he called after me.

But I did not answer. I was not at all sure if I would be coming back.

He raised the great iron grid enough so I could slip under. I walked ahead a few paces and waved back up at him. Chains rattled as he dropped it down again and I resumed my walk down to the Kidron.

It was not long before I could hear the brook. It babbled peacefully, but then I was reminded of the bloody flood that joined this tranquil flow only a short distance downstream. The temple outflow. Water and lamb's blood. First came water, then came blood, just as when the spear pierced his side. *Like the spear that pierced his side*—over and over that thought echoed through the dark chambers of my mind.

Why did Jesus haunt me so? Why did I spit in his face? Why

did I drive in his spikes? Why not some other man? Now I was weighed down with the burden of his death—a death that I brought on.

And what a burden it was! Heaped on what I already bore, this was crushing, as crushing as the round tombstone that left its gouge into the hillside soil. Guilt crushed me. The gouge was too deep—the ponderous weight too heavy.

He was the Son of God. But that profession brought no peace. It was a naked sword aimed at my heart. Surely I would fall on it. Or, now that he was alive, Jesus would drive me into it. Or he would hunt me down. Divine vengeance would surely follow. That was the essence of what Jonas, the tax collector, had said. At the time, I fully agreed with him. But I was implicated right along with Caiaphas and Pilate. They gave the filthy orders; I carried them out.

How could I hope to escape this judgement?

I could rage against Caiaphas, and Pilate, and Herod, too. But when my moment came, I spit in Jesus' face. I, too, played my part in this perverted drama. I played it with all the pent-up, blood-lusting force of hell. It was a force that had been turned loose in Germania, and as the hammer blows rang out on Golgotha, it had come writhing to the surface once again.

I hung my head. I stooped by the brook. I washed my hands in its cool water. But it brought no relief. The stained soul is not so quickly cleansed.

I got up and wandered on. Very soon the olive groves of Gethsemane invited me in. It was a better place to die. The earth here felt cooler on my feet, the shadows darker, the dewy scents of spring were fresher.

By a rock outcropping, I dropped to my knees. I unbuckled my sword and withdrew it from its sheath. I laid it carefully by my side. At the right moment I would take it up.

All about dark silence reigned.

My head throbbed. My heart pounded. Stinging tears welled up. "Why is there no peace? God in heaven… why is there no peace?"

Silence, only dark silence.

I unfastened my cuirass, laid it over to my left.

"God in heaven… why is there no peace?"

Of course, no answer came.

I slid the coin-filled pouch from off my belt. I stashed it in the hard shell of the cuirass. Perhaps the bribe money would be turned over to Zelda, or so I hoped.

Already, in my tormented mind the early morning scenario played through its gruesome images. A Jew, perhaps a young lad, would discover my bloodied corpse. He would call his father. Upon seeing the crested helmet and cuirass of a Roman officer, he would alert the guards at the Messiah Gate. Renaldo would be summoned. In due course, the blood money would be found where I laid it within the cuirass.

I expected Renaldo would do the honorable thing. Zelda would be well provided for.

I looked skyward as the anguished words escaped my lips again. "Why? Why is there no peace?" I fell forward, face to the ground. "Great God in heaven… why is there no peace? Why is there no answer?"

Deafening silence roared through my empty soul.

I lifted my head again and called out into the blackness, "Why don't you hear?" With pleading hands lifted high, in desolate anger, I cried again, "Why don't you hear? Why don't you listen?"

As I did this, my hands came into view. In that moment, I knew the answer. It was my hands. Of course, it was my hands. It was what my hands had done. That was why the great God was silent. That was why my daughter Tara was dead. That was why there was no peace. Blood was on my hands. The blood of a blond-haired girl. And now. Now, the blood of His Son!

295

There was no hope for me; no peace.

In a blur of anguish, I pulled off my tunic. I took up my sword. I fixed the pommel into a depression in the soil. I placed the point of the blade just below the left side of my rib cage. A quick downward thrust of my body would drive it home. I knew exactly how this was done—through the lungs to the heart.

Peace would come. I would find it my way.

As I steadied the blade with the fingers of my left hand, the demons cackled. Their demented laugh echoed off the blackness deep within. Now, only death could bring me peace.

"Tara, I will join you." I whispered.

"Zelda, forgive me," I gasped.

"Boys. Julius… Andrew… forgive me!"

And now, with heaving sighs I sobbed, "Great God in heaven, forgive me. Forgive me! Forgive me for what I have done to your Son!"

"I have," the voice came loud and clear.

It startled me! It startled me so that I dropped the sword.

"I already have," it came again, so distinct, so deep and strong, it took my breath away.

I turned to the left and right. I saw no one. I staggered to my feet and wheeled around, but still there was no one. No one there at all.

But I heard him. I heard him as clearly as I heard his voice when he entered the city. It was the same voice, gentle but strong—incredibly strong. A deep and frightening sense of awe overtook me. I was not alone. He had heard me!

I fell to my knees again and then his first words on the cross came echoing to my mind.

"Father… forgive them… They do not know… what… they are doing."

"They do not know what they are doing," I echoed right back. "I did not know what I was doing. Father God, I did not know what I was doing! I did not know."

I fell back, right flat onto my back. As I my mind grasped his words, his strong but gentle words, an incredible sense of warmth flowed through me.

"But I'm forgiven! I'm forgiven." As I spoke the words, a rush of pure joy flowed right through my soul. It was a surge so strong I thought my head might explode.

"I'm forgiven," I repeated. "I'm forgiven."

I tried to lift my hands in thanks. They were pinned back, right back onto the ground on which I lay.

I lay in the cross position. I lay open before him in the cross position. Open and naked in soul, as naked in soul as he had been naked in body.

I was exposed. Everything was there. Every bit of my past. Every thought. Every intent. Every joy and every sorrow. My eyes closed. I could not force them open.

In the still darkness he touched me. In the cool of this tree garden, the naked shame of Eden was reversed.

I heard him approach, his footfall on the dewy grass. The Christ knelt near me, by my right hand.

While I lay pinned open—while I lay silent—he pressed his nail-scarred hand onto my hand. Four times he did this. Four blows of love.

First the right.

Then he got up and he moved around me to my left. There, he did the same. He put his knee upon my fingers. He pressed the base of his palm onto my hand.

Four more open-handed blows. Four blows like I had done.

Though he was silent, in my mind I heard the hammer ring.

"Xchuuuung!"

"Xchuuuung!"

"Xchuuuung!"

"Xchuuuung!"

I felt his wounds, his ragged piercing wounds.

I felt the blood. His warm blood trickled onto my open palms.

In that moment, I was clean. Truly clean. The residue of evil was expunged. The stain upon my soul was gone! Gone forever!

A fresh surge of joy broke loose. And as it did, the chasm within closed. It closed forever. The hollow man was full—overflowing.

I waited. I waited for him to touch my feet. I tried to form the words on my lips, "Touch my feet, too!" But though I tried, the words would not come out. Then, I remembered! I had not touched his feet. I had not nailed in that spike.

Instead, Jesus got up from my pinned right hand, and he moved to my head. I felt a rush of cool air across my face as he knelt down. Then he pressed his warm right hand to my forehead. This was a yet more gentle hand—the hand of blessing.

And it was peace that came! A wave of peace came crashing through. It surged around me. It overwhelmed my mind. It flowed within. God came within.

He did not say a word. He did not need to. He already had said all that needed to be said.

In due time, he arose. I heard his footsteps as he left.

I lay in peace. Pinned open in perfect peace. How long I lay like this, exposed upon my earthy cross, I could not tell. Delicious joy—hot tears of joy—set no time limit.

I was clean.

When I opened my eyes, the stars, ten thousand stars, shone down. They sang me to my feet, and I walked home, drunk with sober joy. I was new. I felt new, totally new from the inside out!

I crept up the creaking stairs, and pushed open the boy's bedroom door. They slept on in sweet oblivion. I put my hand, my clean hand, first to Andrew's head. Then I moved over to my son Julius, where I did the same. The blessing flowed to them. I turned and pulled the door shut behind me.

Zelda was asleep too. She stirred a bit as I lay down, and then slept on. I joined her quickly. It was a blessed sleep, without interruption, the sleep of the newborn. The blond-haired girl did not visit. I never saw her again. The solution had been found. It had been applied to my hands, to my heart, to my mind, and to my soul. Cleansing had come.

This year, at this Passover, unlike two years ago when Tara died, the Death Angel did not come to my house. The high priest's Passover lamb had been slain, and the blood had been applied—applied to my hands—to my heart.

I did have a future. Jesus, the donkey king, had given me a future, even as he said. And my future was in his hands. They were nail-scarred hands—scars that I put there.

As the rooster crowed, Zelda pressed her warm body close to mine. I smiled. I rolled over and kissed her neck. She smiled back at me. I had so much to tell her, now that the book of life was open. But not right then. Gently, I put my hand to her. In moments she was ready for me. Thus united, we rode to a small outpost of heaven on the face of this dark earth.

These two sparrows would rebuild their nest.

Now, in that penultimate moment, as together we reached the summit of our pleasure, in the house next door, in Renaldo's house, a beggar boy awoke. He raised both his hands—his fully restored hand. And then he let out a wide-eyed scream of pure, unmitigated joy.

This was no dream. It was reality. His hand was wholly restored, without defect, fully functional. Where it had been severed only a faint line was now visible. In that moment, and for years to come, that line would testify to Herod's brutality.

Now, this fully restored hand spoke of another King—a visiting King from heaven's realm.

Of course, Lucas had been right. He was right. This crippled boy vaulted over the wise ones of this world. He was right all along about this man—about the donkey king.

The Kingdom of God had come with power!

Epilogue

HEROD ANTIPAS

Herod Antipas, the scheming Fox, despite his most valiant efforts, never did regain control of his father's kingdom. In 39 AD, the Roman emperor Caius Caligula called Antipas to account for his treachery. Herod had formed a secret alliance with Artabanus, king of Parthia, and Sejanus, a leading military officer. Arms for seventy thousand men had been laid in store for what was to be a coup attempt. Antipas was stripped of all his wealth, and his ruling position as tetrarch. He was banished to Lyons in France (Gaul), and later died in disgrace in Spain.[120]

JOSEPH CAIAPHAS

Joseph Caiaphas may be best remembered for his prophetic words regarding Jesus. Fearing Roman retribution against the temple, as the prophet's popularity grew, he said, *"Don't you know it is better for one person to die for the people than for the whole nation to be destroyed?"*[121] So, for the good of the people, he had the Galilean prophet put to death. He chose the course he thought best. But in 70 AD, when the wood was dry, as Jesus had prophesied, the Roman army swept in. The entire nation and the great temple were destroyed. Not until 1948 was the Jewish nation restored. As for Caiaphas himself, his bones have been uncovered and his stone ossuary is on display in Jerusalem today.[122] A most ironic twist, since his arch rival's bones have never been found, despite him having spent good temple money on bribing Roman soldiers.

PONTIUS PILATE

The Roman procurator of Judea from 26-36 AD lost his position after waging a war against the rebellious Samaritans. The campaign was successful. However, the Samaritans launched a complaint to Vitellius, who gave oversight to the region of Syria. Pilate was called to account before the emperor Tiberius. But Tiberius died before Pilate's arrival in Rome. Caius Caligula assumed the throne in 36 AD. Apparently, the governor of Judea lost his post and was then banished to Vienna on the Rhine. The writer Eusebius claims that not long after, "wearied with misfortunes," Pilate killed himself.[123]

THE CENTURION

Neither the Bible nor history provides us with any account of the centurion's life after his confession before the cross that Jesus was the Son of God. It is, however, worth noting that his confession of faith precisely mirrors that of the apostle Peter.[124] It took Peter two years spent with the Christ to reach this point of faith. It took the centurion just six hours spent at the cross. Jesus went to extraordinary lengths to restore Peter after his threefold denial of the Christ during the trial before Caiaphas. Would the same Christ not show mercy to this centurion? In 40 AD, the centurion, here named Marcus Aureolus, was joined in his profession of faith in Jesus by the centurion Cornelius of Caesarea.[125] The apostle Peter was instrumental in this conversion. It was a monumental event, a pivotal point in the history of the church and the world. God had broken through to the

Gentiles. He broke through to a centurion. It meant the gospel message would encompass the globe.

JESUS OF NAZARETH

Two thousand years after his life and death, more than two billion people on this planet profess that Jesus is the Son of God. In every nation there are men, women and children who freely bow before Him. On the cross He caught a glimpse of His kingdom. It is a glorious kingdom!

Endnotes

[1] Matthew 21:9: The Holy Bible, *New International Version, (NIV).* International Bible Society, Zondervan Publishing House, 1973, 1978, 1984.

[2] After the Christ's betrayal, the Matthias mentioned here was chosen to replace Judas Iscariot as one of the twelve apostles. See Acts 1:15-26.

[3] Zechariah 9:9: The Holy Bible, *New King James Version, (NKJV)* Thomas Nelson, Inc., 1982.

[4] Mark 10:47 NIV

[5] Matthew 21:13 NKJV

[6] Mark 11:17 NIV

[7] *The blind and the lame came to him at the temple, and he healed them* (Matthew 31:14 NIV).

[8] John 7:31 NIV

[9] Matthew 21:16 NKJV

[10] Matthew 21:16 NIV

[11] Matthew 21:27 NIV

[12] *Then some soldiers asked him, "And what should we do?" He replied, "Don't extort money and don't accuse people falsely—be content with your pay"* (Luke 3:14 NIV).

[13] Jesus referred to Herod Antipas as the Fox in Luke 13:32. Whether Jesus was the first person to pin this title on Herod, we do not know. He certainly helped popularize it.

[14] Matthew 22:21 NIV

[15] Matthew 23 in its entirety is a scathing attack on the Pharisees and teachers of the law. *"You snakes! You brood of vipers! How will you escape being condemned to hell?"* (Matthew 23:33 NIV).

[16] Matthew 21:43 NIV

17 *The Romans, for all their efforts to conquer Germany between 12 BC and AD 16, met with only limited success.* Donald L. Niewyk, *Grolier International Encyclopedia*, Danbury, Connecticut, 1991.

18 *At that time a well-known terrorist named Jesus Barabbas was in jail* (Matthew 27:16) New Testament, *Contemporary English Version*, (CEV). American Bible Society, Canadian Bible Society, 1995.

19 *Then he said, "Go and wash off the mud in Siloam Pool." The man went and washed in Siloam, which means "One Who Is Sent." When he had washed off the mud, he could see* (John 9:7 CEV).

20 *They began to spit at him; they blind-folded him, struck him with their fists, and said, "Prophecy!" And the guards took him and beat him* (Mark 14:65 NIV).

21 John 18:29 NIV

22 John 18:30 NIV

23 John 18:31 NIV

24 John 18:31 NIV

25 Luke 23:2 NIV

26 *While he was in Bethany, reclining at the table in the home of Simon the Leper, a woman came with an alabaster jar of very expensive perfume, made of pure nard. She broke the jar and poured the perfume on his head* (Mark 14:3 NIV).

27 John 18:33 NIV

28 Matthew 27:11 NIV

29 John 18:34 NIV

30 John 18:35 NIV

31 John 18:36 NIV

32 John 18:37 NIV

33 John 18:37 NIV

34 John 18:38 NIV

35 John 18:38 NIV

36 Matthew 27:13 NIV

37 John 18:38 NIV

[38] Luke 23:5 NIV

[39] *When he learned that Jesus was under Herod's jurisdiction, he sent him to Herod, who was also in Jerusalem at that time* (Luke 23:7 NIV).

[40] *When Herod saw Jesus, he was greatly pleased, because for a long time he had been wanting to see him. From what he had heard about him, he hoped to see him perform some miracle* (Luke 23:8-9 NIV).

[41] *He* (Herod) *plied him with many questions, but Jesus gave him no answer. The chief priests and the teachers of the law were standing there vehemently accusing him. Then Herod and his soldiers ridiculed and mocked him. Dressing him in an elegant robe, they sent him back to Pilate. That day Herod and Pilate became friends—before this they had been enemies* (Luke 23:9-12 NIV).

[42] Matthew 27:19 CEV

[43] Luke 23:14-15 NIV

[44] Luke 23:16 NIV

[45] John 18:38 NIV

[46] John 18:39 NIV

[47] John 18:40 CEV

[48] *Then Pilate took Jesus and had him flogged* (John 19:1 NIV).

[49] *One of the conscripts picked up a pail of water mixed with salt and sloshed it over Jesus: the stinging brine was a routine way to revive a victim and help stem the flow of blood.* Gordon Thomas, *The Trial: The Life and Inevitable Crucifixion of Christ*, Corgi Books, 1987.

[50] Mark 15:18 NIV

[51] *Again and again they* (the soldiers) *struck him on the head with a staff and spit on him. Falling on their knees they worshiped him* (Mark 15:19 NIV).

[52] John 19:4: The Modern Language Bible, *New Berkeley Version*, *(NBV)* Gerrit Verkuyl, Henderson Publishers, Inc. Peabody, Massachusetts, 1945.

[53] John 19:5 NKJV

[54] John 19:6 NKJV

[55] John 19:6 NBV

[56] John 19:7 NIV

[57] John 19:9 NBV

[58] John 19:10 NIV

[59] John 19:10 NKJV

[60] John 19:11 NIV

[61] John 19:12 NIV

[62] John 19:14 NKJV

[63] John 19:15 NKJV

[64] John 19:15 NKJV

[65] John 19:15 NKJV

[66] Matthew 27:24 NBV

[67] Matthew 27:24 NBV

[68] Matthew 27:25 NKJV

[69] *A certain man from Cyrene, Simon , the father of Alexander and Rufus, was passing by on his way in from the country, and they forced him to carry the cross* (Mark 15:21 NIV).

[70] Luke 23:28 NIV

[71] Luke 23:29 NIV

[72] Luke 23:30-31 NIV

[73] *The cruelty of this form of capital punishment lay in the public shame and in its slow physical torture. Partly as a warning to other potential offenders, the condemned man was made to carry his cross, or the transverse part, along the public roads and to the execution ground, which was nearly always in a public place. There he was stripped of all his clothing. Affixed to the cross, he could not care for his bodily needs, and was the object of taunts and indignities of passers-by.* Pierson Parker, *Crucifixion, Volume 1, The Interpreter's Dictionary of the Bible*, Abingdon Press, Nashville, TN, 1962.

[74] *There they gave Jesus some wine mixed with a drug to ease the pain. But when Jesus tasted what it was, he refused to drink it* (Mark 27:34 CEV).

[75] Jesus prophetic words are about to reach fulfillment. *"But I, when I am lifted up from the earth, will draw all men to myself"* (John 12:32 NIV).

[76] *He was oppressed and afflicted, yet he did not open his mouth; he was led like a lamb to the slaughter, and as a sheep before her shearers is silent, so he did not open his mouth* (Isaiah 53:7 NIV).

[77] Luke 23:34: Good News For Modern Man, *The New Testament in Today's English Version, (TEV)* American Bible Society, New York, 1966.

[78] John 19:24 CEV

[79] Mark 15:29 NKJV

[80] Matthew 27:40 NKJV

[81] Matthew 27:42 NIV

[82] Matthew 27:43 NIV

[83] *Pilate had a notice prepared and fastened to the cross. It read: JESUS OF NAZARETH, THE KING OF THE JEWS* (John 19:19 NIV).

[84] *Many of the Jews read this sign, for the place where Jesus was crucified was near the city, and the sign was written in Aramaic, Latin and Greek. The chief priests of the Jews protested to Pilate, "Do not write 'The King of the Jews,' but that this man claimed to be king of the Jews." Pilate answered, "What I have written, I have written"* (John 19:20-21 NIV).

[85] Luke 23:37 NIV

[86] Luke 23:39 NIV

[87] Luke 23:40-41 CEV

[88] Luke 23:42 NIV

[89] *Adequate exhalation required lifting the body by pushing up on the feet and by flexing the elbows and abducting the shoulders. However, this maneuver would place the entire weight of the body on the tarsals and would produce searing pain. Furthermore, flexing of the elbows would cause rotation of the wrists about the iron nails and cause fiery pain along the damaged median nerves. Lifting of the body would also painfully scrape the scourged back against the wooden stipes. Muscle cramps and paresthesias of the outstretched and uplifted arms would add to the discomfort. As a result, each respiratory effort would become agonizing and tiring and lead to eventual asphyxia.* William D. Edwards, MD; Wesley J. Gabel, MDiv; Floyd E. Hosmer, MS, AMI *On*

the *Physical Death of Jesus Christ*, American Medical Association, 1986.

90 Luke 23:43 NIV

91 John 19:26 NKJV

92 John 19:27 NKJV

93 *From twelve o'clock until three darkness lay on all the land* (Matthew 27:45 NBV).

94 Matthew 27:46 NIV

95 Matthew 27:46 NIV

96 Matthew 27:47 NIV

97 John 19:28 NKJV

98 Matthew 27:49 CEV

99 John 19:30 NKJV

100 Luke 23:46 NKJV

101 *And when Jesus had cried out again in a loud voice, he gave up his spirit. At that moment the curtain of the temple was torn in two from top to bottom. The earth shook and the rocks split* (Matthew 27:50-51 NIV).

102 Matthew 27:54 TEV

103 *Because the Jews did not want the bodies left on the cross during the Sabbath, they asked Pilate to have the legs broken and the bodies taken down. The soldiers therefore came and broke the legs of the first man who had been crucified with Jesus, and then those of the other* (John 19:31-32 NIV).

104 *But when they came to Jesus and found that he was already dead, they did not break his legs. Instead, one of the soldiers pierced Jesus' side with a spear, bringing a sudden flow of blood and water* (John 19:33-34 NIV).

105 *Now there was a man named Joseph, a member of the Council, a good and upright man, who had not consented to their decision and action. He came from the Judean town of Arimathea and he was waiting for the kingdom of God. Going to Pilate, he asked for Jesus' body* (Luke 32:50-52 NIV).

106 *Pilate was surprised to hear that he was already dead. Summoning the centurion, he asked him if Jesus had already died. When he learned from the centurion that it was so, he gave the body to Joseph* (Mark 15:44-45 NIV).

107 *Nicodemus brought a mixture of myrrh and aloes, about seventy-five*

pounds (John 19:39 NIV).

[108] *At the place where Jesus was crucified, there was a garden, and in the garden a new tomb, in which no one had ever been laid. Because it was the Jewish day of Preparation and since the tomb was nearby, they laid Jesus there* (John 19:41-42).

[109] *He was assigned a grave with the wicked, and with the rich in his death, though he had done no violence, nor was any deceit in his mouth* (Isaiah 53:9 NIV).

[110] Matthew 27:63 NIV

[111] Matthew 27:64 NIV

[112] Matthew 27:65 NIV

[113] *There was a violent earthquake, for an angel of the Lord came down from heaven and going to the mouth of the tomb, rolled back the stone and sat on it. His appearance was like lightning, and his clothes were white as snow. The guards were so afraid of him that they shook and became like dead men* (Matthew 28:2-4).

[114] A full account of John and Peter's early morning visit to the tomb can be found in the Gospel according to John 20:1-9.

[115] *Then Simon Peter who was behind him* (John), *arrived and went in the tomb. He saw the strips of linen lying there, as well as the burial cloth that had been around Jesus' head. The cloth was folded up by itself, separate from the linen* (John 20:6-7 NIV).

[116] *At that moment the curtain of the temple was torn in two from top to bottom. The earth shook and the rocks split* (Matthew 27:51 NIV).

[117] *Then the high priest tore his clothes and said, "He has spoken blasphemy! Why do we need any more witnesses? look, now you have heard the blasphemy. What do you think?"* (Matthew 26:65-66 NIV).

[118] *When the chief priests had met with the elders and devised a plan, they gave the soldiers a large sum of money...* (Matthew 28:12 NIV).

[119] Matthew 28:13 NIV

[120] Merrill F. Unger, *Unger's Bible Dictionary.* The Moody Bible Institute of Chicago, 1966.

[121] John 11:50 CEV

122 W. Horburg, *The Caiaphas Ossuaries and Joseph Caiaphas* PEQ 126 (1994): 32-48.

123 Merrill F. Unger, *Unger's Bible Dictionary.* The Moody Bible Institute of Chicago, 1966.

124 *He* (Jesus) *asked them, "But you, who do you say I am?" Simon Peter answered, "You are the Christ, the Son of the living God"* (Matthew 16:15-16 NBV).

125 The full account of the conversion of Cornelius the centurion is found in the tenth chapter of "The Acts of the Apostles."

Bibliography

Bunson, Matthew. *Encyclopedia of the Roman Empire, Facts on File.* New York, NY, 1994.

Buttrick, George Arthur. Dict. ed. *The Interpreter's Dictionary of the Bible,* Nashville, TN: Abingdon Press, 1962.

Editors of Time-Life Books, *What Life Was Like When Rome Ruled the World: the Roman Empire 100 BC–AD 200,* Alexandra, VA: Time-Life Books, 1997.

Edwards, William D. M.D., Wesley J. Gabel M.Div., Floyd E. Hosmer, M.S., AMI. *On the Physical Death of Jesus Christ,* American Medical Association, 1986.

Gardner, Joseph L. ed. *Atlas of the Bible,* Montreal: Reader's Digest Association, 1981.

Geisler, Norman L., Ronald M. Brooks, *When Skeptics Ask,* Wheaton, IL: Victor Books, 1990.

Horburg, W. *The Caiaphas Ossuaries and Joseph Caiaphas,* PEQ, 1994.

Keppie, L.J.F. *The Making of the Roman Army: From the Republic to the Empire,* Okalahoma City, OK: University of Okalahoma Press, 1998.

McDowell, Josh. *Evidence that Demands a Verdict,* San Bernadino, CA: Campus Crusade for Christ, 1972.

Thomas, Gordon. *The Trial: The Life and Inevitable Crucifixion of Christ,* London, U.K.: Corgi Books, 1987.

Unger, Merrill F. *Unger's Bible Dictionary,* Chicago, IL: The Moody Bible Institute, 1966.